I0704050

*To my Phoobs, simply for being the man you
are
and for loving me the way you do.*

dirty little SECRET

LK FARLOW

"I'LL BE BACK!" Orion shouts, kicking his bike and pedaling down the driveway.

I watch forlornly as he gets smaller and smaller the further away he rides, until eventually, he turns out onto the street. "It's not fair," I mutter, sulking on the bottom porch step, my arms crossed over my chest. "Stupid Orion gets to do everything."

"Stelli Bear." My dad sits down on the top step. "It's not safe for you to ride your bike on the road. You could get hit by a car."

"So can Orion." I turn my glare toward my dad. "Or are you magically protected from becoming roadkill when you turn fourteen?"

"Stella Louise!" Dad's tone tells me he's not playing. "I'm not going to apologize for wanting to keep you safe."

"But it's not fair." I sound like a whiny baby, but I don't care. At eight, I'm practically already in double-digits, which is basically a teenager. So...

"Your brother will be back soon."

"With another stinky boy." I stand and plant my tiny

fists on my hips. "Then there will be two of them to pick on me and ignore me."

"If your brother's so terrible, why are you so mad about not being able to tag along?"

I cringe at my dad's word choice—tag along—that's what Orion calls me when he's being a butthead.

"It doesn't matter."

My dad grins, which only makes me madder.

"I'm going to the field." I start toward my bike. "Or is that not safe either?"

"Stop being a brat, Stelli." He stands too. "And wear your helmet."

Begrudgingly, I strap my helmet on before tearing off down the path that leads to my special spot. Who cares if I can't ride my bike on the big road; I can pedal down to the field—my field—and climb my favorite tree and that's better than hanging out with my stupid, smelly brother any day.

The sun is high in the sky by the time I make it to my spot, which means it'll be lunchtime soon, which means I better get to climbing if I want to reach the tallest branch.

I promised Mama and Daddy I wouldn't go up to the tippy-top, but Orion told me you could see all the way across the valley from there and I want to know if it's true.

Plus, he said I'd never make it to the top because I'm a wuss—which is a bald-faced lie! I'm not a wuss!

I plan my route up as I approach my tree. The branches get smaller and farther apart the higher up they go, but I know I can do it. I'm big and brave, almost a teenager—sort of—and definitely not a wuss.

I grab the lowest branch and hoist myself onto it, climbing quickly to the halfway point, where all of the branches shoot out into smaller limbs. This is where it gets tricky.

Slowly, I test the strength of the branch. It seems good—plus it can hold Orion, so it can definitely hold me.

It takes some time, but finally, I make it to the very top... only to realize my stupid brother is a stupid liar. You can't see anything from up here except the tops of other trees.

But still, I made it and that has to count for something. I can't wait to rub it in his dumb face.

"Stella?"

"Speak of the devil," I mutter to myself, not really knowing what it means; but Mom says it a lot, so I do too.

"Smalls, where are you?" I keep super silent. I've always been better at hide-and-seek than Orion. He'll never find me. "I see your bike, so I know you're here!"

"Are you sure she's out here?" I don't recognize the voice, but it must be the boy he went to invite over.

"Yeah, man, she's definitely here. She's just hiding."

"Why is she hiding?"

I can't see them, but I know my brother rolled his eyes. He's always rolling his eyes now. It makes Mom and Dad really mad, so I try my hardest not to do it.

"Who knows?"

I shift myself just enough to be able to see them through the leaves. Orion looks as dumb as ever, but his friend... he's the handsomest boy I've ever seen.

Even from way up here, I can see his tan skin and blond hair. He looks like he lives at the beach and spends all day outside. I've never been to the beach...

"Stella! Mom said to come home for lunch! So, knock it off and come on!"

"Fine!" I call back and both of their eyes fly up to where I'm hiding in the tree.

"Jesus Christ, Stella!" Orion shouts. "What are you doing up there? Are you insane?"

"No, but you're a liar."

"What are you talking about? Just... just come down!"

"You said I could see across the valley from up here and you lied!"

"Smalls, I was just teasing you. I-I didn't think you'd climb all the way up there."

His friend looks worried. "She's really high up, man."

Orion looks sick. "I know."

"Say you're sorry."

"Fine, whatever. I'm sorry. Please, just come down."

"And be careful," his friend adds.

"I'm not a baby."

"No, I know." His blond head bobs. "Even big kids can get hurt."

I start trying to climb down, retracing my way up, but everything seems different. The branches are farther apart now and the wind is blowing harder.

"Come on, Stella!"

I cling to the trunk of the tree, unable to reach the next branch. "I'm stuck."

"You're not stuck, you're just scared. Come down!"

Tears burn my eyes. "I'm stuck!"

"You got up there, I know you can get down."

My heart feels like it's going to break free of my chest and fly away, it's beating so hard. "You can do this," I whisper to myself, but it's no use. I can't reach.

"I'm really stuck," I say, my tears falling so fast they blur my vision.

"Man, should you go up and get her?"

"No." I can just barely make out my brother crossing his arms. "She got up there, she can get down."

"I don't know..." His friend sounds as scared as I feel.

"Quit being so dramatic and come down!" my brother yells, startling me.

My entire body jolts... my grip loosens... and then... I'm falling.

Twigs and branches scratch me as I plummet, but I can't grab any of them.

"Stella!" Orion shouts my name as I make impact and everything goes dark.

I wake to the sound of my brother screaming. "You don't understand! My parents are going to kill me!"

"You should have helped her!" his friend yells from somewhere very close. "Now go get your mom and dad!"

The feeling of cool fingers pushing my hair out of my face has my eyes fluttering open.

"She's awake!" Without ever taking his eyes off of me, the blond-haired boy shouts at my brother. "Go get your fucking parents! I don't care if they kill you!"

My eyes widen. He said the F-word. And he's cradling my head in his lap.

"Are you okay?" he asks, his fingers still stroking my hair.

"Hurts," I mumble, still crying.

"I'm pretty sure you broke your ankle."

I try to sit up to look, but he holds me in place. "Don't move. I don't want you hurting yourself worse."

"I want my mom."

He offers me a sad smile, and I could swear I hear him mumble, me too. "She'll be here soon. You'll be okay."

"Name?" I wanted to say more than that, but my brain and mouth aren't on the same page. It hurts too much to talk. I just want to sleep.

"Samson, and I need you to keep those pretty blue eyes open, okay?"

"Samson..."

"That's right. I just moved down the road."

Through my pain, I try to think of any houses that were for sale, but nothing comes to mind.

He must see my confusion because he says, "I'm living with the Scotts—they're my foster family."

I've never known anyone in foster care before, but I've heard of it. Maybe that's why he wants his mom too.

For some reason, I want to comfort him the way he is me, and I try to snuggle deeper into his lap, but all I manage to do is set off a new wave of pain.

"Ouch!" I wail, fresh tears falling.

"Stay still, Stella." He glances toward my bike. "Your parents will be here soon."

That day was the beginning of the end for my crush on my older brother's best friend. From there on out, the three of us—much to Orion's dismay—were inseparable.

Well, mostly. They still did things without me, but Samson insisted on including me a lot of the time.

And whenever I couldn't tag along—that word quit bothering me after Samson came into the picture—he would always bring me back something from where they went.

My favorite candy from the movies.

A smooth skipping stone from the river.

A quarter-machine bracelet from the mall.

By the time I was ten, I was head over heels in love with the boy—not that he had a clue or felt the same. He was sixteen and the picture of cool.

But even still, he was nice to me. He included me. He never made me feel like a pest.

By twelve, he and I had our own routine—Orion would sneak a girl up to his room, and Samson and I would swing out on the porch. Looking back, it was probably so I didn't overhear anything I wasn't supposed to, but during those late nights, we talked about anything and everything...

"What happened to your parents?" I ask, my legs tucked beneath me while Samson pushes the swing back and forth.

"Um."

"It's okay. You don't have to tell me. Mom said I shouldn't ask—that it's rude."

"You're okay, Luna." That's something he'd taken to calling me lately, but he won't say why. I'm pretty sure Samson Carter has more secrets than the FBI. "It's just not something I talk about too much."

"You really don't have to tell me."

"No, it's fine." He shakes his head and swallows hard. "They... they're dead."

I gasp as tears fill my eyes. I can't imagine my parents not being here. "How?"

"A car wreck."

"I'm so sorry!" I push up to my knees and turn to him. "Can... can I hug you?"

Another hard swallow. "Sure."

I launch myself at him, wrapping my arms around his neck. "I'm so sorry about your parents, Samson. So, so sorry."

I swear, he's crying too, but I doubt he'll ever admit it. Instead, he just holds me tighter, like I'm the only thing keeping him tethered to this earth.

Finally, after what feels like forever, we break apart. "Thanks, Stella. I... I needed that."

"Needed what?"

"A hug."

"Well, you're in luck, Samson Carter."

"Oh, yeah? Why's that?"

My smile brightens. "Because you can hug me anytime you want!"

And he did too. After that night, he hugged me every day.

Secretly, I pretended he hugged me because he loved me like I loved him, which was stupid since he started dating Caroline Arnold that very same summer.

She was pretty, with deep brown hair and green eyes. I begged Mom to let me color my hair brown after meeting her, but she wouldn't let me.

Thank God... hindsight really is twenty-twenty.

I worried he'd forget all about me once he started dating her... that I'd go back to being *tagalong* instead of Luna. But that never happened.

Even when they went out together, he'd bring me something back. And at night, when Orion would sneak girls in, he never asked Caroline to come over.

Nope. He still sat outside with me.

Despite my immense dislike of Caroline, she was as sweet as could be. She was never catty or spiteful like some of the girls my brother brought home.

I still didn't like her.

How could I when she had the one thing I wanted more than anything?

In short, it was the longest, most torturous summer of my life.

But then, one day, she just stopped coming around. I know I should have been sad for Samson, but I wasn't. Not even a little.

In my young eyes, it was time to make my move—my heart never cared about our age difference. It just knew he was the reason for it to beat.

I dressed up in my prettiest Sunday dress, stole Mom's red lipstick, and doused myself in her perfume. Looking back, I probably looked like a damn mess, but ever the gentleman, Samson let me down gently.

To this day, I've never forgotten the words he spoke to me, simultaneously breaking my heart and filling it with hope...

"Luna." *The way he rumbles my name sends butterflies swarming around my belly as I sidle up next to him on the porch swing for our Saturday night ritual.* "You look..."

"Pretty?" I ask, batting my eyes up at him.

When he doesn't answer me right away, I deflate.

Finally, he says, "You always look pretty. Every single day."

"Really? You think so?"

He nods. "I do."

Even at thirteen, I can tell there's more he wants to say. And the way he's hesitating reminds me of when I get into trouble in class and don't want to tell Mom. Whatever he's not saying... isn't good.

"Just spit it out."

He grins. "You're so bossy."

I glare. "It's leadership skills."

"Oh, is that it?" He sounds far too amused for my liking. Here I am, putting myself out there and he's teasing me. God, boys are dumb

"Stop avoiding my question."

"Fine." He stands from the swing. "The lipstick... the perfume... they're not you, Luna. You don't need any of that shit. You're perfect exactly the way you are."

I've read in magazines that women should wear makeup for themselves and not for a man, so now I feel even sillier knowing I put this on special just for him, and he doesn't even like it.

"You don't like it?" I ask, swiping the back of my hand

over my mouth, smearing the red lipstick as I try to rub it away.

"Listen, you asked what I thought and I'm telling you." He leans down so we're eye to eye. "You're beautiful, Stella, all on your own, without a lick of makeup. All you have to do is smile, and you're the prettiest girl in the room."

I don't know why, but it feels like I'm melting. "Samson..."

He takes a step back. "Stella?"

"I like you."

He lifts a brow. "I like you too, Luna."

"No, I like-like you." I wrap my arms around myself. "A lot." I want to tell him I love him, but I don't want to freak him out.

"Oh, Stella." He shakes his head. "You're too young for all of that."

I jump from the swing so quick, the chains rattle. "I am not!"

"Don't be mad, Luna."

"I'm not mad." I blink up at him, tears filling my eyes. "I'm sad."

He wraps me in a hug. "Don't be sad either."

"But you don't like me back." My voice comes out muffled from the way my cheek is pressed against his chest.

"I like you just fine, but I'm way too old for you. You're in middle school and I'm almost twenty. You're still a kid—and before you get all pissy, I'm not saying that in a bad way, okay? You're young. You still have a lot of growing up to do. So, instead of worrying about me, just enjoy being a kid while you can. Because me?" He squeezes me closer before stepping away. "I'll always be here."

"Always?"

Samson cradles my cheeks and wipes away my tears.

"Yeah, Luna. Always."

For the next two years, I tried my hardest to do what Samson told me—to just enjoy being a kid. And for the most part, I think I did.

But the flame I carried for him never died. If anything, it grew stronger and stronger, until finally it was a full-blown wildfire.

And what do wildfires do? They spread.

The change in Samson was subtle at first, as the embers grew.

One day at the lake, his stare lingered.

When he'd hug me, his hands would sit a little lower and he'd hold me a little longer.

Finally, I'd had enough and decided to try my luck again. After all, the worst he could say was no, right?

Like always, we were out on the porch swing, except this time it wasn't late at night and Orion wasn't boning some random girl. This was just your run-of-the-mill Saturday afternoon.

"You look like something's on your mind?" Samson asks, using his long legs to push the swing.

I know he's probably going to shoot me down, but after listening to all the girls at school go on and on about how amazing it is, I know he's the only person I want to experience it with.

"Will you be my first?" I ask, nerves rolling through me like thunder.

Samson's fingers flex as he balls his hands into fists. "Cut it out, Luna."

"Jesus, Samson." I turn away from him, too prideful to run away, even though that's all I want to do. "You don't have to be so mean."

He sighs, and it sounds almost like he's in pain. "You're

too young for all of that."

"All of what?"

"Fucking. Screwing. Sex. Whatever you wanna call it, you're not old enough to do it."

"Samson!" I whirl back around and smack him in the chest. My cheeks feel like they're on fire as I stare at him with my mouth agape.

"Look at you," he murmurs. "Your cheeks are as red as that cherry you're asking me to pop."

An unsettling mixture of embarrassment and something I can't quite name rush through me, making me feel hot all over. "I wasn't... I didn't mean... I just wanted you to kiss me!"

Samson stills. "You've never been kissed?" His eyes drop to my lips of their own accord.

I glare at him. "How could I? Thanks to Orion, guys at school won't talk to me. Plus, even if they would..." I trail off, knowing good and well even if they would give me the time of day, I still wouldn't be interested.

"Even if they would, what?" he growls.

"They still wouldn't be you."

"Dammit, Luna." He sounds mad now and I feel like a fool. Apparently being told no hurts more than I remembered. Or maybe he just let me down easier last time.

"Sorry," I mumble, climbing off the swing. "It was dumb."

"Look at me," he demands, but I don't. "I said look at me." The chains jerk as he abandons the swing and grabs my shoulder, spinning me to face him.

"What in the world?" I shriek right as his lips come down on mine. They're warm and soft and perfect, and even though he doesn't try to french kiss me, I totally see what all the hype is about.

I think I could kiss him forever, I think as he pulls away, rubbing my index finger over my lips as I try to commit the feel of his to memory.

"I wish you could be all of my firsts, Samson Carter," I say before I can think better of it. "I'd save every single one for you."

"Don't say shit like that." He's back to being all growly, but I don't care. Because he. Kissed. Me. Cue the internal confetti.

"Why not?" I cross my arms and glare. "I mean it."

Samson glares right back. "You don't know what you mean."

"Don't you dare tell me what I mean. You don't know my heart, or how I feel, so don't presume to." I pace back and forth on the porch, getting angrier with each pass. "And how dare you try to minimize my feelings. I might be young, but I'm not dumb. I've loved you since I was ten and I love you now. You big dummy."

Ugh. I don't have to stand here and take this. Maybe Mom's right and all boys are from outer space, because he's acting all kinds of crazy. Kissing me and then telling me I don't know how I feel.

My feelings haven't changed, but he's sending all kinds of mixed signals.

I try to make a break for the front door, but Samson blocks my path. "Stella," he rumbles my name and despite how upset I am at him, I shiver.

"Ugh! Just go hang out with Orion. Or better yet, go home!" I shout, my humiliation giving way to tears. I know telling him to go home is a low blow. He's told me over and over how much he hates it at the Scotts'.

"You love me?" he asks, his voice deceptively soft.

I nod, not trusting myself to speak.

"I..." he trails off, unknowingly gutting me.

"It's okay." I will myself not to cry. "I know you don't feel the same way."

"You're too young for me, Stella."

I roll my eyes. "Age is only a number."

"Numbers have meaning. Wanna know another number?"

I nod.

"Twenty."

"What's important about twenty?" Like, are we just throwing out random numbers now? It's not even how old he is.

"That's how many years I could go to jail for touching you."

Worry flashes like lightning in my veins as I shake my head back and forth, my long blonde hair whipping all around me. "No! I don't... I don't want that. I'm sorry, Samson, I didn't know."

Shock quickly follows when he wraps his strong arms around me. "I know you didn't, Luna."

"I'll wait for you then," I mumble against his chest, feeling every bit as hopeful as I do dumb. "If you want..."

He tenses, but then asks, "You'd do that?"

Sniffling, I nod.

"Oh—" The sound of the front door unlatching silences whatever he was about to say.

We jump apart right as Orion steps out onto the porch. "Stella," he says my name in that annoying way of his before turning to Samson. "Is she bugging you?"

"Nah, man. She's fine."

Orion rolls his eyes but lets it drop. "Whatever. Heather called. She and Annabeth are going to the lake and invited us. She mentioned something about new bikinis and wanting *us to inspect them, if you know what I mean." He wags his brows and I nearly vomit on the spot.*

Samson glances my way before I can hide the hurt in my eyes. "You wanna come?" he asks, completely ignoring my brother's answering groan.

"No thanks," I whisper. "Wouldn't wanna intrude."

"Come on!" Orion hollers, already on his way down the steps to his truck.

"Be right there," Samson calls back, keeping his eyes on mine. "What's wrong?"

"Nothing." I've already put myself out there enough to last a lifetime. There's no way I'm about to tell him I don't want him to go.

"Stella."

"It's just... I told you I loved you and you're going off to inspect Annabeth Johnson's bikini. Whatever. It's dumb. This is dumb. Have fun."

I try—again—to shove past him, but he grabs my wrist at the last possible moment. "I won't touch her."

My cheeks lift as I beam up at him. "Really? You're gonna wait for me too?"

"I... we'll talk more about this later, okay?"

And talk about it we did—often and at length. For months and months, we went back and forth, weighing the pros and cons of acting on our feelings.

I was sixteen by the time we reached a compromise—I would be his and he would be mine, in secret until my eighteenth birthday.

Much to my dismay, our agreement came with the caveat that Samson wouldn't lay a single finger on me until after my eighteenth birthday.

But I'd wait forever if it meant I got to call him mine.

"HAPPY BIRTHDAY, LUNA." I blink my eyes awake to the sound of my favorite voice in the entire world.

"Samson," I murmur, sleepily, glancing toward where he lingers in my doorway. Despite us being together and him being a fixture in our house, he never comes inside of my room. He says it's a sign of respect for my dad... whatever that means.

"Up and at 'em, birthday girl. We have plans."

"What time is it? It's a school day."

"Your dad said you could play hooky."

I bolt upright. "What? Really?"

"Yup. So, hop in the shower and get dressed!"

Excitement races through me at the thought of skipping school *and* spending the day with Samson. Talk about the best sweet sixteen ever.

"Okay."

"I'll be waiting in the kitchen." He smiles at me in that way that makes my belly flip. "But, Luna..."

"Yeah?"

"Hurry."

As soon as I hear his feet hit the stairs, I fly out of bed and into my bathroom. I brush my teeth and toss my hair into a loose braid before rushing back into my room to get dressed.

I throw on my favorite jeans and a pink plaid button-down, slide my feet into my boots, spritz on my favorite body spray and call it good.

I take the stairs two at a time, more than ready for my mom's famous cinnamon roll pancakes—they've been my birthday breakfast of choice since I was ten—but when I step into the kitchen, Samson is alone.

"Where is everyone?"

"We're doing things a little different this year."

"What do you mean?"

"I figured instead of pancakes with your parents, I could take you for breakfast."

"Really?"

"Really." He nods and hops off the barstool. "I wanna spoil you today, Luna."

I bite my lip to hide my smile. "You don't have to do that. Just spending time with you is plenty."

"I know I don't have to—I *want* to."

Butterflies take flight in my belly and I have to grip the countertop to keep from flying away with them. "Okay." I nod and start toward the door. "Let's go."

"Hold up." Samson steps closer to me. "Gotta do something first."

"What's that?" I ask, looking up at him from beneath my lashes.

"This," he whispers, wrapping his big, strong arms around me.

I sink into his embrace, loving the way his body feels

pressed to mine as his hands rub up and down my back before finally settling just above the swell of my ass.

"Will you kiss me?" I ask, hoping and praying he says yes.

"God, you tempt me, Luna," he groans, flexing his fingers.

"It's just us..." I whisper, rising up to my tippy-toes. "No one has to know. It can be my birthday present."

"Stella." My name sounds like a prayer on his lips. "Fuck."

"Please." I press my lips to his jaw. "Just one kiss."

"You know I can't deny you." He nudges my face with his nose and then captures my lips with his own.

Despite us being together in secret for months now, this is only our second kiss. And while the first one was pure, sweet perfection, this one is full of forbidden want and need.

He dips his hands lower, squeezing my ass as he sucks on my lower lip.

I've never kissed with tongue before, but I've seen it in enough movies that I feel pretty confident when I slide my tongue against his.

If the bulge pressing against my belly is anything to go by, I think I nailed it. He feels huge.

"Fuck!" He breaks our kiss on a breathless moan. "Go wait in the truck for me. I'll be right there."

"Is everything okay?" I ask, worrying I did something wrong.

"Everything's perfect, Luna." He reaches down and adjusts himself. "I'll... I'll be right there."

I race to the truck with my heart in my throat and my entire body tingling. How is it possible for a simple kiss to make me feel like this? Like I'm flying and falling all at once.

His keys are in the ignition, so I crank it and fiddle with the radio until I find a song I like. It's some top twenty hit that's sure to drive Samson crazy. But he won't complain—he never does.

Finally, after what feels like forever, Samson joins me. "You ready?"

"For what?"

He puts the truck in gear and then rests his hand on my thigh. "The best day of your life."

"That's any day with you." My cheeks burn as soon as the words leave my mouth. *Way to sound like a stage-five clinger*, I think to myself.

"You mean that?"

I hold my breath until we're on the main road, debating how to answer. My mom always says a healthy relationship has no room for mistrust or dishonesty, and I want Samson and me to go the long-haul, so...

"Yeah. I mean it. You're..."

"I'm what?" He gives my thigh a reassuring squeeze. "Tell me."

"You're everything to me, Samson."

"Fuck, Luna," he murmurs, his voice thick like honey.

"Why do you call me that?" I turn in my seat to look at him.

His throat bobs as he swallows. "You really wanna know?"

I nod.

"Because you're the brightest light in my life. Your smile is enough to make the worst day bearable. You steady me, you challenge me, you center me."

Tears—happy ones—fill my eyes, but he keeps going.

"I tried to fight it. Truly, I did. You're too young for me, but fuck if I can stay away from you. You're captivating, and I don't just mean your looks, as beautiful as you are. It's your soul, Stella. Just like the moon pulls the tides, your soul calls to mine, and I am helpless but to answer."

"I..." I swallow hard. "I love you, Samson Carter."

"I love you too," he murmurs, unknowingly giving me the best birthday present of my entire life.

STELLA, AGE 17

I CHECK THE CLOCK—IT'S almost eight, which means Samson will be here any minute. I'm usually still asleep when he gets here, but for some reason, this morning I'm wide awake and more than ready to see him.

"Happy Birthday, Luna."

"Good morning, Samson." I tuck my hair behind my ear and grin as he lingers in my doorway.

"You're supposed to be asleep."

I scrunch my brows. "Why does it matter?"

"I love getting to see you all cute and sleepy." He shrugs. "It's like looking into our future. One day, you'll be waking up next to me like that."

Feeling emboldened by his words, I kick off the covers and stand from the bed.

"The fuck?" Samson shouts, nearly choking on his tongue. "Where are your clothes?"

"I thought you'd like to see my pajamas too." I glance down at my tank top and sleep shorts. "What's wrong with what I'm wearing?"

Samson swallows roughly. "I can see your nipples."

"So?"

"Stella." He pinches the bridge of his nose. "I swear to God."

"Chill. It's not like I'm naked."

"You may as well be."

Giggling, I take a small step toward him. "I think you're being a little dramatic."

"And I think I'm about two seconds away from breaking every rule I've made surrounding you." His eyes move over my body in a way that makes my entire body feel warm.

"Do it," I whisper, knowing good and well I'm playing with fire.

"Stella." He grips the door frame on each side, his upper body leaning ever so slightly over the threshold. "As much as I love seeing you like this, I need you to get dressed for me, okay?"

I pout. "Fine, but only on one condition."

"Anything—you name it."

"You kiss me again."

Samson groans.

"Those are my terms. If you don't like them..."

"I like them just fine." Samson takes a step back. "Maybe a little too much."

"We're all alone." My lips lift into a saucy grin. "You could come in here and show me how much?" I've been testing his boundaries lately, but it always ends the same way...

"Not until you're eighteen."

Only three-hundred-and-sixty-five more days to go.

"That's dumb, Samson."

He cocks his head to the side and stares at me, his eyes never leaving mine. "Is it? Is it dumb?"

I nod, after all—it's my birthday and I can be a brat if I want to.

"I think it's pretty damn smart." He licks his lips. "Do you have any idea the things I'd like to do to you in that big bed of yours? Me not coming into your room is about more than respecting your dad—it's about resisting temptation."

"I tempt you?"

"You know you do."

"Fine." I'm torn somewhere between wanting to see how far I can push him and respecting his boundaries.

I know it's only because he cares about me—because he *respects* me—but he makes me feel all of these things I don't always understand, and every now and then, the reassurance that I affect him just as much as he does me is nice.

"That's right, Luna." He pinches his eyes shut and mutters something to himself before addressing me. "I need you to hear me when I say I want you more than I've ever wanted anything. But I want more than just your body. I want your mind, your smiles, your words, your thoughts."

"Samson..."

"I want your minutes and your hours. I want your days, months, and years. Your whole future, Luna... it's mine. Which is why I can wait. We have forever."

"You really mean that?" I ask, my lip quivering.

He nods and before I can think better of it, I rush him and fling myself into his arms.

"Whoa." He stumbles a little as he catches me, one arm around my middle and the other supporting my ass.

I wrap my legs around his waist and nuzzle my face against his. "Kiss me."

He resists at first, but then his entire body softens against mine as he licks his way into my mouth.

Our tongues touch, sliding together, and it's like time itself ceases to exist.

There's only us. We're reduced down to atoms... molecules... two burning specs of lust and need.

I tunnel my fingers into his hair and shift my hips against his, gasping when I feel the hard press of his erection against my belly.

"Samson," I moan his name, a whole deluge of foreign feelings pouring through me, turning my blood to lava in my veins. "I... I feel..."

"Shh, Luna. I've got you." He reclaims my lips, moving his mouth over mine while sliding me up and down over his rock-hard dick, like our very existence depends on what happens next.

My breaths come in sharp, gasping pants, until finally, I fall apart in his arms.

"Whoa," I whisper in a daze as Samson sets me down on my feet. He grins when I sway a little before steadying myself on the banister.

"Was that your first orgasm?" he asks, an awestruck look in his eyes.

"I... um." I glance away from him and mumble the rest of my reply to my feet. "I told you I wanted to save all of my firsts for you."

As fast as lightning, Samson reaches out and grasps my chin, softly forcing my gaze up to his. "I'm going to be more than just your first, Luna—I'm going to be your only."

Chills sweep over me as a smile turns up my lips. "Yes, please."

Samson grins, looking all too pleased with himself. Which is surprising; I thought for sure he'd feel guilty and lecture me on making better choices.

Which would have been stupid, because his words

would have absolutely fallen on deaf ears. There's nothing, and I mean *nothing*, that could make me regret what just happened between us.

"Happy Birthday, Stella."

I rise up onto my tiptoes and press a soft kiss to his jaw. "Thank you, Samson... for all of it. For everything."

He steps back, once again putting a bit of distance between us. "The day's just getting started."

"What else are we doing?"

He glances down at my barely covered body and fists his hands at his sides. "Get dressed."

I roll my eyes but turn toward my room anyway. "Well, whatever you have planned, I hope it involves cupcakes."

"You know it does. Now, come on before I do something I'll regret."

My shoulders tense at his words—something Samson's keen eyes catch immediately.

"What's wrong?"

"Nothing." I try to shrug it off, but it stings.

"Luna." The tone of his voice freezes me in place, but I keep my back to him. "Talk to me."

"Let me change first," I say, desperate to buy myself some time.

"Look at me first."

I draw in a deep breath before glancing at him over my shoulder. He studies my face long and hard before nodding.

"Hurry."

I bolt into my room, throwing the door shut behind me. How can my body and my brain be in such different places?

My body still feels like it's burning up for him... for his touch.

But my brain, it may as well be in Antarctica, it's so cold.

Did I push him too far? Does he regret kissing me? Is he mad? Disappointed?

I'm torn between hiding in my room until he leaves and going out there and facing him. What if he tells me he wants to take a break?

Surely, he won't, right? Not over a hot and heavy make-out sesh.

I pace in front of my closet before finally pulling on the first outfit I see.

Except, when I step out of my room, he's not there.

"I told your parents I would." I slink down the steps, following the sound of his voice all the way into the kitchen. "Plus, you know it's our tradition."

I know I shouldn't listen in on their conversation, that it's rude, but I find myself holding my breath all the same.

"Sounds like a good time, man. I wish I could be there."

My hackles rise. *Where would he rather be than here? With me?*

He's silent for a minute before a bark of laughter escapes him. "Hey, well, at least without me there you stand a chance."

Dread pools in my gut. I don't know how I know it, but I am one-hundred percent certain they're talking about other girls. Girls Samson wishes he was with, but isn't because he promised my parents he would spend the day with me.

It kind of feels like I'm dying inside, even as I try to rationalize what I'm hearing.

I'm so consumed in misery that I don't make out any more of Samson's words, until he says, "What about me and Stella?" His tone is defensive.

When I was little, Orion was obsessed with super-heroes. We would always pretend we could fly. But right about now, I find myself wishing I had supersonic hearing instead.

"She's my friend too," Samson says, and I blanch at his casual use of the F-word.

I know it's what we are to everyone else, but it hurts a little more than usual after what we just shared upstairs.

"Yeah, well, you don't have to worry about me trying anything with her."

I clench my fist and storm into the kitchen, knowing I'll explode if I have to listen to one more second of this conversation.

"Hey, Stella's ready. Let me let you go."

He's silent for another moment before he shakes his head. "Fuck that. Tell her yourself." He ends the call, pockets his phone, and then looks to me. "You look angry."

"I can't imagine why."

Samson sighs. "Probably because you just listened to half of my phone call with your brother."

I cross my arms over my chest and nod.

"Listen, you know I love you, right?"

Another nod.

"And you know I want us to be together, out in the open?"

"Yeah."

"But we can't yet, Stella. So, if that means I have to lie to your brother—to my best friend—to keep you, then I will."

"It just hurts." I bite my lip, feeling like a brat. "I want the whole world to know you're mine."

"And they will, Luna. One more year and everyone will know we're together, okay?"

"You promise?"

He reaches into his pocket, retrieving a black velvet box.

"What's this?" I ask as he passes it to me.

"Open it," he says with a lopsided grin.

I suck in a deep breath and then flip back the lid, revealing a simple silver band. "Samson?" I exhale his name, all thoughts of secrets and remorse long gone.

"I know it's not much, but it's a promise, Luna." He plucks the ring from the box. "It's a promise that every part of me belongs to every part of you. I love you, Stella. I. Love. You."

Tears burn the backs of my eyes as he slides the ring onto my finger. "I love you too, Samson Carter."

"Next year, I'll get you a real ring. One with a diamond."

I smile up at him, not bothering to wipe my tears. "I don't give a flip about a ring, as long as I have you."

"Always." He leans in and presses a chaste kiss to my lips. "Now, let's go get those cupcakes, yeah?"

3

STELLA, AGE 18

HE NEVER SHOWS.

LUNA

You suck. Like, you really fucking suck. Tonight was supposed to be the night, but you just had to go and ruin it.

LUNA

You told me always. That you'd love me always. That you'd be mine always. What a joke.

LUNA

You're a chicken-shit liar and a thiof.

LUNA

Okay, not a literal thief, but you stole my heart with your blue eyes and silver tongue. I'd like it back, because frankly, you're not worthy of it.

LUNA

I hate you.

LUNA

I want to hate you.

LIKE THE FUCKING masochist I am, I read over the last texts Stella sent for me the hundredth time in as many days. I read the fucking thread every night before bed, just to torture myself.

She's right though. I am a chicken shit. I gave her up out of fear. I ran like a yellow-bellied coward.

Not because I didn't want her, because I did.

Still do.

Always have, always will.

Stella just has this magnetism about her; anyone who spends a minute in her presence, can't help but be drawn to her.

Even as a snot-nosed kid with knobby knees and an attitude bigger than any of us knew how to handle, I always found myself telling Orion to let her tag along.

Not because I was interested in her either—no, those feelings came much, *much* later—but because she was just this fucking ball of sunshine, and as a lonely punk-ass kid, I just wanted to bask in her light.

All she had to do was point her gap-toothed smile my way, and I'd feel lighter. Accepted. Happier. Loved, even, because God knows my foster family didn't have any love to spare for the likes of me.

But Stella... *she saw me.*

And like an idiot, I threw her away.

"Fuck!" I shout, my voice bouncing off the wall of the dingy motel room I've called home for the last six months.

There's so much I could have done better, starting with never taking this damn job.

If it wasn't for my name on that dotted line, I would have turned my truck around the second my better sense kicked in and begged her to take me back.

Instead, I'm two states away, with nothing but my own regret to keep me company at night.

I ghosted her, breaking her heart and mine. She has every right to hate me, but that doesn't stop me from loving her.

It's not going to stop me from trying to win her back either.

Ready or not, Luna, I'm coming for you.

I fucked up when I broke her heart, but I've got less than eighty days left on this contract, and when I get home...

Her ass is mine.

THERE'S something about the feeling of fresh soil squishing between my fingers that centers me. It's been that way for as long as I can remember. From baking mud pies to helping my dad tend to his vegetable garden, I just... love it.

Dad says I have green thumbs; that I can make anything grow. During my freshman year of high school, when all of the other girls were asking for Coach purses and Ugg boots, I was begging my parents for a steel utility cart to haul all of my tools to and from the shed.

There's also something really satisfying about growing something all on your own, about taking a seed and nurturing it into a full-grown plant. It takes patience and dedication, two things I severely lack outside of my seven-by-seven plot.

"You out here, Smalls?"

My head snaps up at the sound of my brother, Orion, calling my name, but I don't bother answering him. He'll see me in two more steps.

"Figured as much."

I stick out my tongue at him and then turn back to the task at hand—pulling weeds. "What's up?"

"Just wanted to see if you planned on coming tonight."

"Coming where?"

He waits until I'm looking up at him to reply. "To my house, for a party."

"Like a dinner party?"

"Nope." Orion shakes his head, grinning in that stupidly annoying way only older brothers can do. "Like an all-out rager."

Shock sends me sprawling back onto my butt. "And you're inviting me?"

I sound redundant, but Orion is the very definition of overprotective.

Thanks to his stifling ass, I'm eighteen and have never been to a real party. Hell, I've never even had a boyfriend.

Unless you count—*nope! Not going there.* He *doesn't get to live rent-free in my brain anymore.*

My point is, even though he's only six years older than I am, my brother is a total mama bear when it comes to me; a totally over-the-top, overbearing, and overprotective mama bear.

"Yeah, of course I am," he says, like it's totally normal for him to invite me anywhere.

Newsflash: it's not.

"Why?" Suspicion overrides the excitement so desperately trying to bubble up inside of me.

"You're eighteen now."

"Riiiight." I turn back to the flowerbed. He's obviously messing with me. It's the only explanation really, because I'm only three months shy of nineteen, so clearly his invitation has nothing to do with my age because he's been as overbearing as ever.

"I guess I'll come." *It's not like I have anything better to do,* I think semi-bitterly.

It's not like I have any real friends. I mean, I didn't eat lunch alone in the library or anything but I didn't get invited to sleepovers or the mall either. The few that tried, either crushed on Orion to the point of obsession or got annoyed by his stifling protectiveness.

"Good. Party starts at nine."

I nod, playing it cool as he turns and heads back up the path toward the house. But the second I round the curve, I tear off my gloves and give a little squeal.

Weeding can wait, I have a party to get ready for.

My goal was to be fashionably late—whatever that means—but by the time I find somewhere to park, it's half-past nine and Orion has already called me twice.

Make that three times, I think as my phone starts up again.

"Where are you?" he asks, before I can utter a single word.

"Ii, Orion."

"Where are you, Smalls?" he asks again, his tone strained.

"Chill. I'm walking up your driveway now."

"I told you to be here at nine."

"It's not like I meant to be late."

He grunts out an unintelligible curse. "Stay, put. I'll come get you."

"Pretty sure I can make it to the backyard on my own."

"And I'm pretty sure you can stay your ass put and wait

for me." He hangs up before I can argue, which I absolutely would have... *the overbearing asshole.*

How is it that I can be old enough to score an invite but too young to walk down his driveway?

I mean, it is a long, dark, and winding drive, but there are literally people everywhere. Like so many people, I can't help but wonder who they are and how he knows them—*if* he knows them. This is seriously like something out of a movie.

Either way, I stay put since my unintentional tardiness seems to have him in a mood; best not to poke the bear after all.

"What are you wearing?" Orion says as he approaches, his face screwing up into a mean-looking scowl.

"A dress."

"Do you have a jacket?"

"It's the middle of summer, so that's gonna be a nope."

He pinches the bridge of his nose, a sure sign that I'm testing his patience. But this time, it's not intentional, because there's absolutely nothing wrong with my dress.

I bought it to wear on my eighteenth birthday, but those plans went up in smoke and I spent the day sobbing into a bucket of ice cream instead. So, I decided tonight was the perfect occasion to bust it out of my closet.

With eyelet lace details, a sweetheart neckline, spaghetti straps, and mid-thigh hemline, it's the perfect mix of sexy and sweet.

"You look like..."

I hold up a hand to silence him. "So help me God, if you say anything other than lovely, I will never speak to you again."

"Stole the words right out of my mouth," he replies woodenly.

"Great."

"Good." He turns and starts walking toward the back-yard, leaving me to follow after him.

"You know, you've gotta let me grow up sometime, right?"

Without stopping, he says, "You're here, aren't you?"

Touché, mama bear, touché.

He jerks to a stop right before the steps leading up to the back deck. "No drugs, no drinking, no hooking up."

I roll my eyes. "Didn't plan to do any of the following."

Orion gives me a long, hard look before nodding. "Good. If you need anything, find me or Ben."

This is technically Ben's house. An old farmhouse fixer-upper passed down to him by his grandpa. He and Orion have been remodeling it for the past two years while living in it. I guess it's a win-win since they own a construction business and there's no mortgage on it. That's what Dad says anyway.

"Okay." He starts to walk away, but I call after him. "Thanks for inviting me."

He tips his chin in acknowledgment before letting the crowd of partygoers swallow him whole.

For a split second, panic threatens to consume me. Everyone here is so much older than me and with so much more life experience. I feel like a guppy in shark-infested waters.

Maybe with a drink in my hand—nonalcoholic, of course—I'll feel a little less out of place.

With a sort-of plan in place, I venture farther into the backyard.

I find the makeshift bar with ease and hop in line. When I finally make it to the front, I snag a bottle of water from the cooler along with a red plastic cup to pour it into. I may not be drinking, but I'm not above looking like I am to blend in.

It's your typical Georgia summer night—hot and muggy —and the sheer amount of people here only adds to the heat. Luckily, my water is ice cold.

I decide to make a lap around the yard. Who knows, maybe I'll spot a familiar face, or at the very least find a quiet corner to hang out in.

Except, instead of finding any of that, I stumble upon the last person I ever wanted to see again. Literally ever.

"Stella," he exhales my name in that deep rasp of his, freezing me in place. "What..." His eyes roam over my body, making me feel hot and cold all at the same time. "What are you doing here?"

Micro-tremors rack my body as I take in the man I once thought was the love of my life. It's only been nine months since he so callously left me, but it feels like a lifetime. "What are *you* doing here?" I ask when I finally find my voice.

"You look good." His voice wraps around me, familiar and comforting, like coming home.

Except Samson Carter isn't my home anymore. He's not my anything.

"Mmm." I nod and raise my cup to my lips.

"Are you drinking?" he asks, his gaze sharpening before dropping to my mouth.

My tongue darts out, swiping across my lower lip; Samson clenches his fists at his sides.

"What's it to you?" Fuck him for thinking he has a say in *any*thing I do. He lost the right when he left me without a single word. He certainly didn't care then, so why should he now?

"You're not old enough."

I force out a laugh. "Wasn't old enough all those times you kissed me either, but you still did." My lips tingle at the memory of his moving against mine, but I force myself not to react.

"I swear to God, Luna." He steps closer to me, but I stand my ground. "You don't want to test me."

"Ding-ding!" I loop my index finger through the air. "We've got a winner."

"That fucking mouth," he mutters.

"But just to clarify further, it's water and I don't want *anything* to do with you." I take a step back. "So, I'll just be going now. Have a nice night. Or choke and die. Either way."

Anger and sadness clash within me, two warring emotions fighting for dominance, as I turn away from Samson. But before I can flee, his big hand clamps down on my shoulder.

"Not so fast Luna."

"Let. Go. Of. Me."

"Not until we talk." His voice holds a note of pleading, like the thought of me being upset with him is unbearable.

A rueful laugh escapes me. Clearly my pain is nothing to him, or he never would have left.

"We have nothing to talk about," I say, refusing to let him sway me. For as long as I can remember, Samson Carter has been my drug of choice, but I'm nine months sober and I refuse to let his reappearance derail my progress.

"We have *everything* to talk about." He steps closer, all the while stroking his thumb over the back of my neck.

I scoff. "We really don't."

"Stella." The way he growls my name sends shivers down my spine.

"Samson?" I spit his name.

"I missed you, you know?" His fingers skate down my left arm, where he grabs my wrist. "You're not wearing it…"

It takes me a second to realize what the *it* he's referring to is.

"You have some fucking nerve, you know that?" Rage boils in my veins, turning my blood to lava. "I don't care if you missed me. I don't care why you're back. The only thing I care about is you staying far, *far* away from me."

With one hand still on my shoulder and the other holding my wrist, he steps impossibly closer. So close I can feel the heat of his body at my back. "You don't mean that."

"Let go."

"Not happening." He presses his face into the side of my neck, inhaling deeply. "Come talk with me."

"I swear to God!" I jerk against his hold, but it's useless —he's easily twice my size.

He cuts me off. "Now, Stella."

"Never, Samson." I punctuate my words with a kick to his shin.

"Ouch!" he shouts, releasing me. The second I'm free, I toss my cup and run like hell. "Fuck! Stella! Come back!"

But I don't… I can't.

I run all the way back to my car, wishing not for the first time for a friend to talk this all out with.

Once upon a time, Samson was that friend. We'd sit for hours on the front porch or my spot in the woods where we met for the first time, talking about anything and everything. He always listened and gave the best advice. He was my everything.

My first love, my first kiss, and my first heartbreak all rolled up into one tall, strong, and devastatingly handsome package.

I loved him with every ounce of my being; served him

my heart up on a silver platter and he tossed it out like two-week-old leftovers. Like it was nothing... like *I* was nothing.

I'm not the same naïve, trusting girl he so callously left behind and if he thinks I'll so easily fall back under his spell, he's got another thing coming.

SOMEHOW, I managed to fuck it all up with Stella.

Again.

At least last night wasn't self-sabotage. Nope, just a good old case of me being an idiot. Which seems to be my default when it comes to her.

I've wanted her for so long, loved her for so long, I can hardly remember my life without her in it. But as we grew closer, we grew reckless. We went from sneaking around under the dark of night to meeting up in broad daylight.

While we weren't *technically* doing anything wrong, our age difference alone was enough to turn heads. I felt the weight of their stares any time we went anywhere together.

But it was overhearing Lizzie Cartwright's innocently whispered words to her husband that sent me running. Without even knowing it, she picked apart every single insecurity I had, unraveling all of the plans Stella and I made.

Like a dumbass, I let the opinions of others get in my head and I left.

I truly believed I was doing her a favor. I wanted her to

have the whole fucking world and worried that tying herself to me at such a young age would only hold her back.

In hindsight, I realize it wasn't my place to make that kind of decision for her. But now, I know better; and I'm damn sure going to do better.

You'd think nine long months of regret and planning, I'd have managed to not fuck up our reunion. But, in my defense, seeing her all dressed up at a party that was sprung on me at the last minute wasn't something I had accounted for.

I figured we would reconnect at her one of her parent's infamous family dinners. And while I had anticipated her anger, I still wasn't prepared for the way her words sliced across my skin. Or for my ring to be missing from her finger.

Foolishly, I thought she'd be pining over me the way I was her. But it feels like I fucked up even worse than I originally thought.

The sound of my front door opening startles me out of my inner thoughts, as Orion lets himself into my house.

"Don't knock or anything," I mutter under my breath, knowing full and well it'll never happen.

"You hungover?" Orion asks, ignoring me as he slings himself down onto the couch beside me.

I'm not hungover at all; I'm brooding, and have been since I woke up, but it's better to let him think my surliness is a result of drinking too much than staying up until dawn obsessing over his little sister.

I grunt out an unintelligible reply.

"I feel you. But it's your first weekend back and the night is young. Let's go out."

"It's almost nine." I frown. "And we partied last night. Let's stay in."

Orion groans. You'd think he was an only child with

how put out he gets over not getting his way. "Come on, one drink."

I glance at him out of the side of my eye. I want to say no, but apparently my brain and body aren't on the same page because I find myself nodding. I guess hitting up a bar is better than sitting around moping over Stella all night.

"Good. I know just the place."

The excitement in Orion's voice should've been warning enough. But just like when we were kids, I find myself happily following along with whatever hair-brained scheme he's cooked up.

And just like when we were kids, I end up regretting it...

"You fucker!" I punch Orion in the shoulder as he pays our cover charge at the door. "You didn't say we were going to a strip club."

Most guys would be down for watching hot women shake their asses, but it's never appealed to me. Especially since there's only one ass I want to get my hands on.

He huffs, shouldering me into the dimly lit club. "ATF is a *gentlemen's* club, Samson. A classy establishment. Plus, I need to scope it out for Ben's bachelor party."

"He's engaged?" I ask, trying like hell to remember if I met his fiancée last night.

Orion rolls his eyes. "Pre-engaged. He plans on asking her any day now."

"That's a thing? Being pre-engaged?"

He nods for me to follow him as he winds his way closer to the stage, and begrudgingly I do. He stops in front of two club chairs with a shared table between them. "This work?"

"I guess."

He drops down into the chair on the left and I claim the one on the right, sliding my phone from my pocket.

As dumb as it sounds, being here feels like I'm cheating on Stella. Which is fucking insane, since we're not together. She's not even speaking to me, and if last night is anything to go off of, she has no desire to.

Still. My guilt is real.

"According to Ben, it is," Orion says as he flags down a scantily clad waitress.

He openly leers at the pretty redhead while ordering us each a beer.

She saunters off, with a wicked sway in her hips. Objectively, she's pretty, and maybe if I'd never met Stella, she'd have caught my eye. But sadly, like the lovestruck fool I am, no one else compares.

"You're really thinking about having Ben's bachelor party here?" I ask once she's out of sight.

"Yeah, seems like as good a place as any. Why? You don't think it's a good idea?"

I shrug. "I don't know. Seems weird to me."

"Weird how? Hot chicks and alcohol... sounds like heaven, man."

"For a single guy, sure. But one who's about to get married probably shouldn't have some random woman's naked tits in his face."

Slowly, Orion nods. "Yeah, you might have a point there."

But before I can say *I told you so*, the music cuts out and the lights flicker. I turn to him with my brows raised in question. He shrugs, as clueless as I am about what's going on.

"ATF, get your wallets ready," the DJ's voice booms

through the club, "because up next is your *all-time favorite,* Birdie!"

Several men vacate their seats in favor of crowding around the stage as the music starts up. Orion and I exchange confused glances as a plucky guitar rhythm resonates through the space.

It's definitely not the kind of music that comes to mind when you think of a stripper, but circumstances aside, it's not bad.

And then the vocals kick in.

"Dude." I nudge Orion with my elbow. "Is that... Britney Spears?"

"It's a cover," he says, his eyes never leaving the stage.

I follow his line of sight to see what has him so transfixed, and while the woman writhing sensuously under the neon lights on the stage does nothing for me, my best friend seems to be totally caught in her snare.

In fact, I'm pretty sure he's two seconds away from rushing the stage and kidnapping her.

Dressed in only a pair of red leather bootie shorts and nipple pasties, the way her body moves seems to defy the laws of physics.

But, she's no Stella.

"Got a little drool," I murmur, nudging him again.

"Shut the fuck up." He bolts up from his seat, and I stand too in case he's actually about to charge the stage.

My worry melts away when he heads for the exit, that is until he makes a sharp turn toward the bar. "Y'all offer private shows?"

The bartender eyes him up like he's a snack. Too bad Orion only likes women, because from the looks this guy is throwing his way, he'd be a sure thing. "Like lap dances? Yeah, we do."

"Does she?" he asks, nodding to the black-haired dancer on the stage.

"Dude." I throw my hands up into the air. "Are you serious?"

"She does." The bartender nods. "Lap, couch, or bed. But no extras."

"Sign. Me. The. Fuck. Up."

I step to the side while Orion puts his name on Birdie's list, scowling all the while. Even if his puppy-like enthusiasm is mildly amusing.

When he's done, he whirls around to face me, a stupid grin on his face. "You want one too? Any of the lovely ladies catch your eye?"

"Nah, man. I'm out."

"You're leaving?" he asks in disbelief.

"I think we both know this isn't my scene." I level him with a glare. "Next time you want to chill, let's actually chill. Being your third wheel at the strip club damn sure isn't my idea of a good time."

"Sorry, man." He has the decency to look remorseful. "I'll see you tomorrow, right? Mom's been asking."

I hesitate before nodding, torn between knowing Stella will be there and also knowing Mrs. C will be too.

Deep down, I know she didn't mean to hurt me. Hell, she wasn't even talking to me, much less about. But words have power, and hers hit me just right.

"Yeah, man. I'll be there."

I'VE SLEPT like shit since coming home—since I left, if I'm being honest—and last night was no different.

If I'm not up all night beating myself up over all the things I could have done differently, then I'm reminiscing about the past, like the sad sap I am.

But this morning, as the clock slowly ticked forward, an epiphany hit me.

Stella isn't just going to let me slide back into her good graces. She's stubborn as hell and is absolutely going to make me work for every inch of ground I gain.

Which is why I'm making a small detour on my way to dinner. I may not remember too much about my birth parents, but I can vividly recall my dad coming home with flowers for my mom every single payday. She would smile and fuss and carry on like he'd given her something precious.

I guess, in a way, he had. Not in the flowers themselves, but in his intention.

Things between Stella and me are murky... my intentions aren't clear. But that's something I intend to change.

She's going to know exactly how serious I am about fixing this goddamn rift I've created, one way or another.

Unfortunately, I've messed things up so badly, I know a pretty bouquet isn't going to cut it—but it sure as hell won't hurt either.

"Welcome to Sweet Peony!" a deep voice calls from somewhere in the shop. "Over here—how can I help you?"

I round the corner to find a man with long dreads arranging a bouquet over a table in the back of the building.

"I need flowers," I say lamely.

He grins. "You're in the right place. Occasion?"

That's a loaded question if there ever was one. "You got anything that says *I know I ruined everything and you hate me, but I still love you and have no plans on giving up?*"

His grin morphs into an all-out blinding smile. "Tricky, but doable."

"Really?"

He nods. "Didn't anybody ever tell you that anything is possible if you just believe?"

"I'm glad one of us is feeling optimistic."

"Do you know her favorite blooms?"

I chuckle. "She actually loves flowers. She has a garden that she tends to damn near obsessively."

"Oh." He hums under his breath. "That changes things. I'm Zach, by the way."

"Samson." I shake his hand. "Nice to meet you."

"You too. Now, what's your budget here?"

I swallow hard. "Budget?"

"Good flowers aren't cheap." Zach raises his brows. "And your girl sounds like she'll know—and appreciate—the difference."

Mentally, I tally my checking account balance, and then

spit out a number. Judging by the awestruck look on Zach's face, it's a good one.

"You must really love her."

I nod. "I do. Oh, and hey! Could you make a small version for her mother?"

"Smart move, my man. Smart move."

Twenty minutes later, I'm at the Cartwrights', hovering on the front porch, wondering if I should knock or just walk in.

Nine months ago, I wouldn't have questioned this—I'd have just walked on in and made myself at home. Because for most of my childhood, this house was my home; or at least more of a home than the Scotts' ever was.

"Fuck it," I mutter as I turn the knob.

The second I step inside, the scent of Mrs. C's cooking tickles my nose. The woman may be a teacher by trade, but she could easily put most of the local diners to shame with her food.

"Orion," she calls from the kitchen, "is that you?"

"No, ma'am." I enter the room.

"Samson Carter!" She shucks off her oven mitts, races around the island, but I stop her before she can hug me, pulling one of the bouquets out from behind my back. "You little charmer! When did you get back?"

"A few days ago."

She grabs a vase from below the sink and fills it with water. "Thank you, these are lovely."

"You're welcome."

"Have you seen Orion already? Oh, Stella's going to be so happy. She's been in a funk ever since you left."

I swallow roughly at the mention of Stella. If only Mrs. C knew the real reason for her daughter's sadness.

"I'm looking forward to seeing her."

She spots the second bouquet. "Are those for her?"

I nod.

"She's in her room. Why don't you go up and take them to her?"

"Okay." An anxious shiver works its way through me.

"Don't take too long—dinner is almost ready."

As I climb the stairs, I only have one thing on my mind —getting Stella to forgive me. Or at the very least, to make her *consider* forgiving me. Baby steps and what-not.

I rap my knuckles against her bedroom door and wait.

"Come in."

I push the door open and lean my shoulder against the frame. "Luna."

"Are you freaking kidding me?" She whips around to face me, her lips curled in an angry snarl. "Why are you here?"

"To give you these." I start to pull the flowers from behind my back, but Stella doesn't give me a chance.

"No." She stalks over to me. "Why are you *here*, in my house?"

"Last I checked, I have an open invitation."

She mimics the words back to me and rolls her eyes. "Well, the last I checked, that was before you shoved a knife into my back."

"I got you something," I murmur, pointedly ignoring her animosity.

"What?"

I pull the flowers from behind my back, loving the ways her eyes widen at the colorful display.

"Oh, wow. These are beautiful." She crosses the room

and snatches the bouquet from me. "But you're still a double-crossing piece of crap liar."

I press my right hand over my heart. "Tell me how you really feel, Luna."

"Don't call me that."

"There's a letter for you tucked in there."

"A letter?" She blinks.

"That's what I said."

She snorts. "Hard pass."

"I get that you're mad, and you have every right to be."

"Damn straight I do."

"But I really think we need to talk—"

"The only thing we need to talk about is you staying the hell away from me. You did it so wonderfully for the last nine months." Stella shoves past me, knocking her shoulder into my chest. "Now, keep it up... I don't know... *forever.*"

With a parting smile that's as cold as ice, she turns and flees down the stairs, taking them two at a time.

I'm not so dumb that I thought an *I'm sorry, please forgive me,* would be enough to get back into her good graces, but I wasn't prepared for her to totally ice me out either.

I guess I should have expected it, but hope makes a fool out of us all from time to time.

But it's all good. I love her stubborn ass and I know full and well that she's more than worth whatever hell she's going to put me through to win her back.

I take a minute to recenter, and by the time I make it back downstairs, everyone is gathered around the table, ready and waiting.

"Can we eat?" Stella asks, her voice reaching the landing.

"Not until Samson joins us."

She sinks back into her chair. "Whatever."

"Sorry to keep y'all waiting," I say, sliding into the chair beside Orion as I take in the spread. "Looks as good as it smells, Mrs. C."

Lizzie beams, while her daughter scoffs.

"We're all glad to have you home, son," Michael says, a smile I can't quite read carving his lips.

"Can we eat *now*?"

"Stella!" Lizzie admonishes. "You're being rude."

She rolls her eyes and then glares at me, as though I'm the sole cause of every bad thing in the world. "So?"

Her mom sighs. "I know you were hurt when—"

Stella shoves her chair back from the table with enough force her place setting rattles.

"What are you doing?"

"I'm not hungry," she growls before turning and fleeing back to the safety of her room.

"Must be on her period," Orion says, scooping a heaping portion of mashed potatoes onto his plate.

"Don't talk like that at the table!" Lizzie screeches, her cheeks turning as red as the tomatoes in the salad.

"Or about your sister," Michael adds, but my best friend only shrugs.

"Always nice to be with family," I murmur, hoping to break the tension, but the only person who laughs is Orion.

"Let's... let's just eat," Lizzie says.

The four of us take turns loading our plates with food before digging in. We eat in an awkward silence—something that never happens at the Cartwright table—and I can't help but wonder if the food I was looking so forward to tastes like ash to them as well.

"Samson," Michael says after polishing off his last bite.

"I hope you'll join us at the lake for our end-of-summer getaway?"

I pretend to mull it over, knowing good and well that I'm going to go. "Yeah, I can come down."

"Good." Michael nods, his gaze boring into mine.

I'm certain if given the choice, Stella would rather me drown in the lake than to spend the weekend with me, but I'm not about to pass on the chance of scoring some one-on-one time with her. Even if I have to lock her ass in the boathouse and make her talk to me.

"HE'S NOT EVEN HERE and he's ruining it," I grumble to myself as I strip out of my wet swimsuit and step under the warm spray of the shower.

While everyone else had a good time today, I sulked and watched the driveway. Even now, as I wash the lake water from my hair, I can't decide if I'm angry he didn't show or relieved.

Definitely relieved.

His sudden reappearance in my life is like a slap in the face—one that still stings weeks later. To make matters even worse, he looks good. Damn good. Certainly not like he's been missing me the way I have him.

But that's fine. It's fine. "Everything is fine." I speak the last words out loud, hoping the universe will hear them and cut me some slack.

I mean, really. Right when I was finally starting to get over him—at least that's what I'm telling myself—there he was, crashing back into my life, unwanted and unwelcome.

And now, I've been avoiding both him and my brother—

because where there's smoke, there's fire and I'm so damn tired of Samson burning me.

"Stop thinking about him," I chide myself as I rinse the conditioner from my hair. "You're going to get a good night's sleep and tomorrow, you won't think about him. Not even once."

"Think about who?" a decidedly male and agonizingly familiar voice asks.

"What in the hell!" I shout, scrambling to turn off the water.

How did he even get here? Was I that zoned out?

"You okay, Stelli Bear?" my dad asks from somewhere outside the bathroom.

"Yup." My voice comes out shrill. "Totally good. Just saw a bug."

He chuckles. "For someone who loves playing in the dirt, you sure do have an aversion to insects."

I force out a laugh. "'Night, Dad, love you."

He murmurs a soft reply before shuffling down the stairs.

With shaking hands, I yank the towel down from where it's draped over the curtain rod and wrap it around my shivering, wet body before tearing the curtain open. "What in God's name are you doing in here, Samson?"

To his credit, his eyes stay on my face. "We need to talk."

I glare at him, torn between wanting to slap his handsome face and kiss his stupid mouth. "And you thought this seemed like a good place?"

He glances down at his feet and mumbles something.

"I'm sorry, what?"

Samson swallows, and I find myself mesmerized by the

bobbing of his Adam's apple. "I said at least you can't run away."

"I guess I learned from the best," I hiss. "Because last I checked, running away was your specialty." My anger and hurt swirl together inside of me, like a living, breathing thing. "You have no right—"

"I know!" He pleads with his eyes for me to understand. "I know I don't. But I'm asking anyway. Please, Luna."

"Don't call me that." I clutch the towel tighter to my chest.

"It's who you are to me," he says unapologetically. "Who you'll always be."

I roll my eyes and swallow down the nasty reply begging to break free.

"Get dressed so we can talk." He takes a step closer to me. "Please?"

"Get out and I will."

He scoffs. "So you can escape? Nah, I'm good."

Slap... I definitely want to slap him.

"Look, I'll turn around, okay?"

"Ugh. Whatever." I quickly dry off before grabbing my pajamas, which are thankfully on the toilet seat and not on the counter, which he's leaning his hip against like he hasn't a care in the freaking world.

I pull my soft sleep shorts up my legs, tug on the matching bralette, and frown. I may as well have stayed naked for how well these cover me. And of course, my robe is in my room.

"You done, Luna? It's late and I'd like to get some sleep."

"By all means, go. Go sleep. I'm not stopping you."

"That mouth," he murmurs, the low, raspy sound sends

a bolt of lust right between my thighs. "I'm turning around in five whether you're dressed or not. Five... four... three..."

"Give it a freaking rest, I've got clothes on."

Samson whirls around and immediately chokes on his tongue when he sees me. "Fucking barely," he growls, his eyes practically bulging out of their sockets.

Despite still being wet, my entire body heats under his appraisal. He looks almost feral, like he's barely restraining himself from reaching for me, as he takes me in. The sad thing is, even though I'm furious with him, if he were to make his move right now... I'd probably let him.

"Are we going to talk in here or can we maybe go some-where with a little more space?"

He cracks the door open and pokes his head out. Once he's satisfied that the coast is clear, he opens it fully and ushers me through. "After you."

I brush past him, making sure to put a little extra sway in my hips as I lead him down the hall to my room, where we'll be totally alone.

He groans and I grin. A case of blue balls is the least he owes me.

"Are you sure this is a good idea?" he asks as I climb up onto my bed.

I snuggle down into the covers and toss him an unim-pressed look. "I don't know, Samson. Was ambushing me while I was naked in the shower a good idea?"

"Well, last time I tried talking to you didn't go so well."

I gasp, pressing my right hand over my heart. "You mean when you cornered me at a party and demanded to know if I was drinking?" I scrunch my nose. "I already have an older brother... not really in the market for another."

He growls and steps closer to the bed. So close his knees brush the mattress. "Not your fucking brother."

"Or do you mean at dinner the other night when you brought me flowers, like they'd fix everything you broke?" I rub my head against my pillow until it's just right. "I threw them away... in case you were wondering."

A lie—I kept them on my bedside table until they wilted and died, but he doesn't need to know that.

"Did you even read the letter?"

"Yep, read every single word."

"And?" he asks, his expression stupidly hopeful.

"And not a single thing you wrote down is enough to erase the hurt you caused. Words on a page don't mean a thing—"

He's on me in a flash, with one knee pressed onto the bed and his arms caging me against the headboard. "Cut the shit, Luna."

I tremble at his nearness, at the fierce look in his eyes, at the way he looks like he wants to devour me whole.

"Samson," I whisper his name, and it's like something inside of him snaps. He lunges for me, claiming my lips in a bruising kiss.

I should push him away, tell him to leave, to stay away from me. I should scream and shout until my dad comes up here and throws him out.

I know I should, and yet the second our lips meet, all the reasons I'm mad at him slip away, leaving me full of an aching need that only his touch can fix.

His tongue swipes over the seam of my lips, begging for entry and like the stupid lovesick girl I am, I open to him.

He slides his tongue into my mouth, tangling it with my own as he climbs fully onto the bed, settling his broad body between my legs. I can feel his erection, even through all of the layers separating us.

I slide my hands through his too-long hair, tugging on

the strands in pleasure when he nips at my lower lip.

He breaks our kiss, moving his attention to my jaw and neck. "Fuck, Luna," he murmurs against my lust-drenched skin. "You feel so good."

I whimper and he presses his hips harder into mine, rolling them in a way that has me shifting and squirming in search of the release my body so desperately craves.

We move together in torturous harmony; our bodies in sync even if *we* aren't.

"Stella." The way he moans my name, deep and low, sends a shiver rolling through me. "Tell me to stop," he pleads, brushing his nose along the column of my neck.

"I can't." I exhale a shaky breath and draw his lips back to mine. "Just kiss me. Kiss me like there isn't an ocean of hurt between us. Kiss me like I'm the only thing that matters."

His brow creases as he cups my cheek, his calloused fingers tickling my skin. "Don't you get it, Luna? You *are* the only thing that matters." His lips feather over mine, but before he can deepen the kiss, I push him away.

He goes willingly, rolling so that he's sitting on the edge of the bed with his feet planted on the floor. "Stella."

I give him a sad smile. "You should go."

With a slow, resigned nod, Samson stands, not bothering to hide the way his erection strains against his jeans. "This isn't over," he says, heading for the door.

I pull the covers up to my chin. "It never started."

After a night of fitful sleep, I'm up with the sun. My dreams were plagued by memories of the man I used to love... that I still love, if I'm being honest. But I've been lying to myself for the last nine months, that I was over him, so why stop now?

One kiss—one soul-shattering kiss—isn't going to change the irreparable damage between us.

We had a plan... an agreement. A promise, and he broke it when he left me.

My body may be eager for his touch, but my heart remembers the pain he left in his wake.

I'm not prone to making the smartest decisions when it comes to Samson Carter. He makes me crazy and desperate and reckless.

Which is why I'm up before everyone else. Avoidance is the name of the game; he can't corner me if he can't find me.

I crawl out of bed and swap my pajamas for a two-piece swimsuit and a pair of jean shorts before tiptoeing to the bathroom to brush my teeth. I throw my hair up into a messy bun and toss my flip-flops into my bag so they don't make noise while I sneak down the stairs.

I'm tempted to make a pot of coffee, but with the guest bedroom being on the first floor, I decide not to risk it. I leave a quick note for my parents and then slip out the back door.

It's not even six in the morning and it feels like it's a million degrees outside, but the destination I have in mind is tucked away, with plenty of shade. It's perfect for a lazy day of hiding... *I mean relaxing.*

The cold lake water tickles my toes as I creep down the shore to where we store our canoes. I grab the first one I see and pull it behind me. Once I'm knee-deep, I climb in.

My oar slices through the water, as I think about everything and nothing all at once. My brain feels like it's going to explode, like I need a sign on my forehead—*caution, contents under pressure.*

After about fifteen minutes, I reach my destination, a little island in the middle of the lake. I paddle as far in as I can before hopping out and dragging the canoe to shore.

I heft my bag over my shoulder, stopping only to slide on my sandals, before venturing into the brush until I find *my* spot.

It's nothing special, just a pile of big rocks, but it's my favorite place at the lake. And more importantly, it's private.

I grab my towel and Kindle, settling in for a day of reading. But before I can finish the first chapter, a shadow falls over me.

"Are you freaking kidding me?" I shout as I set my Kindle down onto the flat rock beside me.

"I said we needed to talk."

"Pretty sure we proved we aren't capable of talking, so maybe we should just stay away from each other."

"I can't stay away from you."

I tap my index finger against my chin. "Could have fooled me."

"Stella," he says my name, as calm as ever.

"Just go!" I shout, my voice echoing all around us. The leash on my emotions is slipping and he needs to leave before I lose it entirely.

"I brought you something."

I follow his gaze as it lowers down to a small cooler resting on the ground at his feet. How he managed to sneak up on me—again—is beyond comprehension.

Closing my eyes, I slowly inhale, fighting against the urge to go off on him. It's not like it would help; he's as stubborn as a mule.

"Fine."

He grins victoriously as he bends to grab something from inside the cooler.

"Is that... coffee?" I ask.

He nods. "I watched you leave without it."

I blink. "You watched me?"

Another nod.

"Do you realize how creepy that sounds?"

Samson widens his stance and crosses his arms over his broad chest. "If you're looking for an apology, you aren't going to get one."

"Clearly." I take a sip of the still piping hot coffee, sighing when I realize he's made it exactly the way I like it.

It's on the tip of my tongue to mention it, but I swallow it down along with another sip. Who cares if he remembers that I like my coffee creamy and sweet? A little bit of cream and sugar doesn't make up for him leaving.

"You said you came out here to talk, so talk."

He reaches down and plucks the mug from between my fingers before lifting me clear into the air. "Samson!" I kick and holler, but he ignores me as he settles down onto my rock.

"What the hell do you think you're doing?" I wriggle like a fish on a hook, trying to break his hold on me but he bands his arms tighter around my waist.

"Stop moving," he growls, burying his face into the crook of my shoulder.

"Let me go!"

"Not happening. We both know this is the only way I can guarantee you won't try to get away from me."

"Or, you could just take a hint and leave me alone."

"Why can't you just see you're mine?"

My eyes bug, because seriously, he didn't just say that. "I'm not yours."

"You will be." He sounds so sure of himself that I almost just give in.

And then I remember all the nights I cried myself to sleep, soaking my pillow with my tears. "In your dreams."

Samson shifts me ever so slightly, pressing a soft kiss to my neck. "Every night, Luna."

Against my better judgment, I sigh and relax back into him. "Just say what you came to say."

A beat of silence passes. "I missed you. I know you don't believe me, but I really did..." he trails off, and then adds, "I thought I was doing the right thing."

"You thought leaving me the night before we were going to tell my brother about us was the right thing?" I grab his wrists and tug out of his hold. "You're either clueless or an idiot."

"Maybe a little bit of both, but I want us to get back to where we were."

"I don't trust you," I whisper, my eyes filling with tears as I crawl out of his lap and stand.

"Let me show you, Stella. Let me prove that I'm worthy of your trust. Of your heart. I swear it, just..."

"How?"

"Give me time," he pleads, his eyes so full of hope.

"What if I said I wanted to go talk to Orion right now?"

Right before my very eyes, Samson's entire body tenses. His jaw pulses and he balls his hands into tight fists.

I let out a dry laugh. "That's what I thought." I shove my Kindle into my bag, not caring about my towel trapped under him. I need to go. To get away from him. And I'll gladly sacrifice some terrycloth to make my escape back to the lake house, where I can hide in my room, which has a door with a lock. "Good to see nothing's changed."

He looks up at me with sad eyes. "It feels like everything has..."

I WASN'T LYING when I told Stella I felt like everything had changed. Gone was the sweet, carefree girl I fell in love with, and in her place is this wild, sexy, angry woman.

Somehow over the last nine months, my Stella grew the hell up and now I'm not sure I know how to handle her. But if she thinks I'm going to give up, that I'm going to walk away—again—she's dead wrong.

It's been a week since the disaster at the lake and I spent all seven days of it trying to figure out a reason to see her again. I thought about just stopping by, since I have an open invitation but after how well my last few attempts to talk to her went, I probably need a better plan.

"How's work?" Orion asks, dragging me out of my thoughts as he cracks open a fresh beer and drops down into the chair beside me on my porch.

"Same as yours but bigger." I smirk, knowing my reply will irritate him. The fucker is competitive as hell and too easy to rile up. Sometimes Stella and I used to take turns, seeing who could make him snap the quickest.

"We use the same tools, dipshit."

"Right, sure. Mine are just bigger."

"Jackass," he mutters, wising up to my game. "You always do this."

"And you always fall for it."

He rolls his eyes and sinks deeper into the chair. "So how was your weekend?"

"What do you mean?" I know damn well what he means, but maybe if I play dumb, he'll drop it.

"You literally spent one night at the lake and then dipped. I saw you for like five minutes and Stella was in a pissy mood and stayed up in her room pretty much the whole time." He pins me with a glare and for a heart-stopping second, I think he's on to me. "Y'all left me alone. With my parents. All weekend. Not cool."

My pulse slowly returns to normal. "Sorry, man. I wasn't feeling too good."

"I thought you had to work." He tilts his head to the side, narrowing his eyes.

I rub at the back of my neck. "Yeah, that's what I meant. I felt bad I had to leave. To go to work."

"Anyone ever tell you that you're a shit liar?"

I lean back into my chair and tilt my head his way. "Once or twice."

Orion's gaze intensifies. "Holy shit!" He's looking at me like he can see my soul. It's unnerving, and not at all the way I wanted this to go down. "Who is she?"

"I can explain—"

He cuts me off, grinning. *Why in the hell does he look so happy right now, I figured he'd want to knock my lights out.* "I bet you can. You're obviously seeing someone." He steeples his fingers under his chin. "The question is who?"

"No one."

He lifts a brow, but I hold steady.

He tips his chin up at me, a sly look in his eyes, like he knows that I have a secret and he's happy to help me keep it. "It's on the down-low. Got it."

I cough to hide my surprise. This conversation is so close to reality—*too close*—that it's not even funny. "Got plans this weekend?"

"Not much. I'm meeting with Ben in a few hours to go over a project and I've gotta help Stella move some furniture at some point. Oh!" He smirks. "And I'm hitting up ATF tonight. You wanna come?"

"Pass." I lean forward in disbelief. "You're still hung up on Birdie?"

"Hell yeah. She's..." he trails off.

I want so badly to give him shit over being hung up on his stripper, but I'm not any better with the way his little sister has me tied in knots.

"Laugh all you want. I'm going to marry that girl."

"You know, right after you learn her real name."

"Fucker," he mutters right as his phone rings. He swipes his finger across the screen and brings the phone to his ear. "What's up, Smalls?"

He cringes, and then asks, "Any way we can do it tomorrow?"

I slide my phone out of my pocket and tap around on the screen, trying to act like I'm not listening to their conversation. Well, the side of it I can hear anyway.

"No, I know I said I'd help you." He snaps his index finger and thumb together. "I've got it. Don't worry, Smalls. We'll get it done."

He ends the call and turns to me. "I need a favor."

"What?"

"Stella needs me to help her at four, but I'll still be with Ben. Could you..."

"Help your sister?" I nod, playing it cool. "Sure."

"You're a lifesaver. I already moved the meeting with Ben once."

"You know y'all live together, right?"

Orion shrugs. "He's weird about these things, likes to keep work separate from pleasure, or some shit."

"Whatever works. Just let me know where to be for Stella and I'll be there."

"Thanks, man." He forwards me the info. "I owe you one."

I wonder how he'd feel if he knew my true motives?

"What are you doing here?" Stella asks before I can even fully exit my truck.

"How about *thank you Samson for coming to help me, that's so nice!*"

She glares. "How about I didn't ask for your help, so please get back in your truck and leave."

I nudge the door shut with my hip and then lean back against it, crossing my arms over my chest. "How are you going to get... whatever that is home?"

"*That,*" she says, all sass, "is going to be a greenhouse for my dorm room."

My lips twitch; at least her love for plants hasn't changed. "It's not going to fit in your car."

"I'll figure it out." She crosses her arms over her chest, mirroring my pose.

"Or you could just let me help. I'm already here."

"Why are you here?" Understanding dawns. "Orion sent you. He couldn't be bothered to help me, so he freaking sent you."

"It's not like that. Well. It is, kind of. He has to meet with Ben for work shit so he asked me."

She sighs, her eyes flitting from me to the large cabinet on the curb, and back to me again. "Fine! Put it in your truck."

I give her a mock salute as I walk around to the back of my truck to lower the tailgate. "Tell me more about this greenhouse thing, because right now, all I see is a cabinet that's seen better days."

She fidgets with the chain around her neck. I can't help but follow the movement, like a hawk watching its prey.

Holy fuck. Holy. Fuck. There, clutched between her thumb and index finger is the ring I gave her.

My mind races as hope inflates inside of me like a balloon. If she hated me, she wouldn't be wearing it in any capacity, right?

Which means... if I play my cards right, I just might stand a chance.

"It's something I saw on a plant blog," she murmurs, drawing my focus back to the task at hand. "It's stupid."

She nibbles her lower lip. "You really mean that?"

"I do."

I can see the battle playing out across her face—she's torn between opening up to me and telling me to fuck off.

"Ugh." She rolls her pretty blue eyes. "It's exactly what it sounds like—a greenhouse for plants. Or at least it will be after some TLC." Her smile grows bigger the more she talks about it. "It will be climate controlled and everything."

"That's pretty cool, Luna."

"Yeah, it's a way to have a little piece of home away from home, you know?"

"Are you excited to live on campus?"

"I'm excited to experience life."

My throat works as I try to swallow down all of my regrets. I went from assuming she'd experience life with me, to worrying I was holding her back. But here she is moving on like it's nothing. And the worst part is, it's my fucking fault.

"Anyway, I need to fix it up... tighten some screws, paint it, install the lighting, and make a distiller unit."

"You have all the stuff you need?" I ask, hoping like hell for this to be my in.

"Not yet."

I decide to shoot my shot. "Why don't we drop the cabinet and your car off and then maybe I can take you to get what you need?"

"I mean..." She hesitates and I know I missed. "I was just going to order most of it online."

"Oh. Okay."

She gives me a small smile. "But maybe..."

"Maybe what?" I sound like an over-eager puppy, but fuck if I care. If she's willing to give me an inch, I'm damn sure going to try and make it a mile.

"Maybe I could text you a picture of it when it's done?"

"Luna, you can text me any damn time, for any damn thing."

"Thanks, Samson." She smiles brighter than the sun before inhaling a deep breath. "And maybe we could grab an early dinner. My treat, you know, to thank you."

Hell yes, my heart hollers, doing a mental fist pump. "Sure thing, Luna, but *my* treat. You know if you go anywhere with me, I'm paying."

"You're insufferable." She doesn't mean it as a compliment, but I take it as one all the same. The fact that she's agreeing to share a meal with me feels like a victory in and of itself.

I shake my head and smile. "Go on, I'll meet you back at your place and then we can go eat. Purple Daisy?"

"Mmm, yes please." She saunters back toward her car. "But, Samson, this doesn't mean I've forgiven you."

I nod, knowing that much already. "That's fair, but it feels like I've got a foot in the door."

She rolls her eyes and pulls out her keys. "Watch it or I'll slam the damn door *on* your foot."

"Drive safe, Luna."

"You too."

<hr>

"Where are you living now?" Stella asks, looking so damn pretty sitting shotgun in my truck, that it's a struggle not to stare at her and hope for the best.

Eyes on the road, I scold myself for the hundredth time. "Not too far from here."

She laughs and I tighten my grip on the wheel to keep from reaching out and touching her. "Vague much?"

"That mouth, Luna." That mouth combined with her body and brain, she's the full fucking package and I'm the dumbass lucky enough to bask in her light.

"Still waiting..." she singsongs.

"Got a place in the North Shore area."

"Oh, that's nice. You should show—" She clamps her mouth shut.

"What was that?" I'm grinning like a motherfucker, because I *know* she was about to ask me to show her my house. I'm half-tempted to push the issue, but she's barely tolerating my presence as it is, so I table it for another day. The last thing I want is to piss her off... again.

"Hmm. Nothing."

"You ready for dorm life?"

She perks up in her seat. "Yeah, I'm really excited. I can't wait to meet my roommate!"

"You might be the only person excited about living in a small ass dorm room."

"Samson." She drags my name out in that way of hers that's always made me smile. "I'm ready to have a social life."

Guilt pricks at me. Between spending time with me and Orion's overbearing ass, she never really had friends her own age. She just had... us. And while I was happy to monopolize her time, I also know I'm part of the reason she's missed out on so much.

"Still majoring in education?" I ask, pulling into the small parking lot.

She laughs. "A lot changed while you were gone, but not that much. I think my parents would have a coronary if I told them I was majoring in something else."

"Hold that thought." I kill the engine, climb out of the truck, and race around to her side to open the door for her. "I think your parents would support you no matter what."

She tilts her head to the right and then to the left. "Yeah, you're probably right, but I really do want to do this. To teach."

"You'll be good at it."

"You think?"

"I know. Some people are just meant for kids, and you're one of them." *I always imagined we'd have a whole bunch.*

job I signed on to. I. Fucked. Up. But, Luna, I'll never stop trying. You're it for me and I don't care if it takes the rest of my life to prove it to you."

She wipes her eyes and inhales a shuddery breath. "Let's just start with the nachos."

HOLY CRAP—TODAY'S *move-in day!*

"Are you sure I can't drive you?" Mom asks, wrapping an arm around my shoulder.

I clutch my keys tighter in my palm and smile up at her. "I'm sure."

"But won't you need help moving everything in?"

"Orion's bringing my cabinet by later, and the rest is just a few bags and boxes. I've got it."

Mom sighs and glances at the clock. She, like all of the women in our family for generations back, is a teacher at one of the local elementary schools. She typically leaves the house at seven-fifteen on the dot and it's already half past.

"You'll still come home to visit, right?"

"I'm literally going to be five minutes away."

She pulls me from her side into a full-blown hug. "I know, but you're my baby."

And therein lies the problem—I *am* the baby. Mom and Dad's baby girl. Orion's baby sister. My small stature doesn't help either. I'm so tired of being the baby. I'm ready to just be Stella.

"You'll still see me all the time."

"I know." She sniffles and presses a kiss to the top of my head before pulling away. "I don't want to leave you."

"It's okay, Mom. I'm good. I'm gonna grab breakfast and then head over to campus."

"Text me once you're there?"

"I will." I hug her again and then walk her to the door.

"And after you meet your roommate."

"I will, Mom."

"And let me know if you need anything."

My lips twitch. "I will, Mom."

"You can come home anytime, okay?"

I lose the battle and my smile breaks free. "I know, Mom, now go or you'll be late."

"Okay," she sighs as she opens the front door. "I love you, Stella."

"Love you too," I murmur, closing it behind her.

Dad and I said our goodbyes last night after he helped me load the bulk of my stuff into my car. He's a big ball of mush and left for work early this morning to avoid watching me leave.

God bless my parents; you'd think I was headed to an out-of-state school and not right down the road. They mean well though, and they love me; even if their love is a little smothering at times.

I bound up the stairs to my room. It's looked the same since middle school, with soft pink walls, pink bedding, and white wicker furniture. It's fine—for a little girl. My tastes have matured a bit since then, so needless to say, when my dad handed me his credit card and told me to get everything I needed for my dorm, I went a little overboard.

Excitement zips through me at the thought of setting up

my room. Sure, it's small and I'll be sharing the space with a stranger, but it will be mine, and that's all that matters.

I give my childhood room one last look, cringing at the explosion of pink before grabbing my purse and laptop. In the kitchen, I scribble a note for my parents on the chalkboard, telling them I love them, and then, I'm out the door and on my way.

To college. *Holy crap! I'm going to college!*

I wipe my hands on my shorts and stand back and assess my work. The oversized purple duvet looks like a dream and my string lights give the small room a cheery glow. But it's the pictures of my family and garden on the wall that I really love.

Because for all my whining about becoming independent, they're still an integral part of me.

My phone dings with an incoming text and I dig it out of my back pocket.

ORION

I'm here. What number again?

ME

303

Five minutes later, there's a knock on my door. I rush through the suite to let Orion in.

"Where do you want this thing?"

"In my room. Back wall, right corner."

He nods and wheels my cabinet in on his dolly, expertly navigating around the furniture in the living area. "What is this thing anyway?"

"A greenhouse."

My brother rolls his eyes. "Only you, Smalls."

"Shut up." I nudge him with my shoulder.

"You shut up." He returns the gesture. "This place is pretty sweet."

"Right?" I bounce on the balls of my feet as another burst of excitement surges through me.

"You met your roommate yet? Is she hot?"

"No, I don't know, and so help me God, you will stay away from her."

"Why? Scared she'll fall for me?"

"More like scared you'll break her heart and then make my entire time here with her unbearable."

He shrugs. "Same thing."

"You're such a dog."

"What?" He cups a hand around his ear. "I'm the best big brother ever? Thanks, Smalls."

"Yeah, yeah. Love you."

He flicks my forehead. "Back atcha. Be good."

"I'll be as good as you," I tease, knowing it'll rile him up.

"Fuck that. You act like me and I'll have Mom and Dad haul your ass home quicker than you can blink."

"You know you have to let me grow up one day, right?"

My brother grins. "But not today."

"Whatever."

"Catch ya later," he says and as soon as he's gone, I race back to my room to set up my greenhouse.

Once I have it up and running and every plant placed just so, I snap a few pictures for Instagram.

And maybe one for Samson. He *did* say I could send him a pic once it was complete, right? So, it's not like I'll look crazy.

I take a deep breath, attach it to a text and send it before I can chicken out.

Not even a minute later, he replies.

SAMSON

Was starting to think you forgot about me.

I snort to myself. *If only.* But forgetting him is like holding your breath—you're fine for a few seconds, maybe even a minute or two, but before you know, you're gasping for air, sucking it down by the lungful.

I guess because for so long, he was my air. My light. My whole freaking world. I want so badly to remain hard—to stand my ground and not let him back in.

He deserves it, but damn if I don't feel myself softening, even if I don't actually want to.

ME

Nope, just been busy. It looks good, right?

SAMSON

Bet it's even better in person.

I bite my lip, wondering if I'm reading too much into his text.

ME

It totally is...

ME

You could come see it... if you want.

Regret instantly presses down on my chest. I can't believe I just invited him over, especially when I'm not even sure if I've forgiven him.

I know he thinks—or thought, I guess—that he was

doing the right thing, but at the same time, I'm not sure how to move past him leaving me.

Or if I ever will, and stringing him along will only end in heartache for the both of us.

When minutes pass and he doesn't reply, I know I read too far into his text.

I feel foolish. Like a stupid lovesick girl chasing after the cool older guy who thinks she's *cute*. Maybe he left because he finally realized he wanted someone more mature. Someone his own age.

Maybe he doesn't regret it at all.

Maybe all of his apologies are empty, meaningless words because he doesn't want things to be weird between us for Orion's sake.

But that kiss at the lake, my subconscious unhelpfully adds. But people can kiss without commitment. It's probably just another thing I read too far into.

Or maybe he's just busy and I'm overreacting?

All I know is I put myself out there and have nothing other than red-hot embarrassment to show for it.

"Don't let him ruin today." I press my thumbs to my eyes, physically holding back my tears. "Don't cry over him. He's not worth it."

I take a calming breath and count back from ten in my head before tossing my phone down onto my bed. I have time to kill and a dorm building to explore.

I feel calmer after checking the entire building. I'm still mad at him—and at myself for jumping the gun—but I don't want to cry into my pillow anymore. I meant it when I said he wasn't worth my tears. No man is and until he can show me that he's serious about us, he can fuck right off.

Outside of my suite, I hesitate, wondering if I should knock. I don't want to be rude, but it's my place too...

I unlock the door and swing it open. Sure enough, there's a beautiful brunette standing in the bedroom to the right. "You must be Emmalyn."

She freezes before slowly looking my way. She's taller than I am, most people are, but it's her eyes that really stand out. They have this haunted look in them that makes my heart thump a little harder in my chest.

"Um. Em-Emmy is fine," she mumbles, not quite making eye contact.

I smile my brightest smile. "Nice to meet you, Emmy. I'm Stella."

She fidgets with the hem of her sweatshirt. "It's nice to meet you too."

Her shoulders curl in as I appraise her, like she's trying to make herself less noticeable, which is an impossible feat, because the girl is gorgeous.

She doesn't seem pretentious like a lot of the girls I went to high school with. If anything, she seems shy—painfully so.

Something tells me we're going to be good friends.

"Sweet. Do you need any help bringing the rest of your stuff up?"

She lowers her gaze and swallows. "Um, no. I... this is pretty much it."

I glance down at the two bags at her feet. *Maybe she put her stuff up already? Or maybe she's a minimalist.* Either way, it's not my place to judge her.

"Well, what are you doing then?"

"The tech center," she blurts out, her cheeks burning bright. "I need to, uh, go there and get my student ID card."

"Perfect. Me too. Let's go!" I grab her wrist and pull her up from her bed. "C'mon, we can grab a bite to eat after."

"So, where are you from?"

Emmy shuffles along behind me. "Texas."

"Long way from home." I can't imagine being that far away from home. "Won't you miss your family?"

She hesitates. "I'll manage."

Gah! Shy or not, this girl's a total badass! "You're stronger than me. I've lived here in Central Valley for my entire life. My parents literally live like five minutes away."

Emmy's nose scrunches. "Then why are you living on campus?"

I laugh and call the elevator. "Wanted the full college experience. These are supposed to be the best years of our lives, right?"

"That's what they say," Emmy replies dryly.

A fuzzy feeling rushes through me as I push the button for the ground floor. It's like my blood is suddenly carbonated in my veins, popping and fizzing as it flows through me.

It's almost like fate put us in each other's paths. I believe that with all my heart; don't ask why, I just do.

I smile at Emmy as the elevator doors open. She doesn't know it yet, but we're going to be best friends.

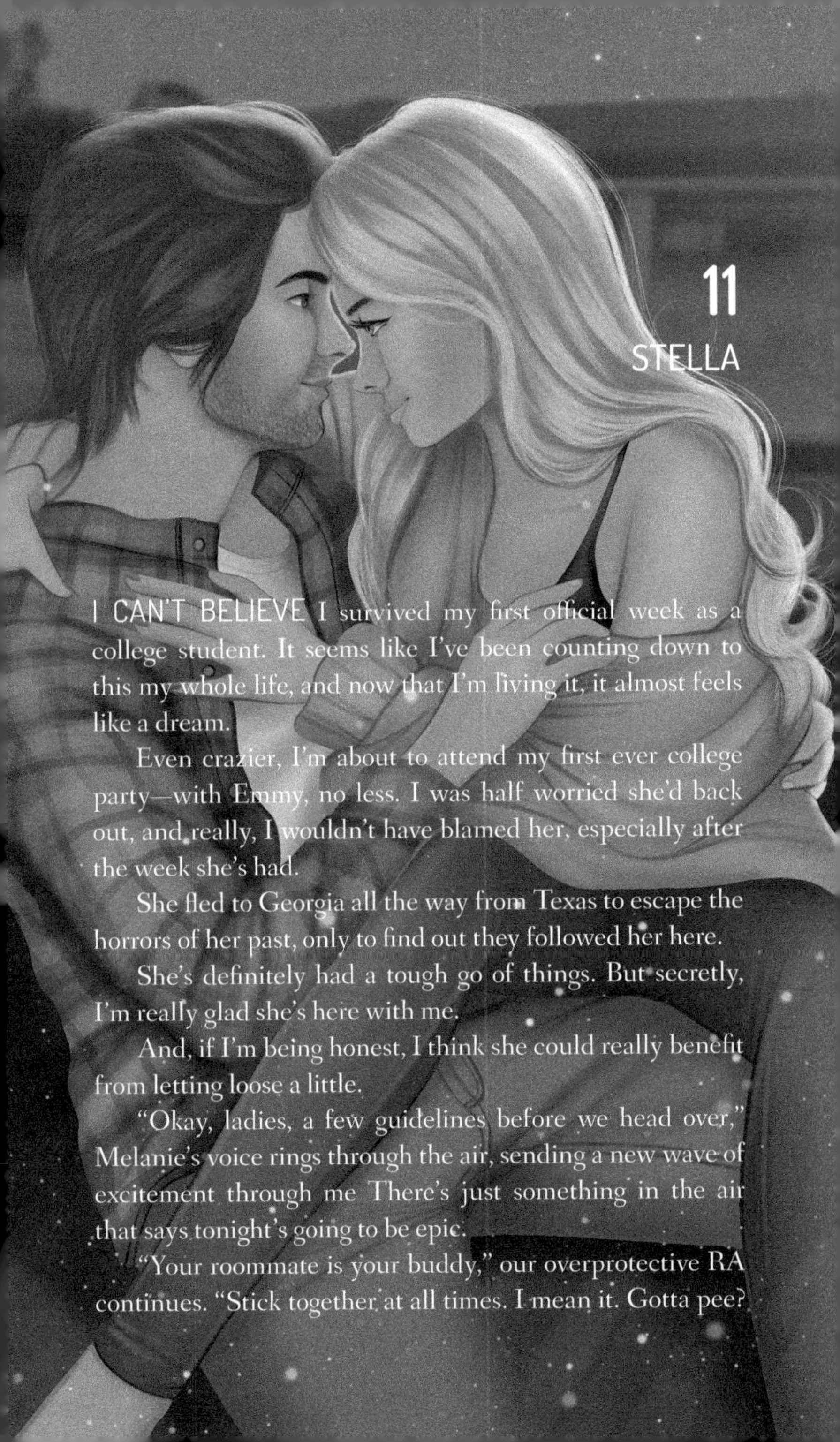

I CAN'T BELIEVE I survived my first official week as a college student. It seems like I've been counting down to this my whole life, and now that I'm living it, it almost feels like a dream.

Even crazier, I'm about to attend my first ever college party—with Emmy, no less. I was half worried she'd back out, and really, I wouldn't have blamed her, especially after the week she's had.

She fled to Georgia all the way from Texas to escape the horrors of her past, only to find out they followed her here.

She's definitely had a tough go of things. But secretly, I'm really glad she's here with me.

And, if I'm being honest, I think she could really benefit from letting loose a little.

"Okay, ladies, a few guidelines before we head over," Melanie's voice rings through the air, sending a new wave of excitement through me There's just something in the air that says tonight's going to be epic.

"Your roommate is your buddy," our overprotective RA continues. "Stick together at all times. I mean it. Gotta pee?

Go together. Gotta puke? Go together. Found a hottie you want to hook up with? Well, maybe don't bring a friend, then, unless that's your thing."

I wrinkle my nose. To each their own and all, but for someone who hasn't even punched their V-card, a threesome is definitely not on the table.

"I'm technically supposed to tell y'all not to drink, but I'm not an idiot. So, while I am heavily suggesting that you not, keep these tidbits in mind if you do. Do not accept a drink from a stranger. If possible, make your own. Do not be the drunkest person at the party. Do not fall asleep at the party. And most importantly, beer before liquor, never been sicker—that saying exists for a reason, ladies."

She fluffs her hair and turns toward the elevator. "Oh, and, ladies, have fun!"

The walk to the Delta Psi house is a short one, but the sounds of the party reach us long before we can see it.

My heart thunders in time with the bass and a fine sheen of sweat covers my skin. This is really it—I'm really about to experience my first ever party.

I've decided Orion's doesn't count since I was there for less than thirty minutes thanks to Samson.

I nudge Emmy with my elbow as we walk up the front porch steps, hoping to ease her nerves. "This is my first party. I wasn't ever allowed to go to any in high school!"

At the door, we're each given a red plastic cup. "No cup, no drinks—got it?"

We both nod and venture inside.

The house is packed. Beyond packed. There are people everywhere and I love it.

"Drinks or dancing?" I ask Emmy, ready to jump into this pool of debauchery with both feet.

"Dancing ple—"

The words aren't fully out of her mouth before I'm dragging her onto the makeshift dance floor.

As soon as we find a spot, the song changes. It's not one I know, but the beat is fast and I move my hips like I'm trying to give Shakira a run for her money.

Emmy, not surprisingly, is a little—okay, a lot—more reserved in her moves, swaying and bobbing her head in time.

But I'm not having it. Dancing is cathartic and if anyone could use a release, it's her. So, I wrap an arm around her tiny waist and pull her body flush with mine.

Together, we dance, twirl, shimmy, and shake, and by the end of the song, we're both riding the endorphin rush.

"You've got moves!" My voice is teasing, but at the same time, I want to know more.

"I used to love to dance," she admits.

"What made you stop?"

The track changes. "I love this song!" she squeals, rolling her hips—a clear deflection.

"Me too!" I shout, letting her off the hook.

By the time the song ends, I'm panting. "I need a drink!"

As I lead Emmy to the kitchen, which is substantially less packed than the rest of the house, I ask her what she's drinking.

She eyes the many alcoholic options before saying, "Water."

Surely, I didn't hear her right. We're at a college party and she wants... "Water?"

Her cheeks burn crimson. "Yup. I don't drink."

That tracks with everything else I've learned about her, so I let it go. "Cool. Let's ask the guy manning the keg where to find you some water."

· · ·

"Hello, ladies," he says directly to our chests. "Two?"

"One." I pass him my cup and bat my mascara-coated lashes and ask him where we can find Emmy some water. "Preferably sealed in a bottle."

He passes me back my cup, now filled with what is undoubtedly cheap beer. "Check the sink."

"You wanna check out the rest of the party while we hydrate?"

"Um." Emmy smirks. "I'm the only one hydrating."

I roll my eyes, loving this show of sass. "Same difference."

We make a loop around the house, and I swear on all that I hold dear, this frat party is every pop culture stereotype come to life and I love it.

By the time we make it back to the living room, my cup is empty and my hips are swaying. I run a hand through my hair and shimmy my body to the beat, loving the freedom being here brings. There's no way I could've ever cut loose like this in high school.

Someone would've called Orion, and he would've gone all mama bear on me, like the overprotective fun-sucker he is.

With my first taste of alcohol rushing through me, I'm really feeling myself and moving to the music like I'm about to work a pole.

I jolt at the feeling of a strong arm wrapping around me. Before I can say anything, I'm hauled back against the owner of the arm. I'm about to give him a piece of mind—that is, until I see him.

He's definitely handsome, with his dark features and chiseled jaw, but... he's no Samson. *No, Stella! We're not thinking about him—the jackass still hasn't replied to your text.*

"I'm going to be right over there!" Emmy yells, gesturing vaguely to the wall behind us. "I won't leave. You don't either."

I nod as I grind back into Mr. Tall, Dark, and Handsome.

We dance for two songs before he leans in and asks me my name.

"Stella."

"Ella?"

"No, Stella."

He nods, his scruff grating against my neck before twirling me around to face him. Dancing with him is fun; easy and mindless, but thoughts of Samson keep creeping their way into my brain.

Thoughts of how much better his hands would feel on my body.

"Don't you wanna know my name?" He wedges one of his thighs between mine. "You'll need to if you're gonna scream it later."

And just like that, I'm out. I stop dancing and push against his chest. "I need to check on my friend. Kthanksbye." I turn and run before he can say anything else.

I head for where Emmy said she'd be, but I don't see her anywhere.

"Where is she?" I mutter to myself, my skin pricking with panic. "She said she wouldn't leave."

And then I see her, slumped over on the dirty floor. "Emmy! Oh my God! Emmy, are you okay?"

Her head flops to the side like her spine's suddenly made of spaghetti.

"Did you take something?" Her glassy, unseeing eyes

send a fresh spike of fear through me. "What's wrong? We need to get you out of here," I tell her, but she's too far gone to answer.

A random guy stops to ask if she's okay, and even though it's risky, I ask him to keep an eye on her while I call for help.

Except... who do I call? My parents would kill me. Orion would kill me, reanimate my corpse and kill me again. Which only leaves one person...

I swipe through my contacts until I find his name, swallow my pride, and hit dial.

Please God, let him pick up.

"GRAB us a booth and I'll get a pitcher," Orion says as we walk into our favorite local haunt—Bandits.

It's a shack of a place that's been here since the dawn of time. Its age shows too, but the music is loud, the food is good, and the drinks are cheap, so we come.

"Sounds good, man." I secure a table near the back door.

The bar's packed a few people deep, so I slide out my phone and settle in to wait on Orion.

I'm half-tempted to text Stella, but she went radio silent after I accepted her invitation to see her greenhouse in person.

I don't know if she regretted asking me or what, but fuck—I didn't think she'd ghost me. It seems like we're the definition of one step forward and two steps back.

It's bullshit. I don't want to play games with her. She means too damn much, but the walls she's built around her heart are as tall as the mountain we live on.

Fuck it. I'm going to text her.

She doesn't get to extend an olive branch only to snap it like a fucking twig.

But before I can type out a message, my phone rings and it's her name flashing across my screen.

I glance toward Orion—he's ordering now—and swipe my thumb across the screen. "Stella."

"Samson. I-I need you." The tremble in her voice sets my teeth on edge.

"What's wrong?"

She sniffles.

"Where are you?"

"A party. Please help me."

Fuck. "Text me the address. I'll be right there." Mad at her or not, I've never been able to tell her no, and I'm not about to start when she's in trouble.

I shove back from the table right as Orion approaches.

"What's wrong?" he asks, placing the pitcher of beer down on the table.

"Man..." I scrub a hand over my face. "I've gotta go."

"What the hell? We just got here."

"I know. I'll make it up to you."

Orion curses me under his breath, but I'm already halfway to the door.

I check my phone as I run to my truck, narrowly avoiding busting my ass, and plug the address into my GPS.

The ten-minute drive seems more like an hour. There's nowhere to park, so I hit my flashers and leave my truck idling at the curb. Stella needs me and there's no way in hell I'm going to waste time looking for somewhere to park.

I cut a path through the front yard, shoulder checking anyone in my way. The kid manning the door calls after me, but I silence him with a lethal glare.

Like heat-seeking missiles, my eyes find their target immediately. Stella's crouched on the floor with a brown-haired girl. She's got the girl's head in her lap and is gently running her fingers through her hair.

Her lips are moving, but I can't make out what she's saying until I'm directly in front of her.

"It's okay, Emmy. I've got you. Just breathe."

"Luna!" I bark her name and her eyes snap to mine.

"Thank God you're here. Help me get her home p-please?"

I'm as relieved as I am annoyed. While I'm happy Stella is safe and well, I'm still pissed that she pretty much ghosted me for a week straight.

Pot, kettle—I know.

"What's wrong with her?" I tip my head toward her friend. She looks almost catatonic.

"I don't know, Samson!" Stella snaps. "Just help me!"

I bite my tongue to keep from snapping back. It's clear she's had a drink or two and now's not the time for us to hash this out.

I lift her semi-unconscious friend into my arms and nod for Stella to follow me. "The hell were you doing at a party anyway, Luna?"

The girl groans as I carry her out to my truck.

"Why do you even care?" Her tone is vicious, which is a whole load of shit, because this time she's the one who left me hanging. "You gonna tattle on me?"

I roll my eyes and gesture for her to open the back passenger door. "You're acting like a brat."

"What can I say?" Stella crosses her arms over her chest. "You bring out the worst in me."

I laugh, because that's a damn lie and we both know it. We're fucking meant for each other. "Get in the truck, Stella."

She's silent the entire drive back to her dorm, which is

fine by me. I don't think either of us has anything nice to say right about now.

My emotions are riding high and she's been drinking, so if she wants to act like a spoiled little snot and throw a fit, fine—I'll let her. For now.

I swing my truck into a parking spot and before I can even get it into park, Stella's on me. "Are you going to help me get her inside or not?"

I grit my teeth to keep from snapping at her. My Luna's normally sweet as sugar, and I don't like this salty as hell side of her. "As long as you keep up your end of the bargain," I say, with a smile that's all teeth. "I'll help."

Stella snarls at me and flings her door open. "You may not think much of me, Samson Carter, but I'm not a liar."

She's trying to pick a fight at this point, but then again maybe I am too. There's no one else on this earth that can fire me up quite like my best friend's little sister.

"You don't have the first clue what I think of you." The question is, have I not made it clear or is she being willfully ignorant?

We both slam our doors shut and I round the truck, meeting Stella on the passenger side. I yank the door open and reach for the girl, who lets out a scream worthy of a banshee.

"Stop!" She kicks at me, clipping me on the chin. "Get away from me!"

"Holy shit, Luna!" I shout, backing away from the truck and rubbing at my sore jaw. "Get your damn friend before she kicks out my teeth!"

"Emmy!" Stella rushes past me, bracing herself against my truck. "Emmy, stop!"

The wailing stops. "Stella?" Her voice sounds small. "What... where?"

"Shh, we'll talk inside."

"Who?"

Stella glances back my way. "That's Samson. He's a... he's someone I know."

That stings.

"He brought us home, and he's going to help get you inside, okay?"

The girl in my back seat whimpers and Stella shushes her softly. "I've known him since I was in diapers." An exaggeration, but sure. "He won't hurt you. Okay?"

She must agree because Stella backs away from the truck and nods for me to try again.

"You gonna try and kick me again?"

She sucks in a deep breath. "No."

I lean in and help her out of the truck, allowing Stella to take over once she's on her feet. I trail behind them, wondering how in the hell this night turned so sideways.

"The door," Stella says, jerking me out of my thoughts.

I look from her to the sensor. "Gonna need your card, Luna."

"It's in my back pocket."

My eyes trail over her, finally noticing what she's wearing—which isn't much.

"Oh my God! It's a freaking pocket. You might graze a little ass cheek. It won't kill you."

I clench my jaw. "It fuckin' might." I try to be all business, in and out, but I can't help but imagine palming her ass under other circumstances. Like her on top of me, bouncing on my dick and screaming my name after I pop her cherry.

Not the fucking time, I shout at myself. And it never

will be if I don't get her to fully forgive me. Sure, I've gained some ground, but I know she's still hurt.

"Whoa!" Stella wraps her arms tighter around her friend. "Are you okay?"

The brunette nods and mumbles something about bed.

"Are you sure she isn't on something?" I ask, scanning the card.

"Positive. Now either help call the elevator or go home. We don't need your negativity."

"No, just my ride," I mutter bitterly as I stalk toward the elevator.

The three of us shuffle into the car and I pop my fist against the button for the third floor. The elevator jerks and her friend covers her mouth as she gags.

"I swear to God, if she pukes on me—"

"Stop being such an asshole, Samson!"

"I'm fine," she says, visibly swallowing.

I follow them to their door and unlock it. "Wait here," Stella orders before helping her friend into the bedroom on the left.

A few moments later, I hear the soft snick of a door closing and I turn to see Stella walking toward me.

"Thank you for coming," she says, but her words don't match her tone. She sounds more annoyed than she does grateful.

"What's your deal?" I ask, tired of her shit.

"Nothing." She puts her hands on her hips. "I don't have a problem."

"Clearly you do, so out with it."

"Fine, you really want to know?"

I nod.

"I freaking invited you over here to see my cabinet and

you just... ignored me. It was hard to put myself out there like that, Samson."

"What in the hell are you talking about?"

She glares. "Oh, sure. Play dumb."

"Not playing anything. I texted you back and *you* ignored me."

"You liar!" she whisper-shouts.

I whip out my phone, pull up our text thread, and thrust my phone in her face. "See? I'm not lying about shit."

"What?" Stella pulls my phone closer. "But I never..." she trails off, reaching into her own pocket for her phone. "See!" She passes it to me.

Sure enough, my text isn't there.

"Well, shit, Luna."

"Shit is right," she says right before she cracks up. "To think, I spent a week pissed off because I thought you were dropping me all over again."

I step into her, gripping her chin between my thumb and index finger. She silences instantly. "Trust me when I say I have no intentions of letting you go. Not now, not ever."

She shivers and steps away from me.

"I mean it, Stella."

"I'm scared," she whispers right as her roommate lets out another ear-piercing scream.

"Is she okay?"

"I hope so." Stella glances toward the door. "Thanks for... everything."

I take half a step toward her and stop. "Always, Luna. Always."

"DID YOU DOUBLE CHECK THOSE MEASUREMENTS?" Saul, my site foreman, asks.

"Yup." I don't bother looking up as I reply.

He nods down to where I'm marking my cuts. "You sure, kid?"

I slide my pencil behind my ear and glare at him, though there's no real heat behind it. Saul's good people—crabby as hell, but a standup guy. "Measure twice, cut one—I know the drill, old man."

"You'd better be sure." He taps his knuckles against the wood in front of me. "Shit's not cheap."

"Promise we're good."

"Don't think I won't take it out of your pay."

"Keep it up and I'll tell Renee you're being mean to me." Saul's wife is his exact opposite—where he's a storm cloud, that woman is pure sunshine.

She cooks for the whole crew at least twice a week and dotes on all of us like we're family.

He crosses his arms over his barreled chest. "You wouldn't."

I grin, knowing damn well his wife would lay into him if she thought he was being mean to any of *her boys*. "Would too."

Saul flicks his wrist in my general direction. "Get back to work."

"I was working, you know, before you interrupted me."

"Yeah, yeah," he mutters, walking off to pester someone else.

Rolling my eyes, I slide down my goggles and ready my saw. Only before I can make the cut, my phone rings, vibrating against my leg.

The sight of Stella's name flashing across my screen has my lips lifting in an easy grin. If she's calling me—on her own accord—maybe she's thinking of forgiving me.

"Hey, Luna, to what do I owe the pleasure—"

"Samson," she whimpers my name, and immediately my entire body is on high alert.

"What's wrong?" I ask, pacing back and forth.

"My... my tire blew." She releases a shuddery exhale. "And Dad and Orion are busy, and I'm sure you're busy too, but I don't know who else to call."

"Where are you?"

"On the side of I-24."

Fuck! Why couldn't she be on the side of some two-lane road with no traffic? "I'm on my way."

"Really?" She sniffles and my heart clenches in my chest.

"Really. I need to hang up for just a second, but drop me your location and I'll call you right back, okay?"

"Okay." Another sniffle. "And, Samson..."

"Yeah, Luna?"

"Thanks."

"Always." I end the call and pull my phone away from my face, waiting for her text to come through.

As soon as it does, I'm off to find my foreman. "Saul!" I holler his name, hoping like hell he hears me over the noise of the job site. "Saul, where you at?"

"Let me guess, you fudged the cut?"

"I gotta go."

"You gotta what?" His voice lowers to a growl as his entire body tenses. "It's not even lunchtime!"

"I know. *I know.* But my girl needs me. You know I'd never just dip, but she's stranded on the side of the interstate. She *needs* me."

"Goddamn young love," he mutters to himself. "Go, but I expect you to make up the hours."

"I will!" I shout over my shoulder, already running for my truck.

As soon as I'm on the road, I call Stella back.

She answers on the first ring. "Samson." Her voice cracks and I swear, my foot mashes the pedal to the floor.

"I'm on my way, Luna. I'm coming. Are you okay?"

"Yes, um. Yeah. These cars are just going by so f-fast, it rocks my whole car."

"You got your flashers on?"

"Yeah."

"Good. Talk to me, and I'll be there soon."

"About what?"

"How are your classes?" I ask, merging onto the interstate.

"They're more challenging than I thought, but in a good way."

"That's because you're smart as hell."

"Whatever. You're just trying to charm me."

"Is it working?"

Stella gasps as a horn blares in the background. "Holy crap!"

"Are you okay?"

"They were just *really* close."

"Jackasses." I squint, looking for her car. "I see you, Luna. Gonna pull up behind you."

"Okay," she whispers.

"Wait for me to come get you." I end the call before she can argue, throwing my truck into park and popping on my flashers.

Car after car rushes by, not bothering to move over or slow down in the slightest as I approach her vehicle.

"Come on," I say, opening the door. "Let's get you situated in my truck and then I'll I get this sorted, okay?"

Stella looks up at me from beneath damp lashes, her cheeks red from crying. "Thank you for coming."

I swipe my thumbs over her cheeks, wiping away her tears. "Always, now come on."

She allows me to help her from her car. I know she's shaken up when she lets me wrap my arm around her as I guide her back to my truck.

"You got a donut in the trunk?"

"Yeah. A jack too."

"Good girl. I'll be right back, okay?"

"Thank you. Again." She looks me up and down—and I mean, really looks at me. "Oh my God! Did you leave work to come help me?"

I stare blankly at her. How is that even a question? "Of course I did."

"Samson! Will you get in trouble?"

"Let's get something straight—I'd have left to help even if it meant getting fired. You need me, I'm there. It's that simple."

Her blue eyes widen. "Did... did you get fired?"

"No, Luna." I give in to the urge and tuck her hair behind her ear. "My boss is every bit as crazy about his wife as I am you, so when I told him you needed me, he got it."

"That's..." she trails off before leaning forward and pressing her lips to my cheek, shocking the hell out of me.

"Damn." I brush my fingers over the spot her lips just touched. "Hang tight," I murmur as I shut her door, heading back to her car before I can do something stupid—like kiss the hell out of her.

I'VE ALWAYS BEEN a sucker for a hard-working man and seeing Samson in his work pants, steel toes, and vest practically has me drooling. Add in the fact that he just dropped everything to come help me, and I can barely remember that I'm still mad at him.

But only a little mad.

It seems my heartache lessens a little more each day, and while I'm not fully over him leaving, I think I'm pretty well on my way.

Plus, if I'm being honest, life without Samson Carter is like a perpetual winter—dull, cloudy, and gray. He's my sunshine, my warmth, and dammit, I'm ready for a little heat.

Speaking of, watching him change my tire definitely has me a little hot under the collar. He's so strong and efficient, and what would have taken me forever, he accomplishes in mere minutes. *Gah!*

He's actually the person who taught me to change a tire —Dad tried, God love him, but I was too busy drooling over

Samson while he and Orion worked in the yard that my dad gave up and asked him to do it.

"Stella?"

"Huh?" I startle, so lost in the memory of that day, I didn't even hear him climb up into the truck beside me.

"I asked if you wanted me to follow you to the tire shop."

"Oh, you don't have to do that. I can figure it out later this week."

He pins me with a hard glare. "If you think I'm letting you drive anywhere on that tire, you're sorely mistaken."

"Samson!"

"The way I see it is, you've got two choices." He holds up a finger. "One, I follow you to the tire shop." He adds another. "Two, I call a tow truck. The choice is yours."

"Not much of a choice," I grumble, only partly annoyed.

He shrugs unrepentantly.

"Fine." I reach for the handle. "Follow me."

Samson nods. "Don't go over fifty."

"Yes, sir," I smart back, secretly loving his protective side. It's one of the things I missed the most when he left.

"Go on, before I find something to occupy that smart mouth of yours."

"It's gonna be a few hours before they can get to it," Samson says, stepping back into the waiting room.

"Hours?" My shoulders slump. So much for my plans.

"Where were you headed?"

"It's... it's not important."

Samson moves closer to me, so close I have to crane my

head back to see him. "The crushed look on your face says otherwise. So, tell me where you were going."

"Target."

"Okay." He nods once. "Let's go."

"You're going to take me shopping?"

His brow furrows. "It's not like it's the first time."

In all fairness, he's right. It's far from the first time he's taken me shopping, and yet, for some reason, the thought has me giddy.

"Fine, but it might take a while."

He grins indulgently. "I think I'll make it."

"Are you sure? Last chance to back out."

"What are you gonna do? Sit here in this lobby for hours?"

"I could Uber back to my dorm."

Shaking his head, Samson loops his thumb through one of my belt loops. "Come on, Luna."

He starts walking back toward his truck, and following after him is all I can do with the hold he has on my pants. "Samson Carter! Let me go."

"Did that once, hated it. Zero stars. Do not recommend."

My cheeks heat, more out of contentment than embarrassment. Maybe we can find a way to work through all of the bullshit after all.

"At least slow down. I'm about to eat asphalt."

But he doesn't let me go. Nope. Instead, he yanks me closer and in some kind of magical maneuver, lifts me into his arms, bridal style.

"Oh my God! Put me down!"

"No can do, Luna."

I squirm in his hold. "Yes, can do. Just let go!"

He swings open the passenger door of his truck and sets me on the seat. "Don't you get it? I *can't* let you go."

"Do you really mean that?" I ask, fidgeting in my seat.

But Samson doesn't answer. He just closes my door and walks around to the driver's side and slides behind the wheel.

The cab of the truck is silent as he turns the key, puts it in gear, and pulls out of the parking lot.

He drives for about a mile before he speaks. "With every ounce of my being."

"Huh?"

"I mean it with every ounce of my being. You're not just in my head, Stella. You're in my heart, my blood, my fucking soul. Do you hear me?"

Gulping, I nod. "Yeah, Samson. I-I hear you."

He glances at me for a long moment and then nods. "Good."

"You don't have to take me shopping," I say, feeling guilty as he turns into the shopping center parking lot.

"I know, but I want to."

"Are you sure?"

"Luna."

"Samson."

He shakes his head and cuts the engine. "Get out or I'll go shop alone."

"Fine!" I draw the word out as I scramble to catch up to him.

Inside the store, I start to grab a buggy, but Samson once again catches me by my belt loop. "What are you doing?" I whisper-shout as he yanks me toward him.

"You always get a cinnamon-sugar pretzel."

"And?"

"So, let's get one for you to munch on while we shop."

I can't explain it, but even with the way he hurt me, my heart still squeezes in my chest with every thoughtful gesture on his part. He said he'd *show* me how he felt, and as much as I'd like to keep icing him out, his actions definitely back his words.

"Thank you, Samson."

"For what?"

"For everything." I shrug, smiling up at him. "For being you."

He skims his knuckles over my cheek. "Thank *you*."

"What?"

He dips down, bringing his lips to my ear. "All the best parts of me are because of you."

I stand, gaping in his wake, as he strides up to the counter, ordering a pretzel for me and a slushie for him. *How does he always know the right things to say?*

For the rest of the day, it's as though Samson never left. We shop and grab lunch at one of our favorite places, talking about everything and nothing all at once—just like we used to do.

By the time he drops me back off at my car, I feel lighter than I have in months.

AFTER A LONG WEEK, all I can think about is getting to my parents' house and getting my hands dirty—okay, and maybe seeing a certain blond-haired god of a man at dinner tonight.

A sense of contentment washes over me the second my house comes into view. Especially when I see my dad working in the yard.

He pauses his raking when I shut my car door. "You're here early, Stelli Bear. Did you come to help me rake?"

I glance at the piles of leaves dotting the lawn. "I can if you want," I say, even though I'd much rather tend to my garden.

He smiles and the corner of his eyes crinkle. "Go tend to your garden, Stelli. Mom's making lasagna tonight."

"My favorite!"

"We missed you last week."

"Sorry, Dad—"

"You don't have to explain."

I smile, grateful for his understanding.

"Now come hug your dad."

Without another word, I bolt toward him, wrapping my arms around his middle.

"I'm proud of you, Stelli."

"I haven't done anything."

"You're growing up," he says, like that's an actual reason to be proud and not just the natural progression of time.

"Okay, Dad." I drop my arms back to my sides and step back. "Enough with the mush."

He smiles down at me. "Go dig in the dirt before I drag out the extra rake."

I press a kiss to his cheek and take off for the backyard.

I stay tucked away in my seven-by-seven plot, weeding and fertilizing, and deadheading my blooms until Mom sticks her head out the back door and hollers my name.

She waits at the door while I put my things away in the shed. "Missed you."

"You too, Mom."

Mom purses her lips, like she wants to say more. Instead, she sends me upstairs to shower and get ready for dinner.

I come back down thirty minutes later, dressed in a pair of leggings and a cozy sweater with my hair in two french braids—comfy but still cute in case Samson comes.

"Smells good, Mom," I say as I enter the kitchen.

"Thanks, Stella." She pats my cheek, right as her timer sounds. "Grab the bread?" she calls out to no one in particular.

"Got it." Orion swoops in, transferring the bread from the oven to the counter in one smooth move.

I lift the lid off one of the pots on the stove. "Did you make green beans too?"

Mom clucks her tongue. "You know I did. Now get away from the food until it's time to eat."

"How much longer?" I whine. After living off of cafeteria food, I'm more than ready for some of my mom's homemade deliciousness.

"We're just waiting on Samson." Butterflies erupt in my belly at the mere mention of his name.

We've texted a few times over the last week; nothing important or life-altering, just small talk but... progress is progress, right?

"Set the table while we wait?" Dad asks, stepping up behind my mom. I look away as he leans in to kiss her. They have the kind of love everyone should strive for. The kind of love I thought Samson and I were on our way to.

As if summoned from thought alone, Samson strolls in through the back door without knocking. The sight of him in a pair of light-wash jeans and a slightly darker denim button-down has my mouth watering. He looks rugged and sexy and like everything I've ever wanted all served up in one hunky package.

"Need help?" he asks, his eyes locked onto mine.

"I've got it."

He smirks. "I meant with the drool."

"Jackass!"

"Language!" Mom calls from the kitchen, and my cheeks burn hot.

"C'mon." Samson steps closer. "Pass me some of those plates."

"Or you could go grab the silverware and napkins."

"You got it, Luna." He walks past me, all swagger, and I

swear to God, just the scent of his cologne makes me weak in the knees.

Samson returns a minute later, with my family hot on his heels, each with a dish in hand.

"Let's eat!" Dad says, taking his place at the head of the table.

We all gather around the table and pile our plates high. Mom really outdid herself, with a massive lasagna, sautéed green beans, a fresh salad, and garlic bread.

"Smells good, Mrs. C," Samson says, shoveling a bite of ooey-gooey-cheese pasta into his mouth. "Tastes good too."

I watch, entranced, as he licks his lips. How is it he can make something as mundane as eating look like a sexual act?

He catches my eye from across the table and winks.

Mom thanks him and then hums thoughtfully. "You know what you boys need?"

Orion groans. "Not now, woman."

Dad reaches over and smacks the back of his head. "Don't disrespect your mother."

"What's that?" Samson asks.

"You boys need to settle down with a good woman."

All eyes fly to me as I choke on my bite of bread.

"You okay, Smalls?"

I nod, my eyes watering as I reach for my glass of tea.

"You sure?" Mom asks.

Another nod.

"Well, if you're sure..."

Dad waves off her concern. "Stelli's fine. Just swallowed wrong, right?"

"Mmm. Yup, great."

"I think I can speak for both of us, Mrs. C, when I say we're not looking to settle down quite yet."

Orion snorts out a laugh. "What Samson actually

means is *I'm* not ready to settle down. He's apparently seeing someone on the down-low."

Samson cuts his eyes at my brother and my heart thunders in my chest.

Somehow, the dinner I was looking so forward to has turned into my own personal hell.

My mom—the unknowing traitor—is trying to set Samson up, and according to my brother, he's already seeing someone.

I chance a look in Samson's direction, only to find his eyes already on me. They're hard, begging for me to understand.

But I don't. I don't understand at all.

Every single time I think we're nearing a turning point something happens and my hope is decimated.

It takes every ounce of self-respect, courage, and willpower I possess to not run from the table crying.

"Let the kids eat in peace, Lizzie," Dad says and I swear, he just became my favorite parent.

"I'm just saying." Mom waves her fork in the air. "Maria —my hairdresser's niece—is a sweet girl. A looker too."

"I'm sure she is, Mom," Orion says in a placating tone.

"Well, one of you boys has to take her out."

I focus on my food, sawing my lasagna—which now tastes like ash—into neat bites. This conversation isn't one I want to participate in. Not in the least.

"Why?" my brother asks, placing his silverware down on the edge of his plate.

Mom sighs. "I already told her you would."

"When?" Orion grits the question from between clenched teeth.

"Saturday."

"I'm busy."

"Samson?"

"Ah, Mrs. C, I really am seeing someone."

"Is it serious?"

My breath stalls in my chest as I wait for his reply. I guess if nothing else comes from this dinner, I'll officially know where we stand. If he says it's serious, I'll know his promises to win me back were nothing more than meaningless words.

Well, I guess that'll be true if he says no as well. Because either way, if he's seeing someone else, he's definitely *not* serious about me.

"It's, um..." Samson's eyes dart to mine, but I look away. "It's new."

"I'm full." I shove back from the table. "Thanks for dinner."

"Stella!" Mom shouts after me. "Where are you going?"

"I-I forgot, um. I forgot about a thing. I'll call... later."

I take off for the door like my feet are on fire, willing my tears not to fall until I'm in the privacy of my car.

"Stella!" Samson yells after me, but I don't stop.

I can't.

Not until I'm safely back in my dorm, where I can let myself feel the hurt of yet another betrayal at the hands of the man I love—no matter how much I wish I didn't.

TALK ABOUT A SHITSHOW.

Last Sunday at the Cartwrights' was one of epic proportions and it had a domino effect on my entire damn week.

I'm sure this fucking blind date won't be any better.

I check my phone—again—hoping for a text from Stella. But she hasn't replied to me since Sunday night when I tried telling her it was all a misunderstanding.

The middle-finger emoji she sent back said she didn't want to understand.

I don't know how I keep fucking up with this girl; it honestly feels like I'm shooting myself in the foot. Over and over.

But I'm going to fix this—fix us—again. Even if I have to limp my way down the path to making her mine.

"Are you Samson?" I glance up from my phone to see a woman standing in front of my table.

She's petite with golden skin, pale green eyes, and caramel-colored hair. By all standards, she's beautiful. But she's no Stella.

"I am." I stand to greet her. "You must be Maria."

There's an awkward moment where I'm not sure if I should shake her hand or hug her; luckily, she decides for me by sitting down in the chair opposite of mine.

"Have you been here before?" she asks, hanging her purse off of the back of her chair.

"Once or twice."

"Okay. Well, um. What's good?"

"Everything," I answer, without looking up from my menu.

"Right." She huffs out a disbelieving laugh. "I knew this was a bad idea."

"What?"

"Listen, Samson, let me be frank with you, okay?"

I nod for her to continue.

"It's clear you're not interested in me, and while I'm sure you're a great guy, the feeling's mutual."

"Then why are you here?"

Maria smiles. "Same reason as you, I suppose."

"A well-meaning but meddling family friend?"

She lifts her hand and flicks her wrist. "Close enough."

"We can just call it a night," I offer.

"Oh, hell no. You're buying me dinner."

I laugh. "Bossy, aren't ya?"

She nods. "My girlfriend certainly agrees."

My eyes widen and Maria grins.

"Oh, yes. Strictly chickly."

"Then why are you here... with me?"

Maria shrugs. "Like you say, well-meaning and meddle-some. My aunt—God love her—thinks I need a big, strong man to take care of me. She means well, but she's a little old-fashioned. I can take of myself, thank you very much."

"How long have you and your girlfriend been together?"

"Four years."

"How's she feel about this?" I gesture in the space between us.

Maria grimaces. "She's not my aunt's biggest fan, but she... she's patient. What about you? How'd you end up here?"

"Best friend's mom."

"You're single?"

I shrug. "It's complicated."

Our waiter comes by, effectively ending our conversation. Or so I thought, because the second we order, Maria pounces. "Tell me about this complication."

I hesitate. How do I even begin to explain Stella? I'm saved from replying when my phone buzzes on the tabletop with an incoming text.

I glance at my phone, swallowing roughly when I see Stella's name.

"Who is she?" Maria asks.

"What?"

"I said, who is she? I *know* that look and it's about a girl. Is it your complication?"

I blink slowly and nod, wondering if she's really intuitive or if I'm as transparent as glass.

"Are you gonna read the text or not?"

"I don't know." I glare at my phone like it's a rattlesnake ready to strike. "Last I checked, she wasn't speaking to me, so I doubt it says anything good."

"Did you do something stupid?"

"Stupid?" I want to bristle, but she's partially right, so I shrug instead.

"Well, you won't know if she's still mad unless you check the text."

When I still don't make a move to grab my phone, Maria heaves out a long-suffering sigh. "I'll tell you something, Samson. Girls don't like to play games—if you want her, go after her. If you don't, let her go."

I scrub a hand over my face and groan, wondering how in the hell my blind date turned into a therapy session. "I want her more than I want my next breath."

Maria smiles. "Then check your phone, dumbass."

I take a deep breath and then grab my phone, pressing my thumb into the screen to unlock it. I pull up her message and my heart practically stalls in my chest. "What the fuck..." I whisper to myself, my eyes memorizing every single detail about the image on my screen.

"What? What is it?" Maria asks.

I lower my gaze down to my screen and then back toward the woman across from me. "It's a picture," I mutter, feeling strangely possessive, like it's an image meant for my eyes only. Which is absurd, given that she's at a party.

"Of what?"

I clench my jaw and force a swallow. "Of her. At a party."

Maria's green eyes shine. "Show me!"

I turn my phone around and pass it to Maria. Her eyes widen when she takes in Stella and her painted-on jeans and skin-tight turtleneck. She whistles low under her breath and asks, "How old is she?"

I bite the inside of my cheek to stop from saying something rude. I should have known this was coming. With one innocent question, she's managed to dredge up the issue that got Stella and me into this whole mess to start with.

Sensing my train of thought, Maria holds up her hands in front of her. "Hey, no judgment here."

"She's eighteen."

I wait for some kind of shitty remark but she just shrugs and smiles softly. "Love is love."

"What do I do?" I prop my elbows on the table and drop my head into my hands.

"I can't really answer that without knowing a little more about y'all." She tips her head to the side. "Y'all's history."

"I'm best friends with her older brother, have been my whole life. She started off as just his annoying kid sister, but one day, something changed. I started seeing her as *more*, and eventually *we* were more. The plan was to tell Orion—her brother—that were together the night of her eighteenth birthday."

She hums under her breath. "Guessing things didn't go according to plan?"

"You could say that. I got too into my own head and started thinking being with me was holding her back, so... I left."

Maria smacks her palms down onto the table. "You left that girl?"

My cheeks burn with shame as I nod. "I thought it was the right thing. Clearly it wasn't and my actions hurt both of us. I'm trying like hell to get her to forgive me, but I keep fucking it up every chance I get."

"Like on purpose or on accident?"

"Like the universe is against us."

"How very star-crossed." Maria smirks. "If it makes you feel better, I'm dating my ex-boyfriend's older sister."

For the first time all night, I laugh. "Yeah, actually. That does."

"So... what are we gonna do?"

"About what?"

She snaps her fingers. "Keep up, Samson. About your girl, about Stella."

"I'm gonna go home, have a beer, and try to pretend she's not at a party surrounded by other guys."

Maria imitates a game show buzzer. "Wrong!"

I arch a brow at her.

"We are gonna go get your girl."

"I'm sorry, what?"

"That's right, lover boy." She pauses as our server places down a burger basket in front of each of us. "Right after I make this burger my bitch."

I shake my head. "You're crazy—this is crazy."

She smiles like the Cheshire cat. "All the best things are. Now, eat up, we have a relationship to save!"

MARIA MANAGED to get the address of the party house from her ex-boyfriend of all people. He played football for CVU and apparently not much has changed since then.

When we walk in, the party is in full swing and there are people everywhere. My eyes move across the room scanning every face until we find Stella in the kitchen, sandwiched between a built blond man and a surprisingly familiar black guy with braids.

She has a red cup in her hand and her hips are softly swaying to the music booming through the speakers in the other room.

I stand frozen, watching her as she tosses her head back and laughs without abandon at something one of them said.

Maria digs her elbow into my ribs. "What are you waiting for? There's your girl!"

But suddenly I feel immobile, like my feet have taken root in the sticky kitchen floor.

"Come on, Samson, don't puss out now."

I glare at Maria but there's no malice in it; it's actually kind of nice to have someone call me on my shit.

"Do you need me to hold your hand and walk you to your first day of class?"

I glare at her. "Ha-ha, you're so funny."

"I'm just saying, you're literally standing here while she hangs out in between two hotties."

"Thought you were into chicks?"

"Oh, definitely. But I can appreciate good looks in anyone and those two boys are fine."

"Whatever," I grumble before stalking toward the keg in the corner of the room.

She trails behind me, cackling in delight at my misery.

I get a cup for each of us. Maria sips hers while I down mine in one go before wiping the foam from my mouth with the back of my hand.

"Forgot how bad this cheap shit tastes."

"There is a reason I'm drinking slowly and it's not because I'm classy."

I huff out a laugh. "Alright, let's do this."

She starts humming—loudly—as we make our way across the kitchen.

"What in the hell are you doing?"

"Oh, sorry. I was making you theme music."

"You're weird."

She lifts her cup into the air. "Hell yeah, I am!"

I set my sights on Stella and stalk across the room to her. "Luna," I growl and she whips around to face me so quickly the ends of her hair slash at my face.

"Samson." Stella breathes my name in a soft exhale before remembering she's mad at me. Then she's all attitude, with her hips cocked and her arms crossed. "What are you doing here?"

"I'm here for you."

"What if I don't want you to be here for me?" She narrows her eyes, an ugly scowl marring her pretty face.

Her attitude doesn't dissuade me one bit. If anything, it spurs me on as I step forward and snake my right arm around her, and palm the back of her neck, tilting her face up to mine. "I'd say that's too damn bad."

"Let me—" I seal my lips to hers in a bruising kiss before she can finish her sentence.

She doesn't put up any resistance. Her lips part instantly, allowing my tongue entry. I run my left hand down her back, stopping just above her ass, and pull her flush to me.

She threads her fingers into my hair, giving just as good as she's getting. Our lips move together, until I lose all sense of time.

This is so much more than a kiss... it's a claiming. I'm letting every one of these fucks know she's mine.

Stella moans into my mouth and pulls me closer. I'm about to suggest we get out of here when a deep voice breaks through the haze. "Wanna introduce your friend, sunshine?"

She pulls back with a dazed look on her face. "What in the hell, Samson Carter?"

"Don't you *what in the hell* me. This was a long time coming."

She screws up her face. "I think you're about ten months too late."

I slip my index finger through one of her belt loops and draw her closer. "There is no too late, Luna. Not for us. We're a forever kind of thing."

"Pretty words," she mumbles.

"Again, who is this?"

I glance to the blond beast of a man. "Samson Carter, Stella's boyfriend." I fucking love the way those words roll off my tongue, but her friend... he seems to take issue with it.

"Interesting." He taps his index finger on his dimpled chin. "She's never mentioned you."

It seems like this dude's trying to measure dicks, but I'm pretty damn confident in what I'm packing.

"Well, now you know," I say, offering him my hand to shake with a smile.

"And you are?"

"I'm Gabe, and that," he nods his head toward the man at his side, "is my boyfriend—"

"Zach. We've met."

Gabe stands taller, crossing his arms over his chest. "When was this exactly?"

"Wouldn't you like to know?"

"I'm not a violent man," Gabe starts, cracking his knuckles. "But I will—"

"Breathe, lover-boy." Zach interlaces their fingers. "I helped with some flowers at the shop."

Gabe nods, seemingly placated.

But I'm not as ready to let it go. "That sure was a lot of macho gesturing over a girl that's not even yours."

He cuts his eyes at me. "She deserves the best."

I hold his gaze. "There's something we can agree on." I release Stella and take a small step back. "This is Maria."

Stella's eyes flare. "You brought your date here and kissed me in front of her? What kind of ass—"

The sound of Maria's laughter cuts her off. "Trust me, neither of us is interested in the other."

"Not even remotely."

Stella pinches the bridge of her nose as she shakes her

head back and forth. "This has been the weirdest night ever."

Maria's lips twitch at Stella's confusion. "You two are so cute."

"Dance with me, Luna?"

Stella looks at me with wide eyes. "Right now? Here in front of all these people."

I run my finger over her cheekbone and draw her lips back to mine for a quick kiss. "Yeah, in front of all these people."

She bites her lip and swallows. "Okay."

I place a possessive hand on her lower back and guide her toward the living room.

Instead of seeking out a spot in the middle of the crowd, I tuck us away in a corner. Not because I'm ashamed to be seen with her, but because I don't want any of these jackasses watching her as she dances.

Stella is mine. Her body is for my eyes—my hands, my mouth, my cock—only. The mere thought of one of these fuckers looking at her... touching her... is enough to make me consider murder.

I crowd her from behind, wrapping my arms around her as we rock our hips to the rhythm.

"You look beautiful." I whisper the words against her neck and she shivers in my hold.

"Why are you here, Samson?"

"Isn't it obvious? I'm here for you."

She sighs but drops her head back onto my shoulder. "I don't even know up from down anymore when it comes to us."

"I want to make things right between us."

She shrugs her shoulders but doesn't pull away from me. "You literally went on a date tonight. And according to my brother—and you—you're seeing someone and it's serious. But here you are, dancing with me, saying you wanna make things right between us."

I spin her so that she's facing me with my thigh wedged between hers. "Come on, Stella. It's you—you're the person I'm seeing. It's always been you; it's only going to be you."

"Why is this so hard?" she asks, twining her arms around my neck.

"The things that are most worth having in life are hard."

"But shouldn't love be easy?"

I grin down at her. "You saying you love me, Luna?"

She tugs on the hair at my nape. "Shut up."

I lean down, brushing my nose against hers. "I love you too."

She pulls back and draws her bottom lip between her teeth. "I don't know if I'm ready for this."

"That's okay, Luna—I can wait."

She pops up onto her toes and seals her mouth to mine.

For a split second, I'm too stunned to react, but I quickly part my lips for her. She tunnels her fingers through my hair as our tongues tangle together.

My hands find purchase on her ass as our hips move together in a rhythm that's as familiar as it is sensual.

God, I want her—no, fuck that—I *need* her. Stella Cartwright is every good thing on this earth and I will spend every single day of the rest of my life showing her that I'm worthy of her.

One song fades into another, and then another but we stay in our little corner, lips locked and hips, until finally Stella pulls away.

Her lips are swollen and red and the glassy look in her eyes says she's as turned on as I am. "Do you... wanna get out of here?"

"Where to?" I ask, knowing good and well I'll go anywhere she wants.

Stella bites her lip and glances at the floor. "I have my dorm to myself... maybe we could go there?"

"Yeah, let's get out of here."

HOLY CRAP! *I can't believe I invited him back to my dorm.*

Clearly, I've lost my mind. That's the only plausible explanation. There's been so much back and forth between us that I think I'm giving myself whiplash.

I can't help but wonder if asking him back to my place was a mistake. But... at the same time, it feels right. Somehow, despite all of the pain and mistrust, everything with him feels right.

"You remember how to get there?" I ask, once he pulls onto the main road.

He glances my way before returning his eyes to the road. "Yup."

Self-doubt slithers through me. "You don't have to come up if you don't want to."

Samson grunts.

"Well, that's reassuring."

He glances my way again before settling his hand on my thigh, the tips of his fingers dangerously close to my center. "Anywhere you are is where I want to be."

"Such a smooth talker," I murmur as he parks his truck in the dorm lot.

Smirking, he kills the engine. "If you don't want me to come up, I won't. Just say the word."

"I do." My hands shake as I unbuckle my seat belt. "I do want you to come up."

He's out of the truck, and opening my door before I can take a full breath. "Then let's go, Luna."

I'm a fidgety, anxious mess the entire journey up to my suite. Tonight feels like a turning point, like something monumental is about to happen.

I let us into my suite and Samson doesn't waste a second making himself at home. He toes off his boots and stows them neatly by the door before heading straight into my room.

He pauses in the doorway, taking it all in, no doubt comparing it to my room at home.

"This suits you."

"Um. Thanks."

"Cabinet is cool as hell too."

"It's on a timer," I say awkwardly.

"Fuck, you're cute." He steps into me, hauling me into him with an arm around my waist. His mouth descends on mine.

His lips move expertly against mine as his tongue licks at my seam, begging for entrance. I part my lips on a moan, and he deepens our kiss.

I push onto my tiptoes and wrap my arms around his neck; Samson takes it a step farther, gripping my ass and hauling me against him. Instinctually, my legs wrap around his waist and we both groan at the contact.

He slides one hand beneath the waistband of my jeans

and kneads the flesh of my ass, pulling me harder against him—and his massive dick.

My hips buck against his, as feelings I've only ever scratched the surface of race through me.

He nips at my lip, eliciting another moan from deep within me.

"Those sounds should be illegal." He hums against my skin as he kisses his way down my jaw and to my neck.

Little moans and mewls escape my lips as he rubs me against him. "Samson," I whine his name.

"I've got you, Luna."

I'm so lost to the sensations racking my body, I don't even notice he's walking until he lowers me down onto the edge of my desk.

"Can I touch you?"

"Please." I'm begging and I don't even care.

He studies my face before reaching between us and popping open the button to my jeans and ever-so-slowly dragging down the zipper.

I squirm in anticipation, desperate and eager for his touch. He leans in, pressing his forehead to mine. "Gonna touch you now."

I nod and he slides his hand down the front of my jeans, rubbing his fingers over my soaked panties.

"Oh, God!" I shift my hips in search of... *something*.

"You like that," he states, dragging his fingers over my seam. "What about this?" He presses two fingers against my clit, rubbing it in quick tight circles.

"Oh! Samson!" My cries turn to unintelligible nonsense as I fall apart in his arms.

"Yeah, you like that," he murmurs as I come down from the high only his touch can deliver.

He steps away and I instantly mourn the loss of his

strong body pressing hotly against mine. He offers me his hand and helps me down onto my feet.

I lift my shirt overhead and unclasp my bra, letting it fall away. "Luna?" My name is a question as his eyes drop to my bare tits, and then to the ring dangling between them.

His eyes flare at the sight of it, and I run my fingers over the warm metal, making sure he sees.

I'm drunk on his touch, drunk and desperate for more.

"Touch me again, Samson." I drag my hands up my body and cup my breasts. "Please." I move one hand to lift the chain and bring the ring to my lips, not caring one bit that I'm begging or that I'm not playing fair.

"Luna." This time my name's a prayer.

"I'm begging you. Touch me." I pinch my nipples. "Make me yours."

"You don't know what you're saying," he growls, taking a step away from me.

Hurt prickles at his rejection, but I'm too far gone to stop now. I've been waiting *years* for Samson Carter to put his hands on my body and now that I've really had a taste of what he has to offer... I don't know that I'll ever get enough.

THIS ISN'T what I had in mind when I went after Stella tonight.

I figured we would talk, hash things out. And now she's standing topless in front of me, her gorgeous tits on display, her jeans undone, her hair all mussed and the scent of her release coating my fingers.

"I'm not a child, Samson Carter." Stella crosses her arms under her chest, pushing her breasts up in the most mouthwatering way.

"Don't I fucking know it," I mutter, willing myself to keep my hands at my sides.

"Then touch me."

"I just did."

She glares at me and shoves her jeans and panties down her legs, leaving her completely naked. I'm pretty sure I blackout for a second, because *fuuuuuck*.

"Goddammit, Luna." I ball my hands into fists, refusing to touch her again, because I know once I do—once I get my hands on her in the way she's asking—I'll never stop. I know once I truly touch her, once I taste her, I'll devour her until there's nothing left. "I'm trying to do the right thing here."

"And the right thing is to leave me wanting?" Stella pouts and I feel my resolve weaken. I never have been good at telling her no.

"If you don't want me..." She drags one hand down her body, following the curve of her waist, all the way down to her pussy. She slides one finger through the neatly trimmed thatch of curls to her clit. "If you don't want me, I'll... I'll find someone else who does."

My mind races and my dick throbs as I wonder who in the hell is this seductress in front of me.

With her finger still playing with her pussy, she steps closer to me. "I'll find someone else to fuck me. To get me off."

A savage growl rips from my throat at the thought of any other man touching what's mine. "If anyone's going to get you off," I whisper, dropping my voice as I crowd her small body with my much larger one, "it'll damn sure be me."

She grins, looking all too pleased with herself.

"You're playing a dangerous game, Luna."

"I'm not scared," she whispers as she comes to a stop directly in front of me, wrapping her arms around my neck. I can feel her heat and smell her arousal. I'm a man on the edge, and I'm not sure what I'll do if she keeps provoking me.

Because that's what this is—she's pushing me to get her way, to get what she thinks she wants. I know she wouldn't go out and let someone else touch her after coming all over my fingers. But still, her antics are *this close* to driving me mad.

"Please, Samson," she begs. "I feel so hot and heavy and

full of need. Please make it better." She ghosts her lips over mine. "I waited for you, you know? Even after what you did, I waited."

And with those softly spoken words, my resolve snaps. I close the minute distance between us in a flash, claiming her soft, supple lips with my own. My right hand gathers her hair in a tight fist, guiding her head just so, and my left slips between us, working my belt buckle with a speed I didn't know I was capable of.

She whimpers as I nip at her lip and I revel in the sound.

This isn't the way I wanted this to happen between us, but knowing that my Luna waited for me, that no other man has touched her, has my baser instincts taking over.

Stella says she wants this, she's going to get it, and I'm damn sure going to enjoy every second.

I walk us toward her bed until her knees hit the mattress. "Lay down, Luna."

She lowers herself down to the edge and then scoots back toward the headboard.

"I hope you know what you're in for," I murmur, shoving my pants down and kicking them off.

"No boxers?" she asks, her eyes glued to my cock.

"Laundry day." I shrug and pull my shirt over my head.

"God bless laundry day."

"Spread your legs, Stella."

Some of her bravado falls away; but she still complies, dropping to her knees. My mouth waters at the sight of her pretty pink pussy, all glistening wet for me. "You're so goddamn gorgeous."

"Are... are you just going to stand there?" she asks, squirming under the weight of my hungry stare.

"Let me enjoy the view." Reaching down, I grip my cock in my right hand and tug.

"Samson," she whispers my name. "Can I... touch you?"

"Soon."

"Why not now?"

I drag my eyes up to hers. "Because if you put your hands on me right now, I'll blow my load before I'm ever inside you."

"Oh." Her chest heaves as her breathing accelerates. "When are you gonna touch me?"

I squeeze myself to the point of discomfort. How is it possible for her to be so innocent and so fucking sexy all at once?

"Put your hands over your head."

She lifts her hands, crossing her wrists over the top of her head.

"Just like that." I press one knee into the bed, and then the other, crawling toward her. "Now, don't move."

I press a kiss to her right knee and then her left thigh, reveling in the feel of her soft skin against my lips.

"What... what are you doing?"

"Tasting you."

"What—" I lick up her seam and suck her clit into my mouth. "—Oh my God, Samson!"

"Watch me eat this pussy," I murmur, waiting for her eyes to lock onto mine before I resume my ministrations.

I lick and suck and swirl my tongue over her sensitive bud. She whimpers and wiggles her hips. "No moving."

"Samson," she whines my name.

I pull back and grin up at her before spreading her pussy lips wide with my thumbs. She's slick, absolutely dripping for me, and I dive in face first, fucking her with my tongue.

When her legs start to tremble, I gently slide my middle finger into her tight, virgin hole, as far as I can without popping her cherry.

It might be kinder to break it with my finger—gentler—but the thought of her blood smeared all over my dick is too damn tempting.

I add a second finger, stroking in and out of her in time with my tongue as I stretch her for my cock.

Her pussy flutters around my fingers, letting me know she's close. I pull back just enough to see her face. A light sheen of sweat covers her forehead and her eyes are pinched shut and her mouth opens in a silent scream.

"Come for me, Luna." I flick my tongue against her. "Come all over my face."

"I..." Stella cries out as I seal my lips around her clit, sucking hard. "Oh—God!"

She gives up on keeping her hands over her head and roughly grips my hair, holding my head in place as she rolls her hips and fucks my face.

The sounds falling from her mouth as she reaches her climax are carnal... decadent... pure fucking heaven meant for my ears only.

Satisfaction swells deep in my chest as she falls apart under my hands and tongue. I lick and kiss and nip at her thighs as the aftershocks of her orgasm subside.

"Samson," she whispers my name so sweetly.

"You sure you want more, Luna?"

Her eyes are slightly unfocused as she nods.

"Need the words."

"Yes, please." She sits up a little. "Make me yours."

I rack my brain, trying to think if I have a condom in my wallet, but I don't. I figured it was best not to keep one on me while she was underage as a way to remove some of the temptation, and then we weren't speaking. *Fuck!*

"What's wrong?" she asks, concern furrowing her brow.

"I don't have a condom."

She nibbles her lip. "Well, you know you're my first and I'm clean—on the pill too. So... if you're clean... you don't have to..."

"Don't have to what?" I ask through gritted teeth.

"Don't have to use one."

I swallow roughly at the thought of taking her with nothing between us. "Are you sure?"

Stella nods. "Positive."

"This... fuck." I breathe out the word on a harsh exhale. "I've never..."

She reaches up and cups my cheek. "Then let me be the first."

The only, my subconscious growls back.

I advance toward her, settling myself between her thighs. "This is going to hurt," I say, drawing her right nipple into my mouth. I suck hard before releasing it with an audible pop.

"I-I know." She stumbles over her words a little.

"I'm going to do my best to make it good, to make you feel good." I give her left nipple the same treatment before placing a kiss directly over her heart.

"It's already perfect because it's you." She loops her arms under mine and pulls me up for a kiss. It honestly shocks me a little—the way she isn't scared to taste herself on my lips. It's hot too.

She's a fucking siren, a vixen, a total minx, and she doesn't even know it.

I part her lips with my tongue, and she opens instantly on a sweet sigh.

My dick is harder than it's ever been, throbbing and aching to be inside of her.

"I hate that this is going to hurt you."

"Just do it, Samson. I-I want it."

I pull back and scan her face for any hint of deception, but she looks every bit as hot for me as I am for her.

With a decisive nod, I reach between us and run my finger over her slit—she's still wet for me, but I want her dripping.

"What are you doing?" she asks, her breath hiccuping when I press my thumb to her clit.

"Making sure you're ready."

"I am. I really am."

"I mean physically."

"Oh—"

I apply more pressure and rub faster, turning her cries into a moan.

"You're gonna feel so fucking good, Luna. I can't wait to feel you squeeze my cock."

"Please," she cries, pressing her hips into mine. "Please just do it. F-fill me up."

Her dirty talk is nearly enough to have me coming before I even feel her heat wrapped around me. This girl really was made for me.

Reluctantly, I pull back from rubbing her clit and wrap my hand around my dick, dragging the tip through her slit. She pushes her hips forward again, and I give in, guiding myself inside of her, stopping when I feel the little piece of tissue blocking my way.

"Oh, um." She swallows roughly. "Wow."

"Are you okay?"

She nods and smiles reassuringly, but it doesn't meet her eyes.

"I'm sorry, Luna. Fuck, I'm so sorry," I say, mostly meaning it. The feeling of her tight, little pussy stretched wide for me is unlike anything I've ever felt before—and I'm not even all the way in.

"Just... just do it."

I lean down and press a soft kiss against her lips before pulling back enough to see all of her. I bring my thumb back to her clit and begin rubbing the sensitive bundle all over again.

I use my other hand to explore her body, skimming my fingers over the dip of her waist and the swell of her breast, whispering encouragement to her all the while.

I touch and rub and play, solely focused on making her feel better—even if it kills me. And right now, it feels like it might. Her pussy may as well be a vise grip around my dick.

"Here we go, Luna." I lean down and claim her lips with mine as I thrust through her innocence, making her mine and mine alone.

A sharp gasp leaves her lips as her eyes fill with tears. "Fuck, Stella. Shit. I'm so sorry."

She tries reassuring me with a smile. "Just..." She exhales slowly through her nose. "Just give me a minute."

I fight the urge to rock my hips. Being inside of her is better than any fantasy I've ever had—and I've had a lot. She's hot, tight, wet, and so fucking perfect.

"Gonna touch you again," I murmur, not wanting to startle her.

"Just kiss me." She looks so shattered, I'm helpless to deny her request.

Cupping her cheek, I bring my lips down on hers, pressing soft kisses to her tear-stained mouth. She opens for me instantly, sliding her tongue into my mouth.

With her hands tangled in my hair and mine softly

exploring her skin, we kiss for what feels like hours, but is probably only minutes. We kiss until she softens beneath me and melts under my touch. We kiss until finally, neither of us can take my stillness any longer.

"You can move." She licks her lips. "You know, if you want."

"More than you know," I whisper, drawing my hips back and pushing into her. When she doesn't stiffen or wince, I do it again.

"You can go faster."

"I don't want to hurt you." Even as I speak the words, my pace increases.

"You're not." She leans up and nips my collarbone. "Promise."

I keep rocking into her, kissing and touching every bit of her skin I can reach, until I can't take it anymore. "Gonna come," I grunt, intending to pull out.

But Stella wraps her legs around my waist, holding me in place as I come harder than I ever have before.

I try to pull out of her, but she clings to me, holding my body to hers. "Are you okay?"

She nods and presses a kiss to my chest. "Perfect."

"Can I get you cleaned up?"

"Just hold me for another minute?"

"I'd hold you forever if I could."

We stay as we are, with her arms and legs wrapped tightly around me. She peppers my skin with countless small kisses until finally, her hold on me relaxes.

"I'm good now."

"Let me help you get cleaned up."

Her cheeks bloom pink.

"Don't be shy now, Luna. I've tasted that pretty pussy

and your blood is on my dick. You're mine in every way, now let me take care of you."

"Okay."

Standing, I lift her into my arms and carry her to the small suite bathroom. I set her down on the plush bathmat and turn the tap on the sink to warm.

Once it reaches temperature, I run a rag under the water and then wring it out before kneeling in front of Stella and wiping between her legs.

Taking care of her like this, it feels right—it's almost more intimate than our sex. There's just something about her allowing me to care for her in this way that sends a burst of male pride through me.

I stand once she's cleaned up, tossing the rag into the hamper tucked between the sink and toilet. "I'll let you have a minute, okay?"

She nods and I pull her in for another kiss before heading back to her bedroom.

"Hey, Stella?" I call, pausing in the doorway.

"Yeah?"

"You gonna let me stay the night?"

She nods again, but as I pull the door closed behind me, I swear I hear her mutter, "I might just let you stay forever..."

EARLY MORNING LIGHT filters through the cracks in the blinds, rousing me from the deepest sleep of my life.

God, it's hot, I think, trying to wiggle out of the covers. Only there's a decidedly masculine arm banded around my middle, holding me in place.

For a split second, panic threatens to consume me, but then realization strikes. The strong chest pressed against my back, the strong thigh wedged between my own, and the very naked erection pushing into my equally naked ass all belong to none other than my brother's best friend.

Because, holy shit! I slept with Samson Carter!

Slowly, I try to shift out of his hold, but it's no use. His arms are like steel bands and his chest a brick wall.

"Stop moving." His chest rumbles as he holds me impossibly closer.

"I need to pee," I wheeze as he squeezes the air out of me.

"Hold it." He nuzzles his face into the crook of my neck. "I like you here."

"You won't like it when I freaking pee on you."

Samson huffs but doesn't move.

"I mean it! Let me up."

He shifts and I think he's finally going to release me. But instead, he digs his fingers into my sides, tickling me mercilessly.

"Samson!" I howl his name, flopping around like a fish on a boat deck. "Oh my God! Stop-stop-stop!"

"But you're so damn cute when you get all worked up."

"Look, if you're into golden showers, fine. I'm not trying to yuck your yum, but since you literally popped my cherry last night, let's maybe slow things down."

"The fuck, Luna?" he asks, his hold on me instantly relaxing.

I crawl out of the bed, not caring one bit that I'm butt naked—I have to freaking pee! "Hold that thought," I tell him, darting out of my room and into the bathroom.

I take care of business in record time, and when I step back into my room, Samson's sitting up, reclining against the headboard, with my purple comforter draped across his hips.

"Golden shower?" he asks, a look of disgust on his handsome face.

"Um." I grab my robe from the hook on the wall and tug it on. "It's common knowledge."

"You were a virgin until yesterday."

"Are we just recapping everything I've already said, or..."

"Don't be a smartass. I'm just trying to understand why and how you know the things you do. You were a fucking seductress last night—all touching yourself and putting on a show. And now you're talking about kink shaming and I... fuck, Stella."

My cheeks heat as memories of my wantonness flash

through my mind. I don't know what came over me last night, other than this soul-deep need for him to claim me.

"Did you not like it?"

"Fuck, no, Luna. I loved it. You were so sexy, but..."

I swallow. "But what?"

"It's just hard to reconcile Sexy Stella with the girl who begged me to be her first kiss when she was only fifteen."

"Is it though? In both scenarios, I pushed you to give me what I wanted, didn't I?"

He mulls over my question for a moment before nodding. "I guess so."

"Exactly, I just begged a little differently last night."

"Why though?"

I shrug my shoulders and move to sit on the foot of the bed. "I don't know. We've just had such shit luck since you've come home, it felt like if it didn't happen then, it never would. I'm... sorry for forcing your hand."

He bolts upright and yanks me against him, plastering me sideways against his chest. "Don't apologize. I loved every second of every minute about last night. It was perfect, Stella, so don't question it or doubt it, okay?"

"Okay."

"It just threw me for a loop, seeing you rub your pussy and tug on your nipples like that."

Despite the wetness gathering between my thighs, I shoot him a dull look. "I've watched porn before, you know?"

His throat bobs as he swallows. "Oh, yeah?"

I nod.

"When?"

"When what?"

"When did you watch it?"

"It wasn't a one-time thing."

His arms tighten. "Did you touch yourself?"

"Some-sometimes."

"What did you do?"

"Samson," I whine his name. I'm practically dripping wet now, which should be impossible given how embarrassed I am.

"Tell me." His voice is deep and low, a carnal growl that ignites a flame deep within my core.

"I would... um..."

"If you don't want to tell me, you can show me."

"What?"

"You heard me." He grabs his phone from God-knows-where and taps around until a familiar website loads on the screen. "Show me."

He rolls me to his side and wraps one arm around me.

"What did you like to watch?" When I don't reply, he adds, "You pick or I will."

"You can." My entire being is a contradiction—I'm burning up for him and freezing all at once; I want to maul him and hide at the same time. I'm turned on and embarrassed as hell. My body is in utter chaos.

He scrolls for a second before settling on a video. There's a short ad from Virtual Kitty—a DIY porn app of sorts—followed by some opening credits, and then, it's all flesh and moans.

My breathing accelerates as the action unfolds on the screen.

"Show me, Stella." Samson props the phone against his thigh, focusing all of his attention on me. "Move your robe to the side and show me how you'd touch yourself."

My heart feels like it's going to beat right out of my chest as I slip my hand beneath the silky material of my robe. I press my index finger to my clit, softly rubbing it.

"I said *show me*." Samson reaches over and tugs the fabric aside, his eyes zeroing in on my finger. "That's right, Luna, rub your pussy."

I spread my legs, hooking my left one over his right, and drag my index finger down my slit to gather some of my wetness.

"What are you thinking about?" he asks, as I begin rubbing my clit again. "Are you thinking about them? The couple fucking in the video?"

"No." I shake my head, rubbing faster.

"Then what?"

"You. I always think about you!"

He groans, but makes no move to touch me.

I can feel myself getting closer, but it's nothing compared to how Samson made me feel. It's like the difference between watching a movie on an old TV versus in hi-def with surround sound. My fingers will get the job done, but Samson... he delivers the full experience.

"You ever slide your fingers into your tight little pussy while thinking of me?"

"Never. I just... rub myself."

"You're telling me I'm the only thing—the only person—to ever be inside you?"

"Yes," I whisper, as I press the heel of my palm in a circular motion over my clit, chasing desperately after my release.

"I want to fuck you so bad right now." He tosses his phone to the floor, the video still playing. "Fuck, Stella, how sore are you?"

I test my opening and wince. "I'll be okay."

"Fuck that," Samson says, knocking my hand out of the way. He thumbs my clit with just the right amount of pressure as he leans in and kisses me. The second his tongue slides into my mouth, I detonate.

My back arches off the bed and I cling to his strong shoulders as he swallows my cries of pleasure with his kiss.

"Fuck, Luna," he moans as he pulls away from me.

"What about you?"

"What?"

I nod down to the very noticeable rise in the sheets, my heart still racing and my legs sticky with my release.

"I'm good."

"But..."

"But what?"

"What if I wanted to?"

"Wanted to what?" He grips his dick over the covers, his knuckles turning white as he squeezes.

"Touch you." I move to my knees and lick my lips. "Taste you."

"You are literally killing me."

"Please, Samson. Please let me."

He shucks off the covers and grabs my hand, wrapping it around his shaft. "Pump your hand up and down," he says, guiding my motions. "A little tighter... yeah, just like that."

With a body crafted by hard labor, Samson is a freaking god. His body is all tan skin and taut muscles and I can't help but want to trace every single divot with my tongue.

"Now, twist your wrist a little as you work the head."

I do as he says, and he groans. The sounds he's making spur me on, and I lean forward, flicking my tongue against the tip.

"Fucking hell!" Samson startles, his hips bucking up.

"I said I wanted to taste you too."

"Stella." I can't tell if my name's a warning or a prayer,

but testing his limits has always been one of my favorite pastimes, so why stop now?

I lean all the way over and draw him into my mouth, licking and sucking him like he's a scoop of my favorite ice cream.

Samson gathers my hair with one hand and palms the back of my neck with the other. "Suck it harder."

I do, and he rewards me with his sexiest sound yet—a deep, guttural moan.

"Keep jerking me off while you suck on me. *Fuck, yes.* Like that."

For a split second, I worry he's going to shove himself down my throat, but he never pushes me past where I'm comfortable.

One of the videos I used to watch pops into my head, and like the girl in it, I reach between his legs and cup his balls. "Oh, fuck! Shit. Gonna come," he warns, tapping the back of my head.

Thanks to countless magazines and articles, I know guys prefer for women to swallow, so I double down my efforts, sucking and rubbing in tandem until he shoots his load into my mouth.

I gag a little at the texture—it's thick and creamy and a little salty. But I force myself to swallow it down, wanting to please him.

"Luna," he breathes my name and then he does something that shocks the hell out of me—he kisses me. I literally just had his come in my mouth, and now his tongue is there instead.

Not that I'm complaining, but I definitely figured he'd want me to brush my teeth or something. But nope, he's kissing me like I'm his lifeline. Which is fitting because despite all of the history between us, he's definitely mine.

After what feels like an eternity, he breaks away from me. "You are..." He pauses and I worry I did something wrong.

"I'm what?" I ask, hating the hint of vulnerability that creeps into my tone.

"Perfect, Luna. You're perfect."

My cheeks hurt from smiling. "What's... what's this mean for... us?" I ask, righting my robe.

"You're mine."

"And you, you're mine too?"

Samson nods decisively.

"Does that mean we can talk to my brother?"

He stiffens at the mention of Orion, and my hopes and heart plummet. "Stella, it's not that I don't want him to know. I just... I think we need some time together. Just the two of us."

I leap from the bed, wrapping my robe tightly around me. "We've had years!"

He stands too and reaches for me, but I take a step back. "Stella," Samson growls my name, but I just glare. "Listen to me, dammit!"

"Listen to what?" I shout. "Listen to you give me some lame-ass excuse? I won't be your dirty little secret, Samson Carter!"

Samson advances toward me, and I retreat, until he has me pinned against my desk. He cups my cheek and holds my eyes on his. "I don't want you to be a secret, Stella. I just want some time that's just ours."

"We've had time," I say, tears stinging my eyes.

"I mean time like this, time where we're allowed to touch, to explore, to love. I want time with the woman you are now. Nine months may not seem like long, but you... you fucking blossomed into this sexy, bold woman, and I..."

"You what?"

"I want time with her. With us, only us, alone. Not because you're a secret, but because I'm a selfish fucker, and don't want to share you. With anyone. Not even your family. You're mine, Stella."

I sniffle. "You promise?"

He draws an 'X' over his heart. "I swear."

"OH MY GOD!" I jump up from the couch when Emmy barrels into our suite. Samson left a few hours ago, and I've been sitting here ever since. I'm so caught up in my own problems that I don't even notice the steam practically pouring from her ears *Looney Tunes* style. "We have so much to discuss!"

"That, we do," Emmy says, wiping her palms against her pants.

"Starting with why your cheeks are so flushed. And why you're wearing a man's shirt."

"Um." She plops down onto the couch, shamelessly claiming my spot as her own. "Well."

"Don't you *um, well* me, babe. I need deets. I spent half the night worried sick about you, you know?"

"Only half?" she asks, and even though her tone is light, a spike of guilt nearly steals my breath away.

Am I an awful friend? My worry over Emmy's out-of-character behavior last night simply slipped away the second Samson showed up.

I didn't even text her to check in—nope, I just let her

leave the party tipsy, and with Sterling no less. The man has been nothing but awful to her since the semester started.

Instead of apologizing for being a crappy friend, I turn the focus back to her. "We'll get to that."

"Okay, fine." She takes a deep breath. "I might have just told Melanie off on my way up."

"What?" I'm torn between throwing her a celebratory party for standing up for herself and putting our monster of an RA in her place and flinging myself down onto the couch next to her to demand more details.

My need for the nitty-gritty wins out, and I plop down beside her. A hiss of pain escapes me as my bottom meets the stiff cushion. *Gah, I knew losing my virginity would hurt, but no one mentioned it would still feel like this the day after!*

"Are you okay?"

I can feel my cheeks heat under her concerned stare. "Mmhmm. Totally fine."

"You sure?" She tilts her head to the side, assessing me with a shrewd gaze.

"Totally fine. Just a little sore."

"Why?"

"After we finish talking about you." I pin her with a look. "About Sterling."

"We talked," she says with a dreamy sigh. "About everything."

Emmy proceeds to tell me all of the details about her night—from drinking to Sterling taking care of her and all of the extras in between.

"Stell, I think... I think he believes me now. Like for real. At first, I wasn't sure if he was faking nice or what, but after last night and this morning, I think he means it."

I'm as excited as I am nervous for my best friend. She

deserves happiness more than anyone I know, but the thought of Sterling—her tormentor and psych TA—being the one to give it to her worries me.

The two have a rich history, steeped in lies and pain and hurt. Their issues make mine and Samson's look like nothing more than a drop in the ocean.

But if he's really turning over a new leaf, and treats her right—then I'll support her in any way I can. And if he hurts her, I'll string him up by his balls.

That's what friends do.

Emmy chews her lip. "I think he's into me, or whatever."

"Of course he is! You're a total catch. Now, why are you wearing his shirt?"

"Nothing like you're thinking," she rushes to say, her cheeks the color of a tomato. "He just let me borrow a shirt since mine smelled like a day-old frat party." She sinks back into the couch. "Now, your turn."

"Well..." I take a deep breath and decide to just go for it. "I ditched my V-card last night!"

"What?" Emmy's brown eyes practically bug out of her head. "With who?"

"You remember my friend Samson?"

"You mean Mr. Mysterious who you'd never spill the details on? That Samson?"

"The one and only."

"Are y'all like an item now?"

My excitement wanes. I'm not sure how to answer her question, because we *are* together, but Samson isn't ready for anyone to know. I feel bad lying to her, but still, I shake my head and say, "No."

"Oh. Um."

"It's fine, Emmy. I got what I wanted, and he made sure

it was good. What more can a girl ask for, right?" Even I can hear the bitterness in my tone.

I get why Samson wants to keep us a secret, but it stings too. He kept me a secret for years, and now that we can finally be together out in the open, him wanting us to hide felt kind of like a knife to my chest.

Emmy clasps my hand in hers. "A lot of things, Stell, a lot of things. But if you're happy, then I'm happy for you."

I offer her a tremulous smile, even as my eyes burn with tears. "I'm over the moon."

It sounds like a copout, but I mean it. I really am happy —last night was nothing short of perfect. Samson was so attentive and considerate, but at the same time, he didn't baby me either.

He made me feel wanted and sensual and cherished.

If it weren't for our talk this morning, I'd probably still be on cloud nine.

A small part of me wonders if I'm making a mistake in agreeing to keep our relationship a secret, but mostly, I'm so happy to have him—in any capacity—that I'm willing to try things his way.

For now, at least.

Because I meant it when I told him I wouldn't be his dirty little secret. If he doesn't man up and talk to my brother soon, I... I don't know what I'll do.

But that's a tomorrow problem. Today, I'm going to snuggle up on this couch with my best friend, watch trash TV, and just... be.

Orion glares at me over the rim of his water glass as I bounce my leg to an erratic beat that only I can hear.

I've been an anxious and excited ball of energy since pulling into my parents' driveway this afternoon.

Even digging in the dirt didn't calm me.

Because tonight will be the first family dinner with Samson and me officially—even if secretly—together.

Mom is in the kitchen putting the finishing touches on the food; I know I should offer to help, but I'm shaking like a sugar addict in need of a cupcake, so I stick to the living room with my brother.

But the way he's watching me only serves to make me more nervous. It's honestly a miracle no one ever suspected anything was going on between Samson and me, since I'm apparently as smooth as a bull in a china shop.

"You're acting weird."

"What?" My eyes fly to Orion. "No, I'm not."

"You are," he insists. "You're like... a fidgety mess."

"Just ready to eat. Pot roast—mmm."

He eyes me like he knows I'm full of it. If older brothers have superpowers, seeing through my shit has always been Orion's. He's always just known when something was bothering me.

"Cut the crap, Smalls."

"What crap?"

"There's something on your mind. Just tell me, maybe I can help you sort it out."

Not likely. And even if I thought he could, thanks to Samson's demand to keep our relationship quiet, my hands are tied. "It's just..."

"Dinner's ready," Mom hollers, saving me from Orion's inquisition.

I spring up from the couch and bolt into the dining room, narrowly avoiding a collision with my dad.

"Whoa, Stelli Bear—slow down!"

"Sorry, Dad, it just smells so good!"

"There's plenty, no need to rush."

"I know." I pull back my chair and surreptitiously check the clock. It's after six. *Where is he?* "Sorry, Dad."

"Smalls has been acting like a spaz all night," Orion says, plopping into his chair on the other side of the table.

"Is something bothering you?" Mom asks, while Dad looks on in concern.

"No." I shake my head. "Nope. Everything is hunky dory."

"You just said *hunky dory.*" My brother crosses his arms over his broad chest. "No one says that."

He's got me there, but instead of admitting defeat, I double down. "Clearly *someone* does." I point both thumbs at my chest. "This girl!"

"You kids knock it off and fill your plates before it gets cold." Mom hands Orion the serving spoon for the potatoes. "Where's Samson at?"

My eyes widen, and then I realize she's asking my brother and not me. But still, I lean in and listen intently as he answers.

"Said he was running late."

"But he is coming, right?" I ask. *Dammit, Stella!*

"Yeah." Orion drags the word out. "Why?"

I smile and stuff a roll into my mouth, mumbling a garbled reply around the buttery bread.

He rolls his eyes and mutters something about me being a weirdo under his breath.

"You two act the exact same now as you did a decade ago," Dad muses, piling his plate high with roast.

"Is that a bad thing?"

"Keeps me young," is all he says in reply.

We fall into a comfortable silence as we eat, which is

why the sound of the back door opening might as well be a landmine detonating.

"Samson's here," Orion mumbles around a bite of carrots.

"Sorry I'm late," he says, his lips tipped up into a charming smile. "Smells good, Mrs. C."

Mom stands to hug him, and Dad to shake his hand. Orion remains seated, so I do too, not wanting to look weird.

"Hey, man," Samson says, greeting my brother as he slips into the chair beside him. "How's work?"

"Busy." He takes a sip of his water. "Good but busy."

"I hear ya. We're breaking ground next week on that new high-rise in downtown and damn—sorry, Mrs. C—I'm already tired and we haven't even started."

Like an eager puppy, desperate for attention, I sit with a smile plastered across my face, waiting for him to speak to me. But... he doesn't.

Not even a simple *hello*.

Once again, my favorite day of the week feels like hell on earth thanks to none other than Samson Carter. *The sexy, stupid jackass.*

"How's school, Stella?" Mom asks, breaking me from my stewing.

"Great."

"That's good, and you like all of your classes?"

"They're perfect."

"Honey, are you okay?"

My eyes flit briefly to Samson. "Hunky. Freaking. Dory."

Mom laughs nervously before turning her attention to the man responsible for my bad mood. "How was your date, Samson?"

His fork clatters to his plate as he chokes on his food.

Dad watches on with a peculiar look in his eyes while Orion pats Samson's back and Mom rushes to pass him a glass of water.

"Yeah, Samson, how was it?" I ask, once he's breathing regularly again.

He glares at me, but I just smile, content to let Karma do her work.

"Maria's such a sweet girl."

I tilt my head to the side, waiting to hear his reply.

"She was very nice, but I won't be taking her out again."

"I figured as much." Mom nods along in understanding. "Well, when do I get to meet this mystery girl you're seeing?"

"After me," Orion mutters, digging his elbow into Samson's side.

Dad snorts.

"What?" Mom asks.

"Nothing. It's just... nothing."

"Is everything okay?" I swivel to face my dad, but he just grins.

"I think everything's exactly as it should be, Stelli Bear. Now, why don't you go grab the apple pie your mom made and bring it to the table?"

I WATCH as Stella shoves her chair back from the table. "One pie coming right up!"

Every molecule of my being wants me to get up and follow her, to demand her attention, but I force myself to remain in my seat.

I made my bed when I walked in here and chose to ignore her, and now, unfortunately, I have to lie in it.

But damn if it doesn't suck.

"So, man," Orion says, pushing his plate away. "What'd you do after your *date* last night?"

I pray for patience as I massage my temples. Honestly, I can't tell if he's baiting me or genuinely wants to know.

Stella waltzes back in, looking like a domestic goddess with a pie dish in one hand and a container of homemade whipped cream in the other.

"It looks good, Mom," she murmurs, but I'm too busy imagining this exact same scenario, fifteen years from now.

Only, we're crowded around *our* table with a few kids of our own. The thought should scare me—she's only eighteen for Christ's sake.

But it doesn't.

It feels too fucking right to scare me.

Life may have a lot of unknowns, but one thing I'm certain of is this: Stella Cartwright is my future, and it's about time I man up and let the world know.

Maybe asking her to hide us wasn't the right idea. A woman like Stella deserves to be shown off—not kept a secret.

Fuck. I'm messing this up all over again.

"This is bomb," Orion says around a mouthful.

"Don't you want any?" Mrs. Cartwright asks me.

"I sure do."

"Stella, honey," her mom prompts.

"What?" The little she-devil looks from her mom to me. "He's a big boy."

Her dad laughs from deep in his belly. Michael Cartwright's a big man. Quiet but with a heart of gold. And Stella is his baby girl through and through. That man would lay waste to entire cities to protect her.

But somehow, I get the distinct idea he'd be okay with the idea of us together.

In fact, sometimes it even felt like he was trying to push us together over the years.

He even tried getting me to take Stella to her junior prom, but we both shrugged it off since I was over the age limit.

"It's fine," I murmur, serving myself the last slice, which is noticeably smaller than everyone else's.

"Stella, what's gotten into you?"

"I don't know what you mean." But the devious curl of her plump lips tells me she knows exactly what her mother means.

"You're being rude to Samson." She gives Stella a disapproving look. "He's a guest in our home."

"Hardly!" Stella gasps out on a laugh. "He's basically a member of the family."

"Stella!"

"Nope." She pushes her chair back from the table again. "I'm gonna get a head start on the dishes so I can head back to campus."

Mrs. C hesitates before eventually nodding. Her indecision is written all over her face. Stella's always been the baby and I know it's hard for Lizzie and Michael to let their daughter spread her wings.

Stella presses a quick kiss to her mom's cheek before gathering the plates from the table and hightailing it to the kitchen.

As soon as she's out of sight, I shove what's left of my pie into my mouth, swallowing in two rough gulps. "I'll help."

Orion smirks. "Well, since y'all have that handled, I'm gonna head out. I've got an early morning." He hugs his mom and gives his dad a slap on the back before heading out the door, hollering a *bye Smalls* over his shoulder to his sister.

"I can take care of those—" Lizzie starts, but I wave off her concern.

"It's the least I can do." *Not to mention, I'm desperate to get your daughter alone.*

"Are you sure?"

"Let the boy help if he wants," Michael says. "Plus, I was thinking we could go for ice cream, just the two of us."

Mrs. C's eyes twinkle. "That does sound nice."

"Good, let's go."

I linger in the dining room while Mr. and Mrs. Cartwright tell Stella they're leaving, hoping that she'll think she's alone.

Something tells me I'm going to need the element of surprise to get her to listen.

"No good stupid jerk," she mutters, plunging her hands into the soapy water filling the sink, as I watch from the doorway.

I approach the kitchen like one would a wild animal—calm and quiet—because if there's one thing I know about Stella, it's that she has claws when she's mad.

And my Luna is fucking furious.

I creep quietly, until I'm right behind her, gripping the lip of the sink on either side of her petite body, caging her in.

"What do you want?" she asks, not even remotely surprised to find me behind her.

"To talk."

"Oh, right." She rolls her eyes. "We're alone now."

"Stella."

"Samson."

"Please?"

She whips around to face me, a feat in and of itself in the narrow gap between my chest and the counter. She shoves at my chest with her sudsy hands. "Why should I?"

"Because—"

"Oh my God, save it." Her eyes brim with tears. "This is what you always do. You reel me in and then just leave me on the hook. I'm tired of it."

"I know." I stare down at her, willing her to *see* how much I mean it. "I know you're tired of it and I know you deserve better—"

"Then give it to me, Samson. Because I'm worth more than scraps."

"I know." *God, do I know.* I've been in love with her since before she was even legal. And yet, now that she is, I'm shooting myself in the foot over and over. "One more chance?"

"Give me a good reason, because from my point of view, I'm struggling to see the upside."

As quick as lightning, I release the counter with my right hand and tunnel my fingers into her long hair. I tug her face up to mine and press my lips against hers in a hard, searing kiss.

Like always, my sweet Stella parts her lips for me.

I pour everything I feel for her into my kiss. My longing, my love, my desire—I give it all to her with my lips, teeth, and tongue.

"Samson," she moans my name as she practically climbs me, wrapping her arms around my neck and her legs around my waist.

I spin us, hoisting her against the island for leverage, dragging my lips away from hers to kiss down the slender line of her neck.

She tugs me closer and I willingly go, nipping at her collarbone. "This, Luna. This is why I need another chance."

"This is just physical." But even as she says the words, she's rocking against me, chasing that feeling only I can give her. Not only because her body was made for mine, but because I'd fucking kill any other man who dared touch her.

"Fuck that," I growl, shoving my hand down the front of her leggings. She's already soaking wet for me when I tug her panties to the side and drag my knuckles through her folds. "This is more than physical."

"Samson." She tries to sound mad, but the way her body bows toward mine... the way she rolls her hips against my hand... I know better. She's turned the fuck on.

I pull my hand back and then palm her hips, sliding her down to her feet. "Don't move."

"What are you—"

I drop to my knees before her, tugging her leggings and panties down as I go. "Showing you."

"Showing me what?"

"That you're fucking mine." I dig my left hand into the soft flesh of her ass and toss her right leg over my shoulder as I lower my face to her dripping pussy. "That every part of you is made for every part of me."

She tries to say my name again, but it comes out as a mangled cry as I dip my tongue inside of her before licking my way up to her needy little clit.

I work her over with my mouth, licking and kissing and sucking everywhere except for where she wants me to. I tease her with my tongue until she's delirious with need... until she's begging.

"Please, Samson." She digs her slender fingers into my scalp, trying to guide me to where she wants me the most. "Please."

"I've got you, Luna. I know how to make you feel good."

She bucks against my face as I finally focus all of my attention on her clit. I alternate between flattening my tongue against the sensitive bundle of nerves and flicking it with just the tip.

"You taste so fucking good, Luna." I speak the words against her fevered flesh. "Like fucking heaven."

Her legs shake from my efforts, and with one last swipe of my tongue, she falls apart as she rides my face.

As she recovers from her orgasm, I press soft kisses to her pussy and thighs.

"Samson." Her tone is firm, and I know it's time to talk.

Gently, I lower her right leg back down to the floor, bracing her while she gets her feet steadily beneath her.

She tugs up her bottoms as I stand, rearranging my rock-hard cock behind the fabric of my jeans.

"As much as I loved... *that*... I'm not sure what you think it proves."

I step into her, craving her nearness. "You're mine. And I can guaran-goddamn-tee there's not another person out there that could make you feel like that. You wanna know why?"

"Why?" She sounds doubtful.

"Because it's not just my body and yours. It's our fucking hearts... our souls. It's every fiber of our beings coming together when we touch because we're made for each other, Stella. You're it for me, and I know I'm doing a shit job of proving it, but I will. I. Fucking. Will."

She sighs and slumps against me, laying her head on my chest. "You keep saying that, Samson. And maybe it's immaturity on my part, but I need you to show me."

"It's not." I lift her gaze to mine. "It's not immature for you to want my actions to back my words."

"Are you sure?" she asks, vulnerability painting her every word.

"I'm positive, Luna."

"Where do we go from here?"

"I messed up when I asked you to keep us a secret." She gives me a *duh* look. "Not for the reason you're thinking."

"Then why?"

"I never wanted you to be a secret, Stella. I wanted time

for us to just *be*. With no weight or expectations. Just you and me, together finally."

"I guess that doesn't sound awful." She drags her bare toes across the floor.

"Yeah?"

"I mean, I like the thought of keeping you all to myself for a minute. But, Samson..."

I cup her cheek. "Yeah?"

"It can't be like tonight. You can't ignore me or make me feel like less than. You have to treat me the same way you always have."

"I promise." I drop a soft kiss to her lips. "Except when we're alone. Then, all bets are off."

She looks up at me from beneath her long lashes. "I think... I think I'm okay with that."

"I bet you are," I murmur, leaning down to kiss her again.

I lick my way into her mouth, but right as our tongues touch, the back door slams shut and we break apart like a wildfire suddenly erupted between us.

"Stella, Samson, what are y'all still doing here?" Mrs. Cartwright hollers as she steps into the kitchen.

Our chests are both heaving and our breathing accelerated as we try to act normal.

"Just the dishes," I say, with my most charming smile.

"That was an hour ago."

Stella grins. "We were letting the pots soak."

Michael walks up behind his wife, takes one look at us and smirks. "Come on, Lizzie. Let the kids be."

"Do y'all need help?" her mom asks, lingering in the doorway.

"Nope." Stella flicks on the faucet and soaps up the sponge. "We're good."

As they head up the stairs, Michael stops and pins me a look. "You two be good."

His words seem normal enough, but it's the loaded look he's aiming my way that says everything his words aren't. The same look he's been giving in regard to his daughter for years. One that says '*Son, you better treat my only daughter like the queen she is or they'll never find your body.*'

I'll never forget the first time it happened. Stella was only fourteen and she wanted to tag along with us to the lake house for the day...

"Please, Orion, please let me go. I won't bother you or your friends or anything! Please?"

Orion looks to me and I nod. I've never minded Stella tagging along. There's something about the little spitfire that centers me. It's crazy really—she's a kid, but somehow, she always knows the exact right thing to say when I'm upset or angry about something.

Sometimes, I wish she were older, because bro-code be damned, if Stella was my age, I'd go after her in a heartbeat—the way she just gets me would be worth the asskicking Orion would dole out.

Other times, I want to kick my own ass for thinking that. She's not even old enough to drive, and here I am wishing I could lay claim to her like a caveman.

My only saving grace is that I'm not sexually attracted to her—yet. God knows, once she... develops... I'll probably be head over ass for the girl. But for now, I'm holding onto the fact that my attraction to her is only a mental thing. It's pretty much the only thing stopping me from feeling like a fucking creep.

"Fine. But Mom and Dad have to say yes too. You know that, right, Smalls?"

She scowls at the nickname. "Mom! Dad" she shouts and both of her parents step out onto the porch.

"What's all the hollering, Stelli Bear?"

"I want to go to the lake too. Can I?"

Mrs. C's eyes cloud with worry but her dad immediately turns to me—not to her brother, but me. His eyes are hard on mine, and his jaw is set as he pins me with his stare.

It feels like he's trying to peer into my very soul, but he must find what he's looking for, because after a while, his lips tip up in a hint of a smile. "Take care of her," is all he says before turning and walking away.

Honestly, it feels like he knew how I felt about his daughter before I did.

"Well, that would have been one way to tell them," Stella murmurs, sounding more than a little relieved.

"You know, I'm pretty sure your dad would be cool with it."

She passes me a plate and I load it into the dishwasher. "You think? No way."

"Bet he would."

"Bet he wouldn't. Don't you remember the summer before high school when he declared I couldn't date?"

"I also remember he let me take you out to dinner the night of your homecoming dance when you didn't have a date."

"Because he wouldn't let me have one," she insists. "Plus, you're you. He thinks of you as another son."

I grin at her as I lean down and start the dishwasher. "Trust me, I'm pretty sure he feels differently when it comes to me."

"And I'm pretty sure your ego is getting the best of you here. He'd send you away just like he would any other guy."

I grip her chin between my fingers. "First of all, I'm not any other guy."

"And second?" she whispers, her wide eyes locked onto mine.

I draw her face up to mine and whisper my reply against her pillowy lips. "I look forward to proving you wrong, Luna." And then, I kiss the hell out of her.

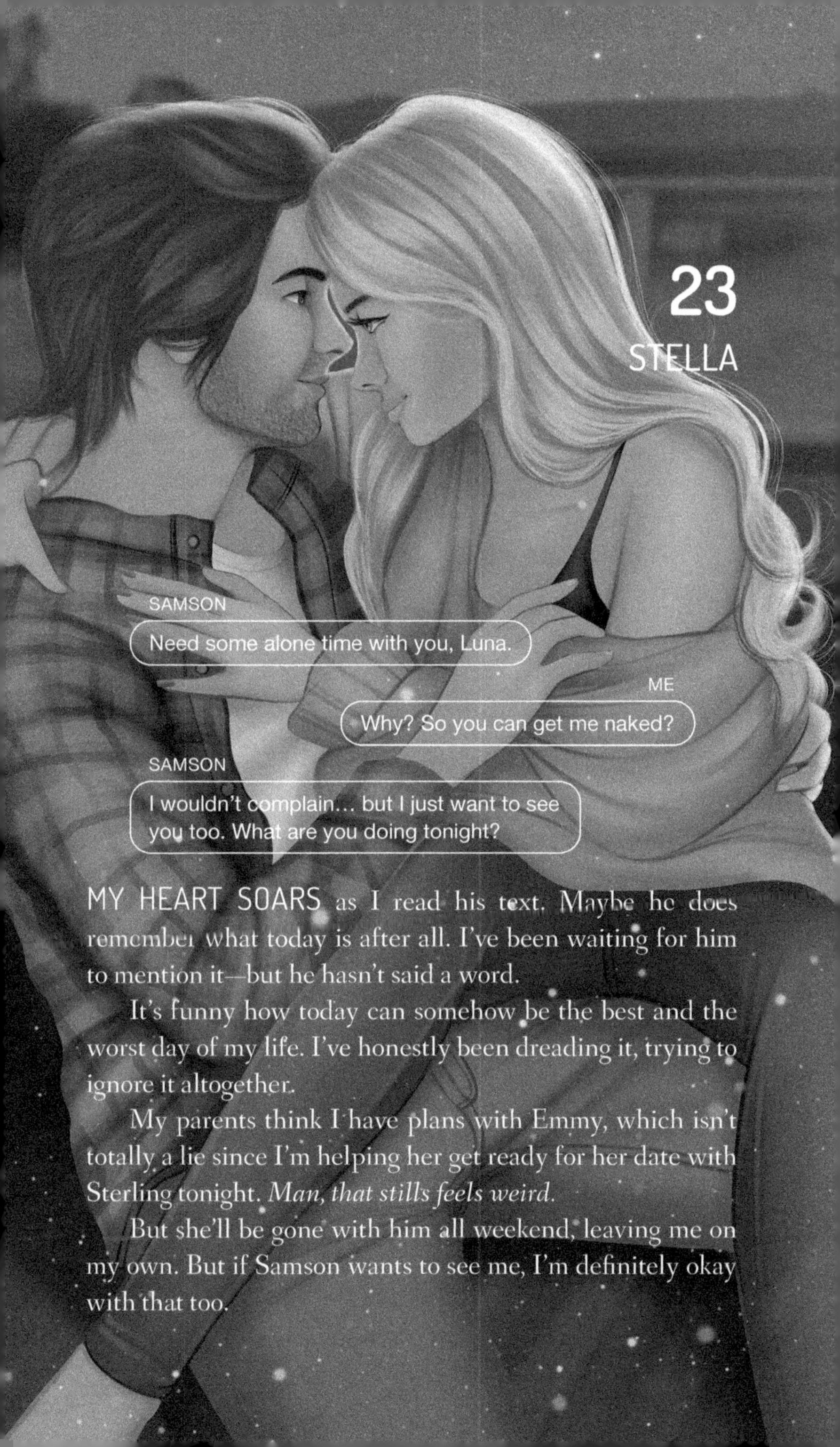

23

STELLA

SAMSON

Need some alone time with you, Luna.

ME

Why? So you can get me naked?

SAMSON

I wouldn't complain... but I just want to see you too. What are you doing tonight?

MY HEART SOARS as I read his text. Maybe he does remember what today is after all. I've been waiting for him to mention it—but he hasn't said a word.

It's funny how today can somehow be the best and the worst day of my life. I've honestly been dreading it, trying to ignore it altogether.

My parents think I have plans with Emmy, which isn't totally a lie since I'm helping her get ready for her date with Sterling tonight. *Man, that stills feels weird.*

But she'll be gone with him all weekend, leaving me on my own. But if Samson wants to see me, I'm definitely okay with that too.

ME

Nothing really… what about you?

SAMSON

Figured I would hit up Bandits with some guys. Grab some drinks.

And just as quickly as it soared, my heart plummets, all the way down to my damn feet.

ME

Cool. Sounds fun.

SAMSON

When do I get to see you again?

ME

idk.

SAMSON

You mad, Luna?

ME

Nope. Talk later.

SAMSON

Talk now. What's wrong?

I know I should talk to him—I should tell him what's on my mind and why I'm upset, but if he doesn't know what today is, then fuck him. And I don't care how bratty that sounds.

ME

It's nothing. I'm fine. I'll talk to you later for real. Emmy needs me.

I turn my ringer to silent and toss my phone down onto the coffee table. As far as the rest of the world's concerned it's just another day—and that's exactly how I'm going to treat it.

It's not like it can be worse than last year, right?

"Are you ready to..." Emmy starts, stepping into the living room. "Hey, what's got you looking so down?"

"Just tired." I force a smile, trying to shake off my melancholy.

She plops down beside me. "Classes, or something else?"

I scooch closer to her and rest my head on her shoulder. "It's nothing important. Is it time to get you ready?"

"Yeah, Sterling will be here soon." Her eyes shine with excitement, and even though I'm feeling pretty low, I can't help but be happy for her. Emmalyn Price deserves all of the good things.

"Let's go then!" I jump up from the couch, thankful for the distraction.

She follows me into my room, planting in my swivel chair while I hunt down my curling wand.

I plug it in and then begin combing and sectioning her hair. "Are you nervous?"

"Yeah. No." Emmy shrugs. "I don't know."

"But it's your first real date, right?" I ask, carefully wrapping a section of hair around the barrel.

"That's weird, right?" She scrunches her nose. "That I'm eighteen and just now going on my first date?"

"I don't think so." I let down the next section of hair and begin curling it. "But what do I know? My brother sure as hell never let anyone take me out."

Emmy grins. "Imagine that... you lost your V-card before you even went on your first date." Her entire body deflates. "Well, I guess we both did."

"Nope." My eyes hold hers in the mirror. "No, ma'am."

I want so badly to toss my curling wand aside and to hug her as tightly as I can, but I force myself not to, knowing that touching her would only make things worse.

She's overcome so much since moving here, but sometimes these dark thoughts still hang over her like a perpetual storm cloud.

"It's true." The words are spoken so softly, so brokenly, that I no longer want to hurl my curling wand... nope... I want to set it to high heat and use it to kill her despicable stepbrother.

Morbid, but true. The sorry sack of crap doesn't deserve to live after the horrors he put my best friend through.

"Good vibes only," I say, forcing pep into my tone. "Today is a good day and tonight is going to be even better, okay?"

"You think so?" Emmy asks, a slight tremor to her voice.

"Yup." I move to the next section. "Physics says so."

"Physics?" She tries to look my way, but I whop the comb softly against her head.

"Yeah. Like, you've had so many awful things happen to you, it's time for good. I'm pretty sure it's a universal karmic law or something."

Emmy giggles and I mentally pat myself on the back. "You're a mess."

"And yet, you love me." I grab my favorite hairspray and coat her freshly curled locks with it.

"More than you know," she says solemnly.

"Do you want me to do your makeup too?"

Emmy waves me off but tells me I can pick her outfit—a task I'm all too happy to take on. After a lifetime of dressing like a good girl, I took great joy in reinventing my style after graduation, much to my entire family's dismay.

I unplug my curling wand before heading into Emmy's room to raid her closet. Her wardrobe is smaller than mine, but I know I can make it work.

Digging through her closet, I grab everything I think could make the perfect date night outfit. Along with some other pieces, which I fold and pack into a weekend bag.

"Um. Stell." Emmy enters the room, her eyes wide and her lips in a perfectly shocked 'O.'

I can't help it—I laugh as I take in the mess. There are clothes everywhere. "I know. I'll clean it up. But I think I've narrowed it down."

"Let's see it."

I proudly display my two final options—a casual look made up of jeans and a cozy sweater versus a long-sleeved maxi dress.

"Jeans for sure."

I grab the bag I packed her and step out of the room for her to change, placing it next to my phone on the coffee table.

The slim device taunts me from the coffee table. With the ringer off, I have no clue if Samson responded to my last text or not. I'm half-tempted to check, but I can't decide which is worse—not knowing, or him not texting.

Uncertainty, my brain shouts as my fingers flex with desire. *Just check it!*

Except before I can give in to temptation, Emmy steps into the living room.

"So?"

I let out a low whistle.

"It's gonna be great, Emmy," I reassure her, right as someone knocks on our door.

"Oh! I still need to pack."

"I took care of it."

Emmy's eyes widen. "Thanks. I think."

"Have so much fun!" I cry, launching myself at her and wrapping her in a tight hug before I can think better of it. She stiffens before slowly returning my embrace. "And remember, I'm only one call away."

"You're the best," she murmurs before stepping away from me, grabbing her bag, and turning toward the door.

I watch as she swings it open, revealing a self-possessed Sterling leaning against the frame.

"Emmalyn." Twin flames of desire dance in his eyes as he looks her over. *Score for the outfit!* "You look gorgeous."

My heart races as she murmurs her thanks. Given their sordid history, these two are the last people I would imagine ending up together, but here they are beating the odds.

Watching them fills me with equal parts hope and dread—not only for them, but for me also.

Hope that Samson and I can overcome our past as well, but dread at the thought of us falling apart.

The idea is almost too much to bear. Especially tonight of all nights.

"You ready?" Sterling asks, taking her bag from her and slinging it over his shoulder.

Emmy nods.

"Then let's go." He's so enraptured with her that he doesn't even notice me standing in the background. It makes me wonder if Samson's focus ever tunnel visions when I'm in the room... if I'm ever all he can see.

"Where?" my best friend asks, but he pulls the door shut before I can hear his reply.

I stare at the closed door long after they leave, wishing like hell Samson was taking me on a surprise getaway for the weekend.

But he's not. Because he's out with my brother, who doesn't know we're together.

Happy-freaking-birthday to me.

DESPITE THE CHILL in the air, I'm exactly where I want to be.

The wind rustles the leaves overhead and the crickets' incessant chirping keep me from feeling too alone.

Even though that's precisely what I am—alone. Like always.

I know I could have made plans with any number of people. I'm not in high school anymore; I have friends now. But none of them are who I wanted to spend today with.

I only wanted Samson, but apparently, he's too busy to even remember. I could have reminded him, but I didn't think I'd need to—I've never had to before.

Growing up, he *always* remembered.

He would always text me at midnight on the dot, wishing me a happy birthday, saying he wanted to always be the first.

And in the mornings, he was always at my house first thing in the morning so he could be the first to tell me in person as well.

He always made a big deal out of my birthdays, especially once things between us shifted. Even before I had a phone, he would always find a way to be at our house bright and early so he could give me my gift and a birthday hug.

My brain wars over what hurts more—not getting anything from him last year other than a broken heart, or him sweeping back into my life only to forget.

Both suck.

He freaking sucks, I think to myself as I roll my blanket out, making myself a cozy little nest to curl up with my latest read. Just because I'm alone doesn't mean I can't have a birthday adventure.

I settle in, leaning against the trunk of my favorite old oak tree—the very same one I fell out of that fateful day—and power up my Kindle.

Before I know it, I'm lost in the pages and I'm no longer a sad girl in a field. Instead, I'm a teenage wolf shifter fighting like hell to keep my alpha status a secret from our new pack.

That is, until a pair of headlights and a familiar engine rumble cut through the field, robbing me of both my solitude and my peace.

I bookmark my place on my Kindle and darken the screen as he kills the engine and opens his door.

"What are you doing here?"

"I knew you'd be here," comes his reply, like that somehow miraculously explains his appearance. "Well, I checked your dorm first."

"I thought you were *with the guys,*" I say, finger-quotes and all.

"Luna, it's your birthday."

"Oh, so you remembered after all. Who clued you in? Orion?"

"You really think I forgot?"

I glare. "I know you did."

"You know, huh?" He's all swagger and I can't help but want to smack the knowing grin off his handsome face.

"Yes." I stand and cross my arms over my chest. "I know. Why else would you go out drinking with my brother? Why else would you not at the very least tell me happy birthday?"

"Maybe I wanted to surprise you."

"Fat chance," I scoff.

"What if I said I could prove it?"

"How'd you even find me, Samson?"

"Because I know you, Luna." He grins. "I know everything about you."

"Oh, yeah?" I throw my arms wide. "Then you should have known how much your stupid little stunt would hurt me!"

He has the good sense to look remorseful. "In hindsight, I can see my plan wasn't the best."

"You think?"

"Are you going to let me make it up to you?"

"How?"

Samson grins. "For starters, grab that blanket and bring it here."

"You want my blanket?"

"Yup." He snaps his fingers. "Move it, Luna."

"Bossy asshole," I mutter to myself as I gather up the blanket and my Kindle.

"Give me the blanket," he says as soon as I'm within arm's reach.

I hand it to him and he pops the tailgate of his truck, climbing up into the bed to smooth it out.

"What are you doing, Samson?"

He looks at me over his shoulder. "Making us a pallet. Now grab the sleeping bags and pillows from the cab."

"Sure thing." *Whatever you say.* I grab everything he asked for from the passenger seat and throw them into the back of the truck.

He gives me a look that clearly says I'm being a brat, but whatever. It's my birthday and I'll be a snot if I want to.

"Grab the cooler and then climb up here with me."

"Anything else you want me to do? Rub your feet? Balance your checkbook?"

"There's a lot of things I'd like you to do, Stella. But none of those are it."

"Like what?"

"Get the cooler."

I cross my arms and plant my feet. "No, tell me."

"Stubborn ass woman," he mutters, but the smile on his face belies his words.

"Here." I grab the ice chest and heft it up toward him before climbing up into the back of his truck. "Now what?"

"That depends—are you hungry?"

As if on cue, my stomach rumbles. "I could eat."

"You didn't go to dinner with your family. Why?"

I wriggle my legs into the sleeping bag and settle back against the cab of the truck. "I wasn't really in the mood to celebrate."

"Because of me."

It's not a question, but I feel the need to answer him anyway. "Yes and no."

"You don't have to explain."

"I want to."

Samson pops open the cooler top and pulls out two growlers, passing me one. "Coffee."

I twist the lid and take a sip. "Mmm. Just right."

His lips quirk. "I know."

"Thank you," I whisper, before taking another fortifying sip. "After last year, I was determined to ignore my birthday. I just wanted to pretend it was any other day. But then you came back... and I kept waiting. Waiting for some kind of acknowledgment."

"And it never came," Samson groans and my belly flutters. I hate that this hurt is still lingering between us. "I shouldn't have tried surprising you like this—I'm sorry."

"It's... it's fine. I was upset, but I can see your heart was in the right place. I guess even though we're trying to move past everything, I'm not quite there yet."

I wish I was though. I wish like hell I could find a way to stop feeling like the other shoe is about to drop.

"I don't expect you to be, Luna. I know I fucked up last year. I'm sorry."

"You don't have to keep apologizing." I take another sip of my coffee before closing the lid and leaning my head on his shoulder. "You really don't. While I don't like what you did, a part of me gets *why* you did it. You got scared—not for you, but for me—and as much as I don't like it, I get it."

"You're pretty wise for your age."

"Yeah, well." I snuggle closer into his side.

"You ready to eat?"

I shake my head. "Yeah, but can you just... hold me a minute first?"

"As long as you want, Luna," Samson says, wrapping both arms around me.

We sit in silence, both lost in our own thoughts for a few minutes. And even though the wind is still whispering through the trees and the crickets are still singing their song, in his arms, I no longer feel alone.

The warmth of his body sears mine, and my heart feels

too big for my chest, like it's thump-thump-thumping against my ribs so it can break free and run to Samson.

"Thank you," I whisper after a while.

"For what?"

"Everything. All of this."

He loosens his hold on me and leans back against the side of the bed. "You haven't seen anything yet."

"WHAT DOES THAT EVEN MEAN?" Stella asks as I reach back into the cooler.

"It means…" I trail off as I fish out the plastic container, presenting it to her triumphantly. "That no birthday is complete without these."

She takes it from me with a dubious look on her face. "Are these cupcakes?"

"Of course."

"From Crumbs?" she asks, referring to her favorite bakery down in the valley. She's been obsessed with their cupcakes since the day they opened.

In fact, I'm the one who took her—it was the summer before she started high school and her parents both had work and Orion was off with some girl.

So, when she came to me with pouty lips and puppy dog eyes, of course I said yes.

We bought one of every flavor—I used every fucking dollar and coin in my wallet to buy them—and then split them. She loved the pumpkin from the start, while I preferred the salted caramel.

I'll never forget the way she smiled and said that was perfect because they were both fall flavors and maybe it meant I'd fall for her.

I laughed it off like she was joking, but *damn*... it only took a few years for Stella to catch me; hook, line, and sinker.

I nod as she pries the lid off of the box.

"Oh my God—are they pumpkin?"

"Your favorite."

"But how did you know?" Her brow furrows. "Even my mom gets it wrong."

"What's it going to take?" I ask, my gaze unyielding, as I beg her to *see* how much I care for her.

She scrunches her nose, completely cute and clueless. "Take for what?"

"For you to get it."

"To get what?" Stella asks, frustration seeping into her tone.

I lift two cupcakes from the box and pass one to her. "To get that I know everything about you."

She readily takes the offered treat, running her finger through the decadent cream cheese frosting—like she always does—before sucking it off. "God, it's so good."

The sight of her tongue wrapping around her finger coupled with her moan has my dick straining against my jeans, but damn if she isn't right. These cupcakes are fucking tasty.

I bet they'd taste even better eaten off her naked body, I think to myself as she goes in for another lick of frosting.

"You're wrong," Stella says, as she peels the wrapper from hers and then tears off the bottom section of cake and presses it into the frosting, making a cupcake sandwich.

"Wrong about what?"

"You don't know *everything* about me."

It's a fight not to roll my eyes at her smart mouth. "Damn close, and the things I don't know, I have a lifetime to learn."

Thanks to the moon high in the sky, I can see the pretty pink blush staining her cheeks. "A lifetime, huh?"

"You think I'm ever letting you go again?"

She shrugs, popping the last bite of her cupcake into her mouth.

"Mark my words Luna—I am *never* letting you go."

"That's an awfully big promise."

"It's always been my promise. Do you remember what I said when I gave you that ring you wear around your neck?"

Her cheeks burn even brighter. "That we belonged to one another."

I nod. "That's right. Even when I messed up and we were apart, you were still mine. The fact that you never took off that ring—not really—proves it."

"You broke my heart Samson, but even then, every shattered piece still beat just for you."

Unable to help myself, I lean forward and cup her cheek. "You're it for me, Stella Cartwright. For as long as I have breath in my lungs and blood pumping through my veins, you're it for me."

"Samson," she exhales my name and the sound of it goes straight to my dick and I want nothing more than to haul her into my lap so I can see all of the other ways I can make her say my name.

But I don't—not yet.

"You forgot something," I tell her, grabbing another cupcake.

"What?"

I produce a candle and lighter from my back pocket. "I didn't sing to you and you didn't get to make a wish."

"Oh, no, you don't have to do that."

"I want to." Truly, I do. Aside from last year, I've never missed singing her happy birthday. My voice is shit, but it's always been something I've done for her.

"Samson." She's all business, trying to convince me not to serenade her.

"Stella." But I'm not so easily swayed. This woman deserves the best, to be spoiled, to know she is so fucking loved that she never questions where she stands with me ever again.

She rolls her pretty blue eyes. "This is so embarrassing."

"What is? Me singing to you?"

"Yes! We're alone in the woods! It's weird."

I scoot closer to her. "That's right, we're all alone, there's no reason to be embarrassed." I stick the candle into the cupcake and light it as I start singing to her.

With every word, Stella's cheeks get pinker, until finally the song is over and they're burning scarlet. "Make a wish, Luna."

She leans in and blows out the candle. "Thank you, Samson," she murmurs so softly I almost don't hear it.

"What'd you wish for?" I ask, as she once again drags her index finger through the frosting.

"Nothing." She swirls her tongue around her fingertip before gathering up another taste of the rich cream cheese frosting.

I grab her wrist and redirect her finger to my lips. "Nothing?" I ask as I draw her finger into my mouth. "Fuck, Stella," I grunt as she climbs on top of me, straddling my thighs.

"It's already come true," she says, sealing her lips to mine.

Her tongue flicks against my lips, and while I'm tempted to take all she's offering, I cup her cheek and pull back. "Don't you want your present?"

"This isn't it?" she asks.

I shake my head as I reach around Stella to retrieve the small gift box I stowed in the corner of the truck bed.

"What is it?" she asks, inspecting the box from all angles before bringing it to her ear and shaking it.

"Open it."

I smirk as she carefully unties the lopsided bow and sets it to the side before tearing off the paper. She's always been this way—saving the ribbon and demolishing the paper. It's one quirk on a list of many that makes her cute as hell.

Her big blue eyes grow comically wider as she opens the box. "Samson?"

"Yes?"

She fingers the key nestled inside the cardboard. "It's... this..."

"It's what?"

Her eyes snap to mine. "It's too soon! Are you freaking crazy?"

"What do you think that's a key to?" I ask, a grin tugging at my lips.

"Your... house?" She phrases it as a question.

"Read the card, Luna."

"Right." Stella nods and tugs the small envelope free.

A smile tugs at my lips as I think over the words scrawled across the card.

HAPPY BIRTHDAY LUNA—
KNOWING YOU, YOU'RE GOING TO SEE THE KEY

AND FLIP, BUT I PROMISE, I'M NOT ASKING YOU TO MOVE IN. NOT YET.

NO, THIS KEY GOES TO THE SHED IN MY BACK-YARD. IN IT, YOU'LL FIND EVERYTHING YOU COULD EVER WANT TO GARDEN, AND IN CASE I MISSED ANYTHING, THERE'S A GIFT CARD TUCKED INTO THE TOP DRAWER OF THE DESK INSIDE.

WHILE I KNOW WE'RE NOT READY TO LIVE TOGETHER, MY BACKYARD IS YOURS. PLANT ANYTHING AND EVERYTHING YOU WANT... EVERY SINGLE INCH OF SPACE IS YOURS TO DO WITH WHAT YOU WILL.

I... YOU'RE NOT READY FOR WHAT I WANT TO SAY HERE, BUT SOON.

—SAMSON

"Are you serious?"

I nod. "Deadly."

"Samson, this is too much." Her pretty blue eyes shine with unshed tears.

"It's not enough." I would give anything to see her smile, especially knowing that for a time, I was the reason for her tears.

She grabs the key, slides it into her back pocket, and flings herself at me, peppering my face and neck with kisses. "Thank you!"

"There's one more thing," I say once she settles down, sitting sideways across my lap with her head on my chest.

"You can't be serious." She tips her head back to look up at me. "This is already perfect."

Pride swells within me at her praise, but I know I can do better. "I'm as serious now as I was the last time you asked."

"Deadly?" Her lips tip up in the prettiest of grins as she idly plays with the strings to my hoodie.

"That's right."

"Okay." Her throat works as she swallows. "What is it?"

"Do you have plans next weekend?" I already know she doesn't thanks to some sleuthing on my part, but I ask anyway.

"No..." Stella hedges. "But something tells me I'm about to."

"Aren't you perceptive?" I skim my index finger over the apple of her cheek.

"You're about as subtle as a freight train."

"Choo-choo."

"Oh my God!" Stella's laughter lights me up, like electricity in my veins. I would make a fool out of myself anywhere, anytime, to hear that laugh.

"Don't you wanna know our plans?"

She extracts herself from my arms and moves so she's straddling my lap. "If I say yes, are you actually going to tell me?"

I pretend to think it over. "Nope."

"Okay, then."

"You're just going to let it go? To roll with it?"

Stella shrugs. "Nope. I'm going to pester you and wear you down until you tell me."

"Not gonna happen."

"Maybe I'll bribe you with sexual favors?"

Yes, please, I think to myself. "Pack a bag and be ready to head out around lunchtime Friday."

"Bossy." She bites her lip in that way of hers—sexy and innocent all at once.

"You fucking love it."

"I—wait, pack a bag?" She searches my gaze. "Are we going somewhere?"

"We are."

"Where?"

"Are you always this hard to surprise?"

"Can I have a hint at least?"

"Clothing's optional?"

She smacks at my chest, her eyes shining bright. "A real hint, Samson Carter!"

"No can do." I tug her into my side.

"Then how will I know what to pack?"

I whistle innocently. "Like I said, clothing's optional."

"ARE you going to tell me where we're going?" Stella asks as we head north on I-75.

"Nope," is all I say, forcing my focus to stay on the road in front of me—a feat in and of itself when all I really want to do is drink in the woman sitting next to me.

It feels like I've been sporting a semi for seven days straight over the thought of having Stella to myself for an entire weekend—and now that she's riding shotgun in my truck, I'm counting the miles and the minutes until we're well and truly alone.

It's more than the physical stuff though; I'm just as eager to just relax with her, to unwind and for us to stay up all night talking like we used to.

That's not to say I don't want to fuck her on every available surface of the cabin I rented, because I do. I want to make her scream my name so loudly that even the bears in the woods know she's mine. But I also want to cuddle her and talk and just spend time with her.

"Ugh. Well, how much longer until we're there?"

I risk a glance her way as I merge onto TN-66. "In this traffic? About an hour or so."

"We're going to Gatlinburg?"

"We are."

"What are we going to do there?" she asks, her eyes burning a hole in the side of my face.

"Anything you want."

"Anything?" Stella sits up a little straighter in her seat.

"So, if told you I wanted to stay naked in bed the entire time, we could?"

I grip the wheel a little tighter. "Fuck. Yes."

"And if I said I wanted us to sleep in separate beds and to go hiking every day, we could do that too?"

"Sure could," I reply mildly, hoping like hell she's only messing around.

"Hmm." She leans forward and fishes a tablet of some kind out of her bag. "I'm going to read until we get there."

I drive in silence as she reads, smiling as she laughs every couple of pages. Finally, I can't stand it anymore, and I ask what she's reading.

"Do you really want to know?"

"How can I buy you books and shit if I don't know what you like?"

"You... you want to buy me books?"

"I want to get you anything that makes you smile and laugh like you have been for the last ten minutes."

"It's a rom-com about a country music star and an adult summer camp."

"Adult summer camp... that's a thing?"

I see her nod from the corner of my eye. "Apparently."

"And what's happening to make you giggle like that?"

"Um." She flexes her fingers in her lap. "Do you really want to know?"

I nod.

"It's kind of hard to explain—um—the hero and heroine are at an anything but clothes party at camp and they're going skinny dipping, and—"

"There's an idea," I murmur.

"What?"

"Skinny dipping." I turn to her and wag my brows. "Is this the same book you were reading on your birthday?"

She giggles and I swear to God, the sound penetrates all the way down to my heart. "No. I've read like two books since then."

"That's... a lot of reading."

"But I love it."

It's on the tip of my tongue to tell her that I love her, but I swallow it down. We're not there yet. "Books and gardening. What else do you do for fun now that you're all grown up?"

Stella taps something on the screen on her tablet before powering it down. "You act like you were gone for years rather than months."

My heart thumps painfully against my ribs—this is the first time she's mentioned my absence without malice or hurt. "Maybe, but sometimes it feels like you're a totally different person."

Stella makes a little sound of protest, so I rush to add, "I don't mean that in a bad way, Luna. You've grown into this fierce, sexy woman who knows what she wants and isn't afraid to take life by the horns. You're smart and funny and—"

"Are you saying I wasn't all of those things before?"

"Yes and no," I answer honestly. "You're harder than you were before, and I know—and hate—that it's my fault. But at the same time, I think you know yourself better. You know your wants and needs and worth. It kills me that I hurt you, but I think... now, you're no longer willing to settle. Now, you're more than willing to demand what you *know* you deserve."

She reaches over and clasps my hand. "Being with you was never settling, Samson."

We lapse into a comfortable silence for the rest of the drive. My mind, however, is working overtime, trying to think of ways to make sure Stella knows exactly how I feel about her.

Telling her I love her won't cut it—I have to *show* her. *You could tell her brother about y'all's relationship,* my brain shouts, but the driveway for the cabin comes into view before I can give the idea much more thought.

"We're here," I murmur, pulling onto the winding gravel trail.

"Samson!" Stella shouts when our cabin comes into view. "Are we staying in a freaking treehouse?"

"We are."

"Oh my God! This is so freaking cool!"

"Just wait until you see the inside," I murmur, throwing my truck into park.

Stella's unbuckled and out of the truck before I can think about opening her door for her. "Come on! Hurry up, old man!"

Smiling, I grab our bags from the back seat and join her. "I'm not that much older than you."

"Old enough to go gray first!" She sticks her tongue out.

"I'll show you old," I mutter, taking a menacing step toward her.

She giggles and darts away, running toward the steps leading up to our treehouse.

I take off after her, and even though I could easily overtake her, I make sure to let her keep the lead—the view of her tight ass bounding up the stairs is worth losing, no questions asked.

"Beat you!" Stella crows when she reaches the door, mere steps ahead of me.

"Pretty sure I'm the winner," I retort, dragging my eyes over her body with deliberate slowness.

"Perv."

"Only for you."

"Whatever." She shakes her head like she thinks I'm joking. I'm not though, *I'm so not.* "Let's go inside?"

I retrieve my phone from my back pocket, punch in the lock code, and swing the door open.

"Wow," Stella exhales the single word as she crosses the threshold. "Samson, this is..." She spins in a wide circle, taking in the white shiplap walls, the iron spiral staircase, and the high ceilings. "Beautiful."

"You are," I agree, only I'm looking at her, because like always, anytime Stella's around, she's all I can see.

"So, what do you want to do first?"

It's on the tip of my tongue to say *you*, but there's plenty of time for that. "This weekend is all about you, so I'm down for whatever."

"What's there to do around here?"

"Aside from the tourist-y crap, there's supposed to be some good hiking on the property."

Her eyes brighten. "I love hiking!"

"I know you do. Let's put our stuff down and we can head out."

"What's that sound?" Stella asks as we near the end of the trail.

"There's a creek that cuts through the property."

Stella grins and then takes off toward the sound of the bubbling water.

By the time I catch up to her, she's standing at the creek bed in just her bra and panties. "What are you doing?" I ask, cutting my eyes left and then right, even though I know we're on private property. The thought of anyone else seeing my Stella like this makes me feel murderous.

She turns to look at me over her shoulder and grins, unclasping her bra. "Thought you wanted to skinny dip?"

"Stella."

"What?"

I damn near swallow my tongue when she shimmies out of her little panties. "It's gonna be freezing." There's only a slight chill in the air, but I know the water has to be icy.

She turns to face me, her supple, tanned body on full display. My gaze greedily eats up every inch of exposed flesh and my mouth waters at the thought of sucking on her tightly beaded nipples. "You'll keep me warm, right?"

"Fuck, Luna." I tug my shirt over my head as she steps one foot into the water.

"Yes please," she murmurs back as I toe off my boots and socks before stripping out of my pants. "Come on, it's not too bad."

I stride toward her with purposeful steps, that is until I step into the water. "Fuck!"

Stella giggles.

"Laugh it up, but I'm pretty sure the Titanic sank in warmer waters than this."

"Come here, you big baby." She crooks her index finger

at me, and despite my good judgment and the ball-shriveling temperature, I wade out to her.

By the time I reach her, I'm pretty sure my junk has receded up into my fucking body. "Told you it'd be cold."

"It's not that bad," she stammers out between shivers.

"Pretty sure your nipples could cut glass." I reach between us and drag my thumb over one of the hardened buds.

"Samson," she moans my name as she wraps her arms around my neck and her legs around my waist. "Kiss me."

I lean down and capture her chattering lips with my own. Our tongues tangle together as we cling to each other for warmth. Stella's hips rock against mine, and while my dick twitches with interest, it's just too damn cold.

"You know there's a hot tub on the deck, right?" I ask, breaking our kiss.

"What? No! Why are we out here freezing?"

"You're the one that stripped and ran out into the water like a crazy person."

She pouts. "You said you wanted to skinny dip."

"I am always down to get naked with you, but I'm not opposed to continuing this somewhere warmer."

"Yes please." She releases me and heads for the shore.

"OH MY GOD!" I moan in delight as I lower myself into the warm, bubbling water. "This is so much better."

Samson drops down beside me, stretching his arms out wide against the edge of the hot tub. "Agreed." His fingertips dance over my shoulder, causing me to shiver as gooseflesh erupts all over my skin.

His touch has always had this kind of effect on me—platonic or not—but there's something about knowing I can touch him back now that makes even the slightest brush of his skin against mine so much better.

"This is nice," I say after a while.

"What is?"

"Us, together." I tip my head toward him, licking my lips when he looks down at me. "Alone."

"It is," Samson agrees, wrapping his arm around my shoulder and tugging me even closer.

"You know," I drawl out the word as I twist myself to straddle his thighs, his semi-hard dick bobbing in the water between us. "Now that we're warm, we should finish what we started in the creek."

Samson moves his hands from my hips, over the dips in my waist, all the way up to my breasts, where he cups and kneads the sensitive flesh. "Should we?" he asks, his tone pure sin.

"Please." I punctuate my request with a roll of my hips that has us both groaning.

"Didn't I tell you; you never have to beg with me? You want me to fuck you? I'll fuck you. You want me to lick your pussy until your legs are shaking, I'll do it with a smile on my face. You want to snuggle and watch a movie? I'll do that too, Luna. I'll do anything for you." He grips my chin and holds my gaze to his. "There's a catch though."

"What's that?" I grind down on him again, his cock now fully hard between us.

"You have to tell me what you want."

I raise up onto my knees, bracing myself with one hand on his chest while I snake the other between us. "Or I could show you." I grab his dick and line it up so I can rub myself against him.

"Fuck me," he rumbles as I press my hips into his.

"Soon," I whisper my promise against the heated skin of his neck before flicking my tongue over his damp skin, licking my way up to his mouth. "But first, I want to kiss you and touch you and rub you into a frenzy. And then, when you're on the verge of combusting, I want you to take me inside and fuck me."

Samson grips my hips and begins guiding my movements, pulling me up and down against his dick a few times before stilling me completely.

"What's wrong?" I ask, worried I did something wrong.

"Turn around," he murmurs, a heated look in his eyes.

"Why?"

"Because I told you to, Luna." He leans in, presses a

fast, hard kiss to my lips. "Turn around, put your knees on the seat, and your elbows on the edge."

Despite my trepidation, I do as he says.

"You're so beautiful." His praise is a rough growl that has my whole body tightening with need. "So perfect." He leans over me, crowding me from behind. "So. Fucking. Mine."

"Yes," I agree, as his lips meet my spine and he kisses away all of my earlier doubts.

"Say it." He palms the tops of my thighs from behind, digging his fingers into the soft flesh. "I want to hear the words."

"I'm yours, Samson."

"Hell yeah, you are." He thrusts against me, his dick gliding against my pussy lips. "You trust me?"

"You know I do."

He nuzzles his face into the crook of my neck, nipping at the skin as he shifts his right hand between my front and the wall of the hot tub.

"What are you—oh, God!" I shout, as the water from the jet pulses against my clit.

"You like that?" Samson asks, thrusting against me once again.

I'm not sure *like* is a strong enough word—it's like my showerhead turned up to twenty. Or maybe the added pleasure comes from Samson. Either way, it feels amazing.

"Yes." I circle my hips, desperate for release.

"What about this?"

Something—his thumb—presses against my asshole, causing my entire body to jerk to attention like a steel cable pulled too tight.

"Relax," he whispers, peppering my neck and shoulders with kisses.

I take a deep breath and nod. I know he'd never do anything to hurt me. So, if he thinks I'll like this, I'm willing to try.

I will my muscles to unclench as he rubs his thumb against me, applying the barest hint of pressure. The combined effect of his dick sliding against my wet folds, his thumb rubbing tight circles, and the jet swirling against my clit sets off wave after wave of dark, unexpected pleasure.

"Samson," I moan his name when the sensations become too much—and yet, not enough. "I need you. I need you inside of me."

He thrusts harder from behind me, a growl rattling loose from his chest. "Not until you come."

"I'm so close," I promise him, nearly delirious with need.

"Get there." He brings his left hand around to pinch my nipple. With the added touch, I detonate, shooting off like a rocket leaving Earth's atmosphere. "That's right, Luna, scream as loud as you want to. No one can hear you but me."

"Please, please!" I beg, as I come down from my orgasm knowing the next one he gives me will be even better.

"Let's go inside." Samson backs away from me, stepping out of the hot tub. He extends a hand toward me to help me up and over the side of the tub. "Bedroom's up the stairs," is all he says, and like the desperate horny girl I am, I make it there in record time.

Despite being right behind me, by the time Samson ascends the steps, I'm laid out in the middle of the bed, my legs spread with one hand cupping my breasts and the other fingering my clit.

"You get the party started without me?" His eyes move over my body, my skin heating under his intense stare.

"I was imagining what you were going to do to me when you got up here." I've never spoken to anyone like this in my whole life, but it works in porn and the way he's looking at me right now, tells me it works for him too.

He stalks toward the bed like a predator with prey in its sight, but am I really his prey when I'm all too willing to let him feast on me?

"What were you imagining?" he asks, the bed dipping beneath his weight.

I swallow roughly, willing my nerves away. Knowing my words turn him on is well-worth stepping a little outside of my comfort zone. "I was imagining your lips on my pussy."

"You want me to lick you?" His tongue darts out, wetting his lips.

I spread myself with two fingers. "Please."

"Move over," he says, claiming the spot I just vacated. "Come up here." He pats his chest.

"What?" I can feel my cheeks burn as the implication of his words fully sink in.

"You heard me."

Acting braver than I feel, I crawl up his body until I'm straddling his chest.

But in one single motion, Samson slides his arms beneath my thighs, grabs my ass, and pulls me onto his face.

The sudden movement causes me to wobble, and I have to brace myself against the wall behind the bed. "Samson," I hiss his name.

"You remember when we danced at that party?" His hot breath tickles my sensitive flesh, making me squirm.

"Yeah..." My breath saws in and out of my lungs as I balance over him.

"Dance like that now."

"What?" I ask again, as my entire body flushes with an odd combination of embarrassment and need.

"You heard me, Luna. Move your hips and rub that pretty little pussy on my face."

My heart thunders so loud in my chest, I swear I can hear it as I tentatively swivel my hips. The feeling of his stubble alone is electric but when he flicks his tongue against me on my next rotation, I damn near see stars.

"That's right, fuck my face, Stella." Samson grips my hips with his big, strong hands, guiding my movements in time with his ministrations, until my legs are trembling and my body is on fire.

"Come for me. Come all over my face. Let me taste your desire."

His rumbled command sends a flutter through me and before I know it, my thighs are clamped tight around his face as my second orgasm barrels through me.

"Taste so fucking good, Luna." The feel of his lips moving against me sends aftershocks racing through me.

"Samson," I whisper his name. "How do I get down?"

"I've got you," he says and the next thing I know, I'm flat on my back on the opposite end of the bed with him settling between my legs. "You liked that?"

How is that even a question, I think to myself as I nod. I'm pretty sure I came harder than I ever have before.

"Words, Luna."

"It was so good."

"Next time, you can suck my dick while I eat your pussy."

His filthy words send a new pulse of desire rushing through me. "Like... a sixty-nine?"

He smirks down at me. "Just like that."

"I'm willing to try." And I mean it, because that's the

thing about Samson Carter—there isn't much of anything I wouldn't do for him.

Samson reaches between us, gripping the base of his cock and lining it up at my entrance. He rubs the blunt head over me, once... twice... before pushing inside of me with agonizing slowness.

"Fuck, you feel good." He draws his hips back, almost pulling out of me before slamming himself back in. "Like you were made for me."

"Yes," I cry, clawing at his chest. "Only you."

He continues his brutal pace. My body is caught somewhere between pleasure and pain as he fucks me into the mattress.

"You want to come again?" Samson asks, slowing so we're grinding together, creating the most delicious friction.

"I... I don't know if I can." I feel wrung out, drunk with pleasure.

"You can, and you will," Samson says, pulling out of me completely.

"What are you doing?" I ask, as he settles himself back against the headboard, his right leg out straight and his left bent at the knee.

Samson crooks a finger at me. "Come sit on my dick."

"Oh... okay."

I move to straddle him, but he stops me. "Put your back to me and hold on to my left leg."

Self-consciousness ripples through me as I position myself on top of him. But the second I slide down onto him, it melts away into mind-numbing pleasure.

My breathing shallows as I test the position, bracing myself against his leg as I rock my hips.

"That's right, Stella. Use me, get yourself off, come all over me, so I can fill you the fuck up."

Every nerve ending in my body is on fire as I undulate against him, chasing my third orgasm.

"Lean back," he instructs me, his voice tight. "Put your hand on my chest."

"You're so deep," I moan at the new angle, rotating my hips even faster while Samson's calloused hands explore every inch of my skin he can reach.

"Touch yourself," he demands, flexing his hips beneath me.

I press my two fingers to my clit, rubbing the sensitive bud in tight circles. "I'm gonna—" is all the warning he gets before my pussy grips him tight as I come for the third time.

"Fuck yes, Luna. Milk my dick." Samson grips my hips and stills me as he flexes his hips up off the bed and spills himself inside of me. "One of these days, I'm gonna put a fucking baby in you."

"I..." *I don't know how to respond to that.* Is he still dirty talking or does he really want me to be the mother of his child one day?

"Hey, are you okay?" he asks, noticing the change in me immediately.

I have a million questions I want to ask him, but I can't seem to get my mouth and my brain on the same page.

"Stella, baby, talk to me."

On still-quaking legs, I slide off of him. "Do... do you want kids?" I finally ask.

"Why don't we get cleaned up?" he asks, and my heart sinks. *Clearly it was nothing more than bedroom talk.* The thought hurts more than it probably should, but for as long as I can remember, every game of house I ever played, he was the dad.

"Sure," I whisper, following behind him into the en suite bathroom.

I stand here silently while he turns on the shower. My heart thumps painfully in my chest as his release slides down my thighs. *How are we still not on the same page?*

"Come on," he says, once the water is warm.

As soon as I step beneath the spray, the tears I was holding at bay fall, mingling with the droplets from the showerhead as they roll down my cheeks unchecked.

"Stella." He steps up behind me. "Look at me."

I shake my head, but he persists.

"Turn around. Now."

Slowly, I pivot to face him, letting him see the rainstorm in my blue eyes.

"Dammit," he mutters before scooping me into his arms. "I need you to listen to me, okay?"

I nod, keeping my eyes trained on the water circling the drain.

"Need you to look at me too." Samson grips my chin and directs my gaze up to his. "You're it for me. I want you to have my last name, my ring on your finger, and I damn sure want to put my baby in your belly."

"Then why... why did you brush me off back there?"

"Stella," he breathes my name like I'm the most precious thing in the world to him. "You're only nineteen. The last thing I want to do is scare you away when I just got you back."

"I'm not scared." I soften against him. "Every future I see for myself involves you."

"Fuck yeah, it does." He leans down and kisses my lips. "We can have a whole baseball team's worth of kids if you want, Luna. After you finish school and get your degree."

I giggle, despite my earlier sadness. "Maybe not that many."

"However many kids you want," he vows. "You know I can't say no to you."

"It's not only about me, Samson. I know you're trying to make up for leaving, but I... I think it's time we leave the past in the past and focus on our future—one where we do things together. Decide things together. One built on love and respect and communication and compromise."

I reach up to cup both of his cheeks. "Does that sound good to you?"

He drags his teeth over his bottom lip before giving me his best smile. "Sounds fucking perfect."

"YOU COMING OUT TONIGHT?" Orion asks.

I pull my phone away from my ear to check the time.

"Depends. What are you doing?"

He hesitates.

"I swear to God, if you say ATF."

"Fine. I won't say it."

"Bro, you're obsessed."

He scoffs. "Like you're one to talk. Whoever this mystery chick you're banging is must have a magical pussy because it feels like I hardly ever see you anymore."

It's on the tip of my tongue to tell him off, but he's partially right.

In the week since our trip to Gatlinburg, Stella and I have been damn near inseparable. Any time she's not in class or with her roommate, she's with me.

When she isn't here tending to her newly planted garden, she's parked on my couch studying, and I fucking love it. I love having her in my space.

If it were up to me, she'd be here full time. But I know

she needs to be able to experience all life has to offer, which means living on campus while she's in school.

Swear to God though, the day she graduates, I'll be loading her shit into the bed of my truck and moving her into my place.

But before we can do any of that, the man I've called my best friend my entire life needs to know the truth about us.

I was hoping to tell Orion about us this weekend—for us to talk man-to-man, since Stella's camping with friends, but she begged me not to. She said she wanted to be there too, and while I still think it should just be Orion and me, she batted those long lashes of hers up at me, and I found myself agreeing to wait for her.

Maybe that makes me pussy whipped—so be it. Stella Cartwright is well worth it.

Since I can't say any of the things I want to, I settle on, "It's more than fucking."

"You have feelings for her?" he asks, his tone riddled with confusion. "Like, it's something serious?"

"Yeah, man. She's... she's the one."

"Damn, Samson." He laughs. "Never thought I'd see the day."

"Stranger things have been known to happen."

"I don't know, brother, I've never even seen you seriously date anyone and now you're saying you're with some chick and it's serious, but I don't even know her fucking name."

I run a hand through my hair, tugging on the ends. *You know her, brother, you've known her your whole life.* "Yeah..."

"It's almost like you're trying to hide her from me or something." A beat passes. "You're not seeing Birdie, are you? Fuck, man, is that why you never want to come? You know how I—"

"Chill. I'm not seeing your stripper."

I can hear him exhale his relief. "Thank God."

"You're still obsessed with her?"

"Stalker level. I actually bought a membership to the club."

"You ever think of just… asking her out?"

Orion laughs, but it's void of any humor. "Man, like a girl like her would ever give me the time of day."

"You never know, man. Objectively, you're a catch."

"But she's a fucking queen."

I shake my head, not knowing what to say to my friend. "You have fun tonight, man. I'm going to stay home. But think about what I said."

"About asking her out?" he asks and then shrugs. "Maybe. See you Sunday?"

"Hell yeah—I'd never miss your mom's cooking."

"We're actually going out. Mom won an award. But she wanted me to make sure you knew you were still invited."

"Send me the details and I'll be there."

As I end the call, I see a text from Stella blinking at me from the notification bar.

STELLA

I wish you were here.

Me

Me too, Luna. You having fun?

STELLA

Yeah, we are. The guys are pitching tents.
Hey… do you think there are bears out
here?

ME

Uh… probably.

STELLA

WHAT?!?!?!

ME

Chill, you'll be fine. I'm sure people camp there enough that they stay away.

STELLA

You think so? Now I really wish you were here!

ME

You'll be fine, Luna. Just keep the fire going all night and make sure you don't leave any food out.

STELLA

Okay… Well, everyone wants to hike, so talk later?

ME

You know it.

I toggle out of my text screen, with a smile on my face. For as much as she loves her plants, Stella isn't the biggest fan of the great outdoors.

I pull up the app for my TV remote, ready to binge-watching some *Property Brothers* to pass the time. I don't know what it is about their show, but I fucking love it.

Three episodes later, my phone rings, with Stella's name flashing across the screen. I slide my thumb across the screen, pathetically eager to hear her voice.

Except before I can get a word out, a deep, masculine voice greets me. "Samson?"

"Who's this?"

"Gabe, we met—"

"I remember. Where's Stella? Why are you calling me from her phone?"

"We're at Central North—"

"What?" I shout, jumping up and grabbing my keys. "Why?"

He chuckles. "If you'd stop interrupting me, you'd know."

"Fine. Speak."

"She tripped at the campsite and twisted her ankle pretty bad. We're in the emergency waiting room and she keeps asking for you."

"I'm on my way."

Fifteen minutes later, I fly through the automatic doors, my heart jackhammering in my chest as I scan the waiting area, looking for Stella.

"Sir, can we help you?" the nurse behind the desk asks, right as I spot my girl.

"I'm good," I say with a tight smile, as I head toward Stella.

She's sitting in a wheelchair, looking smaller than ever, squished between the chairs Gabe and Zach are occupying on either side of her.

"Samson, you're here."

I kneel down beside her. "If you're here, I'm here, Luna. Are you in pain?"

Sniffling, she nods.

"What happened?" I ask, pinning both men with a hard glare.

Zach cuts his eyes to his boyfriend. "Ask him."

I stand, focusing all of my attention on Gabe, not caring

one bit that he could probably crush me single-handedly—which is saying something, I'm not exactly puny. "What. Happened?"

"Samson," Stella whispers, but I keep my eyes locked on the man in front of me.

"We were goofing around and she fell."

"Gonna need more details."

"Fine." Gabe rolls his eyes. "I was chasing her. It was an accident."

I'm ready to tear him a new one when Stella reaches over and takes my hand. "Leave him be. I was antagonizing him. It really was a stupid accident."

Like always, her touch soothes me; which is bullshit, because I should be the one comforting her.

"Make some room," I say, not caring which of them moves, as long as I end up next to Stella.

Gabe stands with a resigned huff. "Take a seat, caveman."

"Gladly."

"Be nice," Stella begs, her blue eyes brimming with tears.

"I'm sorry, Luna. I know I'm being an asshole, but seeing you hurt... fuck."

Gabe grumbles something under his breath, but Zach jabs him in the ribs with his elbow. "Ignore him. When I got a concussion last year during a soccer match, he acted just like you." He tips his head to the side and his long braids follow. "Maybe worse."

"Excuse me for loving you."

"I love that you love me," Zach says, patting Gabe's knee. "And I love you too. But quit giving Samson shit for acting the same way you do."

"Whatever."

Zach exchanges a glance with Stella. "Alpha men."

She giggles and lays her head on my shoulder; then and there, I decide Zach's all right in my book.

"Did they say how long?"

"Haven't said shit," Gabe replies, still surly.

"How long have y'all been here?"

"We called right when we got inside."

"It could be a while then," I say, glancing around the busy waiting room. "Y'all can go if you want."

The two men trade looks.

"We'll stay," Gabe declares.

"Or," Zach hedges. "We could grab food for everyone since we didn't get to eat."

"We'll do whatever Sunshine wants."

Stella yawns and snuggles in as close as the armrests between us allows. "Y'all can go if you want. I hate the thought of keeping y'all here."

"We don't mind."

"Seriously, Gabe. It's fine. Samson's got me. Y'all should go back to the campsite or out for dinner, something better than sitting here in this freezing-ass hospital."

"Are you sure?" Gabe asks, looking down at her.

"Positive."

He stares hard down at Stella, before finally relenting. "Text us updates."

Stella nods her agreement and the two head out, leaving us alone to wait.

"Are you hurting?"

"Yeah." She clutches the hem of my flannel. "It's throbbing."

"You want me to see if I can get you something? Some Tylenol?" I glance down at her ankle. "It's pretty swollen."

"I hope it's not broken." The despair in her voice guts me.

"Twisted, sprained, or broken, I'll take care of you, Luna."

She tips her head back to look up at me. "Promise?"

As gently as possible, I lean down and press my lips to hers. "I swear."

Stella falls quiet as we wait to be called back, but I keep murmuring to her, reassuring her that she's going to be okay and that I'll take care of her.

"Stella Cartwright?" We both glance toward the sound of the masculine voice.

"Come on, Luna, let's get you fixed up."

I stand and wheel her toward where the nurse is waiting, clipboard in hand.

"Right back this way," the nurse says as we approach, leading us through a set of double doors and down a short hallway. "Let's get you up onto the bed and then we can go over everything."

He steps forward to help Stella, but I beat him to it, gently lifting her out of the chair. I brush a kiss across her forehead before placing her down on the small mattress.

"Okay, then," the nurse says, smiling down at his clipboard. "My name's Liam, and you are..."

"Stella Cartwright."

"Perfect." He proceeds to ask a whole host of questions, from her date of birth to her last menstrual cycle. "Alright, that's everything. Let's get your foot elevated and I'll be right back with an ice pack and something for the pain, okay?"

As soon as Liam steps out of the room, Stella reaches for me. "It hurts," she sniffles, trying to keep the tears at bay.

I glance down at her ankle; the skin is puffy and

bruised. It pains me just looking at it. "I know." I lean down and press a kiss to her temple.

"Don't," she whispers as I move to stand, clutching at my shirt like it's her lifeline. "Don't go."

"I'm not going anywhere, Luna." I smooth her hair away from her face. "I've got you."

Ten minutes pass without Liam returning. Logically, I know he's busy and we're not his only patients but watching Stella whimper in pain cancels out any bit of logic I have.

The only thing stopping me from storming the nurses' station is my unwillingness to leave her side.

Finally, after what feels like a lifetime, a knock sounds from the other side of the door.

"Sorry about that," Liam says apologetically. "Tell me if this hurts." He drapes a towel over her ankle and settles the ice pack on top of it.

Stella's hold on me tightens as she winces in pain.

I listen intently as he goes over the pain meds he's administering, explaining the dosage and possible side effects. "If you begin to feel nauseated, don't hesitate to hit the call button for some Zofran. The doctor should be in shortly."

"Thanks," Stella murmurs, her eyelids heavy as hours of pain give way to exhaustion.

The sound of the door opening rouses Stella from the first bit of rest she's had all night. "Samson?" she mumbles my name, searching for me in the dimly lit room.

"I'm here, Luna," I assure her, squeezing her hand for good measure.

"Sorry to wake you, Stella. I'm Dr. Gardner. If you could just confirm your date of birth for me really quick." She verifies the date Stella gives against her paperwork. "Perfect. Tell me about what's going on?"

"I was camping with friends, and fell."

"On a scale of one to ten, how's your pain?" she asks, gently removing the ice pack and towel from Stella's ankle.

"Before meds, an eight. Now it's more like a six."

"Can you rotate your ankle?"

Stella shakes her head no.

The doctor runs her through a series of other tests, checking the pulse in her foot, along with her range of motion. Stella, despite her obvious discomfort, handles the whole thing like a champ.

"Okay, Stella, I think we need to send you for X-rays." Dr. Gardner places the towel and ice pack back over her swollen ankle. "I'm going to put the order in and someone will be by to wheel you down to radiology shortly."

"Thanks," Stella whispers, before allowing herself to sink back into the thin pillow propping her up.

"Are you okay?" I ask, threading my fingers through hers.

"Just tired. And hurting." She turns her head to look my way. "And tired of hurting."

"I'm sorry," I say, but she's already drifted back into a fitful sleep.

As I watch her rest, I'm torn between texting Orion to let him know she's hurt and keeping it to myself. Her family —especially her mom—would want to be here with her, but how can I explain my presence without outing us to her family?

At this point, my loyalty lies with Stella; and plus, what's one more lie where her family is concerned?

Countless minutes pass before another knock sounds.

"Come in."

"Stella Cartwright?" a young-looking nurse asks.

"Huh?"

The nurse smiles. "Are you Stella Cartwright?"

My girl nods sleepily.

"I'm here to take you down to radiology. If you could verify your birth date, please?"

Stella groans as she wiggles herself into a more upright position before replying.

"Okay, great. We're going to move you into the wheelchair and then we'll be off."

The nurse looks like a strong wind would blow her over, so I take charge and transfer Stella from the bed to the chair.

"Sir, you're welcome to come with, but you'll have to wait outside of the actual imaging room."

"Got it. You lead the way, I'll push."

Twenty minutes later, we're back in the room waiting for the doctor to let us know the damage.

Now wide awake, Stella is restless and her pain level is slowly creeping back up. "I want to go home."

"We'll be out of here soon," I tell her, not knowing whether it's true or not. Judging from how the night's gone so far, we may be here for a while longer, but telling her that when she's already miserable isn't an option.

"Has anyone texted me? I told Emmy I would keep her updated."

"I'm not sure. Do you want me to get your phone?"

She nods and then shakes her head.

"I don't know what that means, Luna."

"You get my phone and text her. My hands feel shaky."

I stand and retrieve her phone from her bag on the other side of the room. "What's your passcode?"

A small grin brightens her otherwise pale face. "Both of our birth months."

"Oh, really?" I tap in the code, grinning like a lovesick fool.

"Shut up."

"You really love me, huh?" I wag my brows at her and then promptly freeze when Stella nods her head and says, "Yeah, Samson, I really do."

"Love you too," I whisper, my voice barely audible and my heart lodged in my throat.

Before either of us can say anything else, Dr. Gardner steps into the room.

"Okay, Stella, the good news is, it's not broken."

"And the bad news?" she asks, her voice raspy.

"It's a fairly severe sprain."

"What does that mean?"

"Since it's so swollen, we're going to wrap it and set you up with a pair of crutches. Until you can follow up with an ortho, I'm going to suggest you follow RICE—rest, ice, compression, and elevate, okay?"

Stella nods.

"All of the aftercare information, along with your follow-up appointment, will be in the discharge paperwork. So, hang tight and we'll get you wrapped and on your way."

As soon as the doctor closes the door behind her, Stella bursts into tears. "How am I going to get around campus on crutches?"

"Hey, no." I slide her phone into my pocket and wrap her in my arms. "Don't cry."

She pulls out of my embrace and wipes away her tears. "God, I don't even know why I'm crying."

"It's been a rough day, Luna. You're hurting and tired. But I've got you."

"You've got me?" She blinks up at me through tear-soaked lashes.

"Always. Once they discharge you, I'm gonna bring you back to my place and nurse you back to health."

Her lips tip up in a weak grin. "That sounds kind of dirty."

I tsk her. "We can role-play when you feel better."

"Thanks, Samson."

"Always, Luna."

"DO YOU NEED ANYTHING?" Samson asks, for what feels like the millionth time. "Water? A snack? Something for the pain?"

"Samson." I try to rein in my exasperation, because I know he's only trying to care for me; but for the past day and a half, the man's been treating me like I'm made of glass. "The only thing I need is for you to sit down beside me and to relax."

"Are you sure? Because if you need a new ice pack or a blanket—"

"Positive." I cut my eyes at him and pat the mattress beside me. "Now sit."

He glances longingly toward the kitchen, like he's considering making a break for it to refill my water. But finally, he relents and crawls into bed beside me.

"Are you sure you're up for tonight?"

"You mean dinner?" I clarify.

"Yeah. Do you think you should stay home? Well, here?"

I warm at the thought of calling his house home. *Maybe one day...*

"Do you not want to go?" I ask, indecision rippling through me. On one hand, my ankle hurts—a lot—but on the other, tonight's a special night for my mom and I know it would hurt her feelings if we both missed it.

"I told your brother I'd be there, but that was before you got hurt."

I angle my body toward him, well as much as I can without moving my leg. "Tonight's too important to miss. If it was just a run-of-the-mill Sunday dinner, I would consider it, but we're celebrating her tonight and I need to be there. *We* need to be there."

"Fuck. I know." He inhales deeply, holding his breath a beat, before slowly exhaling. "I just... getting the call that you were at the hospital, it rattled me, Stella."

Forget being warm, this man has reduced me to a puddle of goo. "I'm sure it was scary, but aside from some tenderness and discomfort, I'm fine, Samson." I grab his hand and bring it to my lips, kissing my way across his knuckles. "Plus, you've taken really good care of me."

"Okay, we'll go." He nods to himself. "But only if you agree to sleep here again tonight."

I grin up at him. "You've got yourself a deal."

Four hours later, we're idling in the parking lot behind 1885 —my parents' favorite restaurant. "You sure you're up for the walk?"

I cut my eyes at Samson, glaring. "It's less than a block. We are literally on the other side of the building."

He glances toward my crutches, which are laid across

his back seat and holds up his hands in surrender. "Okay, okay. Sorry."

"Ugh, I'm being a snot. I'm sorry."

He grins. "I love you anyway."

My heart races and then slams to a stop. "You what?" Is he really doing this right now? In what universe does this seem like the time to tell me he loves me? Maybe I misunderstood?

"I love you," he says, his voice strong and clear and his words so full of intention that I can feel their weight.

"Samson," I whisper his name, trying to process this development.

It's not that I don't love him, because I do. Oh my God, I do. I have since before I was old enough to give a name to my feelings. But I never imagined him telling me like this.

I never imagined him confessing his love for me in a parking lot, moments before facing my parents. My parents, who have no clue we're even together.

"Is everything okay?" He searches my gaze. "Are you hurting? Do you want to go home?"

"You said... you said you love me."

"Is everything okay?" he asks, his brow creased in concern.

"You. Said. You. Love. Me."

"Stella, I'm not seeing the—oh..." He shakes his head, a sad smile turning down his lips. "I think I get it."

"Get what?"

"You don't remember, do you?"

"Samson," I plead with him. "What don't I remember?"

"You said you loved me in the ER. I thought... *fuck*."

My heart rattles in my chest. *I told him I loved him?*

"Listen." He reaches out and takes my hand in his. "It's fine. You were pretty out of it. I get it if it's too soon. But what I said stands—I love you, Luna. You're my heart. My fucking soul. You're my past, my present, and my future. You're the person I want to grow old with."

He squeezes my hand before interlacing our fingers. "I love you, and I know you love me too, but if you need some time, that's fine. I'll give it to you." He smiles, and this time, it reaches his eyes. "What's a little bit longer when we have the rest of our lives together?"

"I…" I trail off, blinking rapidly to keep my tears at bay while I attempt to arrange my spiraling thoughts into words.

"Stay put and I'll come help you down," he says, killing the engine. "We're already ten minutes late."

"I love you too," I whisper, but he's already out of the truck.

My heart is still beating erratically when he opens the back door to retrieve my crutches. I want to scream and shout how I feel for him, but he's right—we're already late for dinner.

But tonight, once we're home, he and I are going to sit down and have a serious talk. Because the thought of him thinking I'm not ready for his love… it's unacceptable.

He opens my door and offers me his hand. "Careful getting down, the ground's a little uneven."

I place my hand in his, trying to ignore the butterflies flapping around in my belly. It's like, now that I *know* he loves me, I'm looking at every interaction under a new lens.

Even the simplest of gestures, like helping me down from his truck, are done in love, and holy crap, if that knowledge doesn't set me on fire.

"Thanks, Samson." My voice sounds breathy even to my own ears, but if Samson notices, he doesn't call me on it.

"Anything for you, Luna."

We walk—okay, he walks, I hobble—down the sidewalk that leads around the backside of the building, cutting through the patio toward the entrance.

Samson holds the door, allowing me to approach the hostess stand first. "Hi, welcome to 1885. How many?"

"We're meeting my family." I scan the dining room, my eyes instantly settling on my dad, who is staring at Samson and me with a laser-like focus. "I see them, thanks."

"Enjoy!" she says before directing her focus to the next patron.

Samson reaches out and gives my hand a quick squeeze. "After you, Luna."

Nerves swim through me as we near the table, between Samson's declaration, the way my dad was staring us down, my injury, and Mom's award, I feel like I'm walking a tightrope.

I've never been the kind of girl that lies to her parents, and knowing I'm keeping something so momentous from them leaves me feeling slimy, but I know—and respect—that Samson wants to talk to Orion first.

My brother would feel blindsided if he wasn't clued in beforehand. So, as much as I'd love to spill the beans tonight, I won't.

Plus, it's Mom's big night, and it would be selfish of me to take the focus away from the reason we're here—to celebrate her.

God only knows, my sprained ankle will be enough of a distraction as it is.

"Stella!" My mom's smile drops as soon as she notices my crutches. "What on earth happened?"

I laugh lightly, trying to calm her. "Just sprained it. No big deal."

"No big deal? Stella!" Mom shoots out of her seat and rushes toward me. "When did this happen?"

"Friday night."

"Friday! It's Sunday. Who's been taking care of you?" I glance back over my shoulder toward Samson, who's looking everywhere except at me and my mother.

"It's under control. Promise."

"Lizzie, if Stelli Bear says it's handled, it's handled." Dad shoots me an indecipherable look. "Now, everyone take a seat."

Samson places a steadying hand on the small of my back, helping me to the table before pulling out my chair. Once I'm seated, he grabs my crutches and stows them out of the way.

"Such a gentleman," Mom coos, staring at the man I love with hearts in her eyes. "One day you'll make some woman very happy."

"Sooner than you think," Dad mumbles, coughing into his hand.

I whip my head around to face him. "What?"

"I said I don't know what I want to eat."

"You always get the chicken." And I do mean always. For as long as they've been eating here, he's ordered the Springer Mountain Farms chicken, with grits and green beans.

"Well, there you go." He smiles indulgently. "I'll get the chicken."

Ignoring his absolute weirdness, I ask, "Where's Orion?"

"Right here." My brother flicks the back of my head as he walks by. "Now the party can begin."

"You loser."

"Takes one to know one."

"Whatever."

"Both of y'all stop," Samson says, grinning. "Tonight's about celebrating Mrs. C."

I swear to God, my mom swoons. "Such a good boy."

"He's not a dog, Mom."

"It's fine, Luna." He knocks his elbow into mine. "Everyone loves a good scratch behind the ears every now and then."

"You're so weird."

He winks before focusing his attention on my brother. "How you been, man?"

Orion narrows his eyes at Samson, his gaze darting between the two of us. "Good. Where's your car, Stella?"

"Oh!" Mom exclaims. "You didn't drive here with your ankle, did you?"

"Um." I snatch my glass from the table and gulp it down, buying myself time to formulate a response. "Well—"

"How's the house coming?" Dad asks, cutting me off.

"Pretty much done now," Orion says, forgetting all about me and my missing car. "All that's left is to finish the hall bath and the master closet."

"Has Ben proposed yet?" Samson asks.

"Any day now."

"Where will you live when they get married?" I ask, content for us all to keep grilling him, so long as it keeps the spotlight off of me.

"Oh, you can move back into your room at home!" Mom says, clearly already imagining having one of her kids back under her roof.

I grab my glass again, hiding my laughter with a well-timed sip.

"Now, Lizzie," Dad says. "Let's not be too hasty. I'm

sure Orion has other places he'd rather lay his head than his childhood bedroom."

Mom bristles, but doesn't remark.

"I could always crash at your place, right, man?" He levels Samson with a glare.

To his credit, Samson doesn't even flinch. "Things are getting pretty serious with... my girl, but a night or two would be fine, man."

"Is everyone ready?" our server asks, unknowingly saving us all.

Once we've all placed our orders, my dad proposes a toast. "To my darling Lizzie—may your love for teaching continue to change lives."

We all raise our glasses, clinking them together.

"And to my sweet Stella," Mom says, dabbing at her tears with one hand and raising her glass with the other. "For following in my footsteps. I know you're going to do amazing things."

"Mom!" I duck my head even as I raise my glass, embarrassed for the spotlight to be on me.

"I mean it. I can feel it right here." She presses her hand over her heart.

"Thanks, Mom," Orion says, his tone laced with sarcasm.

"Oh, hush, you. I am every bit as proud of you as I am your sister. You two are my babies. Well, you three—you may as well be a second son, Samson."

As she looks to the man at my side with such tenderness in her eyes, I can't help but wonder how she'll react when she learns that Samson's feelings toward me aren't very brotherly.

Despite the rest of the evening passing without any hiccups or drama, I'm exhausted and more than ready to go home—I mean, back to Samson's place—put on my jammies and snuggle up in his king-size bed.

"Are you okay to get home?" Mom asks as we all head toward the door.

I'm tempted to look toward Samson, but force myself to keep my eyes ahead of me. "I am. Promise."

"Okay, but Dad and I don't mind you coming home with us."

"I'm good, Mom." I pause beside her in the doorway and press a kiss to her cheek.

"And you'll come next weekend, right?"

"I wouldn't miss y'all's anniversary dinner for the world. Love you, Mom." I step out onto the sidewalk. "Love you too, Dad."

I linger off to the side while Samson and Orion talk, watching my parents cross the street to their car.

I'm about to head to Samson's truck on my own when I hear him say, "I'll get up with you later, man." I glance over my shoulder in time to see them slap their palms together. "Drive safe."

"Yeah," Orion says, staring hard at me. "Y'all too."

Oh, crap... he knows. He totally freaking knows.

"You ready, Luna?" Samson asks once it's just the two of us.

"He knows."

"Who knows?" He presses his hand to the small of my back, positioning himself between me and the busy street.

"Orion. He totally knows about us."

"No way." He steps around me to open my door. "Why do you think that?"

"He literally just *y'all too* when you said to drive safe."

Samson stares at me like I've grown an extra head. "Because he wants us both to be safe."

"Wrong!" I let Samson help me into the passenger seat and then wait for him to climb behind the wheel. "He said it because he knew we were leaving together."

"Stella." He grins at me as he cranks the engine.

"Samson."

He shifts into gear and then takes my hand. "He doesn't suspect a thing. Orion's too caught up in his life to think twice about what's going on between us. But we do need to find a time to tell him."

"I know. Maybe next weekend?"

"Sounds good. Everything's going to be fine, Luna. Just trust me."

My stomach flips as a sense of unease zips through me.

Famous last words...

I COULD WAKE up next to Stella Cartwright every day for the rest of my life and die a happy man.

The feeling of her soft curves pressed into all of my hard is... it's fucking indescribable.

There's nothing better than this... *nothing.*

Even her soft snores, sleepy mumbles, and the little bit of drool on her cheek do it for me.

"Stella," I murmur her name, skimming my nose along her cheek. "Wake up."

She wiggles her shoulders and presses her cheek deeper into the pillow. "Go away."

"It's time to get up."

"Ugh." She tugs the covers over her head.

"Come on, Luna. You have your ortho appointment in a few hours and then class." I lean in and kiss her neck, sucking and nibbling at her soft skin. "I want to spend time with you before you go."

"Fine." She shoves the blanket down. "But I want some coffee."

"I have something that can wake you up better than coffee."

"I'm sure you do, but..."

She doesn't finish her sentence, but I already know what she's thinking. We're both worried about hurting her ankle more, and I told her fooling around was off the table until after her ortho appointment.

Luckily, my right hand took the edge off this morning in the shower while I let her sleep in a little.

"I'm gonna take a quick shower."

I kiss the tip of her nose before standing. "I'll make coffee."

"Samson," she calls my name as I walk toward the door.

"Yeah, Luna?"

"Thank you for taking such good care of me."

"Always." I commit the way she looks, her blonde hair splayed across my pillow and her lips stretched into a sleepy grin. She's as flawed as anyone else, but to me, she's perfect.

In the kitchen, I decide to do one better than just making a pot of coffee; my girl deserves a full-out breakfast.

I grab the eggs and bacon from the fridge and bread from the pantry. The coffee is percolating and I'm whisking the eggs when I hear the shower turn on.

The thought of her all soapy and naked almost makes me renege my no-fooling-around decree, but I know it's for the best. If I somehow made her injury worse, I'd never forgive myself.

I set the eggs to the side and start the bacon, frying it extra crispy, just like Stella likes, when I hear my front door open.

Instantly, I'm on high alert.

"Smells good," Orion says, casually planting himself onto a barstool.

"Uh, thanks, man." I plate the bacon and pour the eggs into the pan. "What brings you by?"

"Can't I stop by and see my best friend?" He sounds calm, but a quick glance in his direction tells me he's anything but.

His eyes are narrowed to slits and his mouth is set in a firm line. I guess Stella was right after all, but there's no way in hell I'm copping to shit unless he comes right out and asks me.

"Just seems odd," I say mildly.

The shower cuts off and he smirks. "Got company?"

I scratch the back of my neck, wondering how to play this. I don't want to lie to him, but—

"Something smells good," Stella says, stepping into the room, clad in only a towel. "You didn't have to go to all —Orion."

"Hey there, Smalls." Orion's glare pins her in place.

"Um." She tightens the towel, her gaze dropping to the floor.

"Um," he mocks, crossing his arms over his chest. "Let me guess... it's not what it looks like?"

"You're not being fair," Stella whispers.

"No!" Orion shoves away from the bar, sending the barstool he was sitting on to the floor. "No way. Fuck that. What's *not fair* is rolling up to my *lifelong* best friend's house and finding my baby sister fucking naked."

I shove the pan off the burner and place myself between Stella and her brother. "Watch it."

"You watch it!" He paces back and forth, running his fingers through his short hair. "Whatever happened to the bro-code?"

"We didn't mean to keep it from you," Stella says, clutching the back of my shirt.

"Oh, right. You just accidentally started fucking my best friend and forgot to tell me."

"Please stop." Her voice breaks. "Please. Just..."

"Just what?"

"Just let us explain."

Orion stomps into the living room and slams himself down onto the couch.

I turn to Stella, gathering her into my arms. "Shh, don't cry, Luna." I press a chaste kiss to her quivering lips. "Go get dressed. I'll deal with your brother."

"Be nice," she pleads.

"Of course." But if he says one foul word about Stella, all bets are off.

She scurries back into the bedroom while I join a still fuming Orion, taking a seat in one of the chairs across from the couch.

"I take it she's who you've been seeing?"

Wordlessly, I nod.

"That's fucked up, man." He relaxes back into the couch, some of the anger seeping from his body. "How did this even happen?" He clenches his fists, flexing his fingers. "Like, I knew y'all both had stupid little puppy crushes on each other, but—"

"What?" I ask, cutting him off.

"Dude. I'm not an idiot."

I hold my hands up. "I'm not implying that you are. I'm just... confused."

"Join the club." He laughs, but it holds no humor. "Her crush was obvious—like a flashing neon sign, but do you really think I never noticed the soft spot you had for her? The way you always asked me to let her tag along? The way you spent time with her even when I wasn't around? The way you ignored all of the girls throwing themselves at you? Seriously?"

I chuckle and shrug my shoulders. "I mean, I guess when you say it like that."

"How long has this been going on?"

"Let's wait for Stella. She really wanted to be a part of this conversation."

"Fine."

We lapse into a tense silence, neither of us willing to give an inch while we wait.

"It seems like y'all are making good progress," Stella says lightly as she clomps into the room.

"C'mere." I pat my lap.

She glances at Orion before propping her crutches against the wall and hobbling over to me.

I help support her weight as she lowers herself down onto my lap, and then wrap my arms around her waist, holding her close.

"Don't you two look cozy," Orion sneers. He scrubs his hands over his face. "Fuck. This is really hard for me."

"Do... do you not want us together?" Stella asks, her voice thick.

When he doesn't immediately reply, Stella's tears fall.

"I love him, Orion. I love him with all of my heart and soul."

"Love?" My best friend's brow quirks. "How long has this been going on?" he asks again.

Stella and I exchange glances, and then she dips her head, signaling me to take lead. "Before I answer that, I want you to know, I never touched her until she was eighteen."

Orion exhales as loudly as a raging bull.

"Like you mentioned, Stella's always been in my orbit.

There's always been something special about her. At first, she was just a goofball kid that made me smile, but as she grew up, my feelings changed."

"How old?" Orion asks through gritted teeth.

"I was fifteen when I confessed how I felt about him," Stella whispers.

Her brother pinches the bridge of his nose.

I probably should keep this next bit to myself, but decide I might as well go for broke. "I kissed her that day—"

"You what?" In a flash, Orion's on his feet, pacing the length of my living room. "You put your hands... your mouth on my underage baby sister?"

I slide out from beneath Stella, placing her down on the chair. "It wasn't like that."

"Then what was it like?" He advances me, until we're chest to chest, squaring off in the living room like it's a WWE ring. "Because I'm having a really tough time understanding any situation in which it would be okay."

"I love your sister. I. Fucking. Love. Her. And I'm sorry if that's hard for you to hear, but you better get used to the idea. Because one day, she's gonna be my wife. I want us to stay friends, but, Orion, if you make me choose..."

"It won't be me," he finishes for me, all of his anger leaving his body. "Got it, man."

"You're hearing me?"

He shakes his head, his eyes flashing to Stella. "Loud and clear, man. I'll see myself out."

"Orion!" Stella tries to follow after him, but isn't able to keep up on her injured ankle.

"Let him go, Luna." I cross the room to her and pull her into my arms.

She clings to me, burying her face in the fabric of my shirt. "He's so angry."

"He just needs time to adjust." I speak the words against her hair, tightening my hold on her as she trembles in my arms.

"You can't."

"Can't what?"

She wriggles out of my hold. "You can't choose me over him. He's been your best friend for your whole life."

I step back enough to wipe away her tears and lift her gaze to mine. "And you're my whole world. Orion will come around, I promise. And if he doesn't, as shitty as this sounds, I'd rather lose him than you. I love you, Stella. With every ounce of my being, I love you. Until we're old and gray, I love you. Until the day we die, and in the next life too, I love you."

"I love you too." She offers me a watery smile. "But I hate coming between y'all."

"You won't. I know it feels like it now, but give him time to cool down, okay? He's feeling betrayed, and I get it. But you know your brother... he's a hothead. He needs time, okay?"

She breathes out a shaky exhale. "Okay."

"Are you ready to head to your appointment?"

Stella nods.

"Wait here and I'll grab your stuff. Are you sure you have a ride to campus?"

"Yeah, Mom's coming to get me. Crazy lady got a sub and everything just so she could come to this appointment with me." Stella's entire body goes ramrod straight. "Do you think she'll say something if she sees me get out of your truck?"

"Luna," I say her name softly. "If Orion hasn't already told her, she'll know soon enough. Not to mention, your mother loves me. But if you want..." I swallow roughly, hating the words I'm about to speak before they even pass my lips. "...I can drop you off a bit down from the door."

Immediately, she shakes her head no. "You can drop me off *at* the door, and if she says anything, I'll just tell her like it is."

I can't help but smile at her reply. "And how is it, Luna?"

"That we're together."

"In love."

"No matter what they say."

She leans into me. "It's you and me."

"Always." *For fucking always, Luna.*

AFTER DROPPING Stella off at her ortho appointment, I call Orion—unsurprisingly, he sends me straight to voice mail.

He can try to avoid me all he wants, but I know him like the back of my hand, and I will find his surly ass and make him talk this out with me.

Because while I meant it when I said I'd choose Stella over him, I'm damn sure going to do everything in my power to avoid having to choose.

Orion's more than my best friend—he's like a brother to me... the family I never had.

But Stella... she's the fucking air I breathe.

I try Orion's number again as I drive past his house— voice mail again.

He thinks he can hide from me, but he's definitely in one of three places. And seeing as it's barely noon, I highly doubt he's at ATF or Bandits, which means he's at his parents' house.

At least I hope he is, because I'm really not trying to

hash this out with some chick's naked ass shaking in my peripheral.

Sure enough, when I pull into their driveway, Orion's truck is parked right next to his dad's. I park perpendicular to their tailgates, blocking them both in.

It might make me an asshole, but he's going to talk to me, one way or another.

I rap my knuckles against the front door before pulling it open. I don't see them, but I can hear them and follow the sound of their voices into the kitchen, where Orion's pacing like a caged animal.

"I was wondering when you'd show up," Michael says, nodding his head in greeting.

"You're not welcome here," Orion says, jerking to a stop directly in front of me.

"Am I not?"

"Not anymore," he spits the words, anger lacing every syllable.

"Now, son—"

"Don't you *now son* me—do you even know what he did?"

"I know he's like family, not just to you, but to all of us, and the way you're speaking to him isn't how we speak to *family*."

Orion scoffs. "Yeah, he feels really *brotherly* toward Stella."

"Look," I start, "I know you're mad—"

"You're damn right I'm mad. You went behind my back. With my sister."

"Son, what part are you mad about?"

"Huh?" Orion's eyes narrow in confusion.

"Are you mad that Samson's seeing Stella, or are you mad they weren't upfront with you about it?"

Mr. Cartwright poses a good question—and if I had to guess, he's more upset about being kept in the dark than he is our actual relationship.

"I..." He starts pacing again. "I don't know."

"Listen, you're like the brother I never had." I drag out a barstool and plant myself on it. "And that means something to me. I don't have any family or loved ones outside of y'all. I just happen to love your sister a little differently."

I pinch the bridge of my nose, but press on. "I get that we could have gone about things a little better, but we did what felt right at the time for *us*. We never meant to hurt you."

"You lied to me. You've been lying to me. For years." He turns to his dad. "You're really okay with this?"

He nods. "I couldn't think of a better man for my Stelli Bear."

"And you're okay with the fact that they were basically together in secret before she could even drive?" Orion crosses his arms over his chest and smirks, like he's played a trump card.

But Michael just laughs. And laughs. And laughs.

"What in the hell is so funny?" Orion shouts.

"Anyone with a set of half-functioning eyes can see how those two feel about each other." His dad shrugs. "Love doesn't always have a neat and tidy timeline, son. It's complicated and messy and frankly, doesn't care what other people think. If I didn't think Samson was good for Stella— if I for even one second doubted his intentions with her—he wouldn't have been allowed to come around. Plain and simple. But sometimes... sometimes two people are just meant for each other and that's all there is to it."

Michael rounds the island and wraps his son in a bear hug. "I think you need to take a step back and think long and hard why you're so mad." He releases him and heads for the back door. "I'd hate to see you throw away y'all's friendship over something that's a good thing."

The kitchen is silent, save for the sound of the back door shutting. We're both stewing, only willing to see things from our own point of view, and I know if I'm not the one to bow, there's a very real chance our friendship could break.

"I'm sorry."

"For which part?" he asks, settling onto the stool next to me.

"For not telling you from the start." I prop my elbows on the island and angle my head toward his. "I'll never apologize for loving Stella."

He mulls over my words for a minute. "You really love her?"

"With all that I am."

"Then... I guess I'm good with it." He pins me with a hard glare. "I don't like that you went behind my back or that you lied to me, but Dad's right. You're good for her. And she's good for you."

I visibly deflate as relief courses through me. "Thanks, man."

"But if you hurt her..." Orion slings his arm around my neck, clamping his hand down hard on my shoulder. "I'll fucking end you."

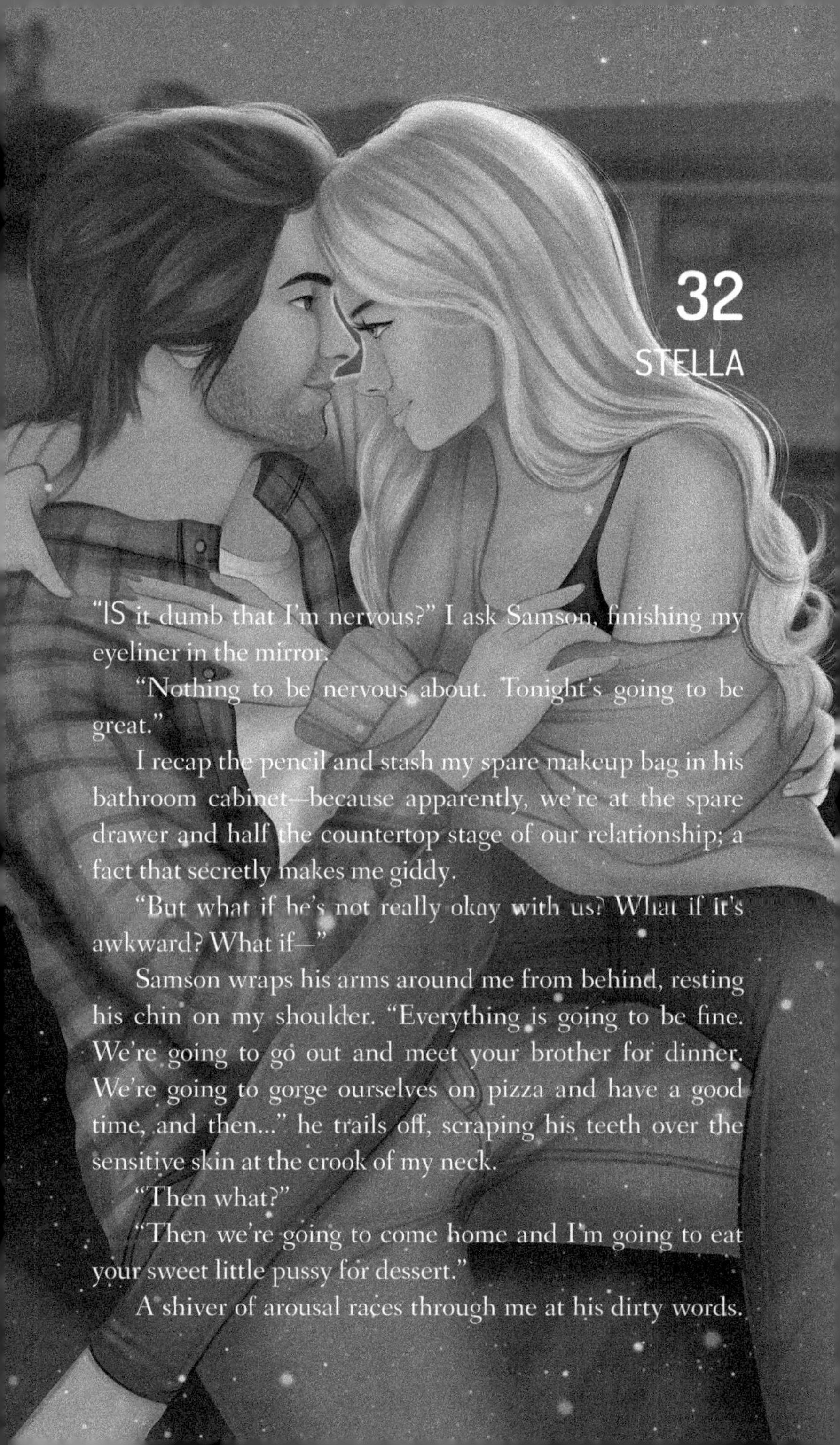

"IS it dumb that I'm nervous?" I ask Samson, finishing my eyeliner in the mirror.

"Nothing to be nervous about. Tonight's going to be great."

I recap the pencil and stash my spare makeup bag in his bathroom cabinet—because apparently, we're at the spare drawer and half the countertop stage of our relationship; a fact that secretly makes me giddy.

"But what if he's not really okay with us? What if it's awkward? What if—"

Samson wraps his arms around me from behind, resting his chin on my shoulder. "Everything is going to be fine. We're going to go out and meet your brother for dinner. We're going to gorge ourselves on pizza and have a good time, and then..." he trails off, scraping his teeth over the sensitive skin at the crook of my neck.

"Then what?"

"Then we're going to come home and I'm going to eat your sweet little pussy for dessert."

A shiver of arousal races through me at his dirty words.

I push my ass into his groin, my panties already damp with my desire.

"Get dressed, Stella, or we'll be late."

"So?" I raise a brow at him in our reflection in the mirror.

He skims one hand up my body and beneath the silk of my robe to cup my breast, while the other sneaks between my legs.

"So wet already." He rubs his finger over the front of my panties, rubbing my clit through the drenched fabric.

"Samson," I moan his name, desperate for him to push the material to the side, so I can *feel* him, flesh on flesh, but he never does. Nope. He just rubs and rubs at me until I'm ready to combust.

"Please," I beg wantonly, rolling my hips the best I can in the stupid walking boot the ortho gave me. "I need you. I want to feel you. For you to make me come."

He groans and rubs me harder, faster, and I swear to God, I can feel the start of my orgasm. I'm so close, I just need a little more... *something*. "Oh, God, Samson."

My legs shake with need. "A little more. I'm almost—"

"Not yet," he says, stepping completely away from me.

"What?" I cry, frantic for the release he's just denied me.

"Be a good girl, get dressed, and let's go to dinner."

"Samson!" I'd stomp my foot if I thought I could manage it. "You're seriously not going to finish what you started?"

"Not until after dinner." He grins darkly, promising me pure pleasure if I play by his rules.

But I've spent my entire life following other people's rules, and I'm more than ready to make my own. "Fine. I'll finish myself off then."

"The hell you will!"

I whirl around and lean back against the counter, trying for casual despite the twinge in my ankle—and the lustful inferno lighting me up from the inside out—and untie the sash to my robe.

His eyes turn molten as he takes in my bare breasts and tiny lace panties.

With my eyes locked on his, I tease myself over the top of my panties, before sliding my hand beneath the soaking wet material.

"Mmm," I moan, pressing my index finger to my clit.

"Stella," he growls my name as he knocks my hand out of the way and shoves my panties down.

He rubs circles over my clit with his thumb while his fingers explore my folds. "Whose pussy is this?" he demands, sliding his index finger deep inside of me.

"Yours," I gasp, pleasure almost robbing me of my voice. "It's yours."

"You're goddamn right it is." He curls his finger inside of me in time with his thumb working my clit.

"Samson!" I moan his name, my entire body tensing before the most glorious pleasure rushes over me, consuming me, until all I can hear, see, and feel is him.

He holds me, supporting my limp body against his while whispering all kinds of filth into my ear as I recover from my orgasm.

"You're feeling pretty proud of yourself right now, aren't you?" I ask once the fog clears.

He shrugs. "Would've been better if you waited like I wanted you to."

"But I didn't want to." I sound like a bratty child, but I'm still too blissed out to care.

After making sure I'm steady, Samson steps back.

"Sometimes, the best things are worth waiting for. You're lucky I don't punish you."

For some inexplicable reason, my core clenches at the thought. "Punish me?"

"Spank your ass red."

"Samson," I hiss his name, my cheeks burning bright.

"You'd like that, wouldn't you?" he asks, running his tongue along his bottom lip.

"I..." I suck in a deep breath. "I don't know. Maybe?"

He breathes out a laugh. "I bet you would."

"Maybe when we get home... you can... try?"

"Fuck, Luna." He balls his hands into fists at his sides. "You can't say stuff like that."

"Why not?"

"Because it makes me want to tie your ass to my bed and never let you leave."

I grin, wondering if that would really be such a bad thing...

As if reading my thoughts, he groans again, backing himself toward the door. "Get dressed."

"Where are you going?"

"Away. Away from you before I say to hell with our plans."

I grin, loving that he's as tempted by me as I am by him.

He shakes his head before giving me one more long look. "Hurry up, Luna. I'll be in the truck."

"You're late," my brother says as Samson and I approach, his eyes lingering on our interlaced fingers.

"I'm so sorry! We—"

He holds his hands up in front of him, stopping me mid-sentence. "I don't need to know."

"It's nothing like that," I start, my cheeks burning because it *totally* is something like that.

But Orion shakes his head. "Don't want to know."

Samson grins, his gaze pinging between the two of us. "Cut her some slack, man."

"Yeah, yeah, whatever. Why don't you lovebirds take a seat and we can order." He nods toward the empty chairs we're awkwardly lingering in front of.

"You mean you didn't order already?"

Orion smirks. "Nah, I wasn't sure what y'all would want."

Samson gives him a funny look. "We've been eating here for years and have literally ordered the same every single time."

My brother shrugs his shoulders. "A lot of things have changed recently... I didn't want to make any assumptions."

"Oh my God!" I bury my face in my hands, hating the way I feel put under a microscope by my own brother.

But the jackass only chuckles. "You're way too easy to rile up, Smalls."

My head snaps up, my gaze locking on his mirth-filled eyes. "That was mean, you jerk!"

He brings his draft glass to his lips and takes a sip. "You deserved it."

"Did you really not order?" Samson asks, like food is the most important thing we're talking about.

"Chill, I ordered."

"Thank fuck—I'm starved."

I cut my eyes toward Samson. "Seriously."

"What?" He raises his brows. "A man's gotta eat."

"Oh, God," Orion groans, smacking his forehead with the back of his hand as he rolls his head back.

"Oh, God," I mimic back. "Now you know how I felt every time I walked in on you feeling up some random girl on the couch back in the day."

"Totally different." He points a finger our way. "None of those girls were your friends."

"Let it go, dude."

"For real though," Orion says, propping his elbows on the table. "I'm happy for y'all. And even though it weirds me out a little, I'm glad you're together. I'm not gonna lie though, it's gonna take time for me to adjust, so maybe hold off on the PDA. Like, forever. But, truly, I'm happy."

"That means a lot to us, man," Samson says, placing his hand on my thigh under the table, giving it a reassuring squeeze.

"There's definitely worse people she could end up with."

Samson chuckles darkly. "Over my dead body will she *ever* end up with anyone else."

I jam my elbow into his side, even though I'm secretly delighted by his words. "Put it away, caveman, we both know I'm all yours."

My brother gags and Samson and I laugh.

Things might not be completely back to normal between us all, but they're on the way and knowing Orion supports us... I feel lighter than I have in days.

"SHOULD I have gotten your parents a gift?"

"For their anniversary?" Stella asks.

"Yeah." I continue inching down the road the Cartwrights live off of, low-key wondering if I have time to hit up the mall before dinner. "I was reading online that thirty years is pearls—whatever that means—but all I have for them is a card and the knowledge I'm sleeping with their only daughter."

I can tell she tries to fight it, but judging from her red cheeks and rolled lips, it's a losing battle. My girl cracks up.

"It isn't funny, Luna."

"It kind of is." She reaches over and takes my hand. "Plus, I put your name on the card for my gift."

I glance at her out of the side of my eyes. "That seems like a big deal."

She does this cute little shoulder shimmy and grins. "We're a big deal, Samson Carter. Now, put your foot on the gas or we'll be late."

I press my foot down harder on the accelerator. "Thirty years is a long time."

"It is," Stella agrees, but I can tell something is on her mind.

"What's wrong?"

She looks toward me and frowns. "Nothing."

"Something."

She huffs. "Fine. I was wondering if you envisioned us making it that far."

"Stella." I swing my truck into their driveway and throw it into park. "What part of *always* don't you get? You're. Mine. I have every intention of putting a ring on your finger and a baby or two in your belly. I've said this more than once—but I'll say it as many times as it takes... I love you. My future is with you. Only you, always you. Got it?"

She smiles softly. "Yeah, Samson, I got it."

"Good." I put the truck back into gear and continue down the driveway.

I pull in next to Orion, kill the engine, and then rush around to help Stella down from my truck. I've suggested taking her car countless times, but she insists on me driving my truck, with the excuse of me being too tall to fit comfortably.

"Can you grab the gift bag from the back seat?" She pulls her jacket tighter around her body as the wind blows.

"Of course." I retrieve the gift and then offer her my arm for added stability.

"You ready?" she asks as we approach the front door.

I look down at her, my cheeks lifting as I grin. "Hell, yeah I am."

And I am—in more ways than one. I'm ready for tonight, but I'm ready for the rest of our lives together too. I'm ready for Stella to take my last name and to call my house home. I'm ready for us to have a whole gaggle of kids that look just like her.

I'm ready for it all with Stella Cartwright.

"Mom, Dad, we're here."

"In the kitchen," her mom calls. "And who's we? I didn't know you were bringing—" Mrs. Cartwright's jaw clamps shut when Stella and I enter the room, hand in hand. "Oh... oh my."

"Hey, Mrs. C." I give her my best smile. "Happy Anniversary."

"Hello, Samson." Her eyes dart back and forth between her daughter and me. "This... this is new."

"Not as new as you think," Orion says, moving to the left of his mom to grab a glass from the dishwasher.

"What?" She whirls around to face him.

"I'm just saying." He shuffles over to the fridge and pulls out the pitcher of tea. "It threw me for a loop at first too, but it's not *new*."

"Use ice, I just brewed the tea." She turns back to us with her hands on her hips. "Someone needs to explain this to me."

The back door opens and Mr. Cartwright steps into the kitchen. "I thought I heard your truck." He turns to his daughter, oblivious to the tension brewing. "How's your ankle?"

"It's good. A little sore, but good." Stella shifts on her feet. "Honestly, this boot makes my knee and hip hurt more than anything."

I watch as understanding dawns on Lizzie's face; she whips around to face her husband. "Did you know?" she hisses.

Stella tightens her hold on my hand and tugs. "Samson."

I lean down so she can whisper to me. "What's up?"

"I don't think my mom is happy." The disappointment in her voice guts me.

"She's not mad we're together, Luna. She's upset she was the last to know."

"You think?"

"How could no one tell me?" Mrs. Cartwright throws her arms wide, glaring at all of us.

"We're sorry, Mom."

"As you should be," Lizzie says.

"Are... are you angry?" Stella's lower lip wobbles.

A fact her mom notices immediately. "Oh, Stella, no."

"You sound mad." She's clinging to me now, like I'm the only thing keeping her upright.

Lizzie races around the island to us. "Stella, sweetheart. I'm not mad. Not at all. Well, not at you anyway." She glares at her husband over her shoulder. *Looks like Michael's in the doghouse for not spilling the beans.* "I'm delighted you and Samson are together. Truly, I couldn't think of anyone better for either of you."

She turns to me. "But I would like to speak with Samson—privately."

Orion and Michael don't waste a single second making themselves sparse.

"Okay. I need to call Emmy anyway. I promised I'd help her with her outfit for tonight."

Mrs. C gathers her daughter in a crushing hug. "Come back down to help with the salad in about twenty, okay?"

"Yes, ma'am." Stella turns toward the stairs, but I stop her.

"Are you good to get up the stairs on your own?"

She nods and I press a kiss to her forehead before sending her on her way.

"Let's sit," she says, nodding toward the dining room.

I pull her chair out for her before sitting down across from her.

"So, you and Stella?"

"Yes, ma'am."

"Since when?"

"Since always?" I wince and run my hands through my hair. "I know that sounds bad, but there's always been something special about her to me. But I want you to know, I never acted on my feelings until she was—"

Mrs. Cartwright waves a hand in the air, silencing me. "I'm not worried about any of that. You're family to us, Samson. I couldn't be happier for the two of you. I just wish someone had thought to tell me."

"If it makes you feel better, Orion and Mr. C just found out."

"That does help. A little." She taps her nails on the tabletop and levels me with the kind of look only a mother can give. "But I need to ask you a question, and I expect an honest answer."

I swallow roughly. "What's that?"

"When you left—is that why Stella was so hurt?"

"Um." My skin feels hot and tight. This isn't a conversation I ever expected to have, much less ever *wanted* to have. "Yes. Stella and I... we, um, had plans to let everyone know we were together the night of her eighteenth birthday."

"But you left." Lizzie nods knowingly, like the final pieces of a puzzle are finally falling into place.

"You hurt her. She was devastated."

Fuck. "I know."

"Why?"

I parrot the question back to her.

"Why did you leave? Why did you hurt her?"

Deep breath in and here we go. "I realize I messed up.

Knew it the second it happened. I overheard some things I wasn't supposed to, got in my own head, and made a bad judgment call."

"She was crushed. Cried for days, Samson. Wouldn't leave her room."

I hang my head in shame. "I know."

"What did you overhear?"

"Um." I rub at the back of my neck, wishing someone —*anyone*—would come in and save me. "I... heard you talking to someone, saying how proud you were of her for focusing on school and not boys. And how getting attached to someone at such a young age could be detrimental to their future. I was already psyching myself out, thinking I was holding her back, and then..."

"And then you heard me running my mouth." She reaches out and takes my hand in hers. "Oh, Samson. I'm... I'm sorry."

"No, ma'am. You don't need to apologize. The only person responsible for my actions is me."

Her blue eyes, so similar to Stella's, shine with unshed tears. "Still..."

"Nope. No stills and no apologies. I own my actions, as idiotic as they were, and I'm more than willing to spend the rest of my life showing your daughter how much I love her. Because I do. Love her."

"What's not to love?" She laughs, but the sadness still lingers. "But, Samson... you break my baby girl's heart again, *for any reason*, and I'll castrate you without a second thought."

My entire body stills at her sweetly delivered threat. "Hearing you loud and clear, Mrs. C."

She stands from the table and pats my cheek twice.

"Such a good boy. Why don't you head upstairs and make sure Stella gets down safely?"

"Of course," I say, but she's already back in the kitchen.

As I approach Stella's room, the sound of laughter filters out into the hallway. I knock lightly before pushing the door open.

Stella glances at me over the top of her phone. "Okay, I better get going. I need to go help Mom chop vegetables for the salad."

"She's making the dinner?"

Phantom pain erupts at the sound of her roommate's voice—the girl kicks harder than a damn horse.

"Oh, girl, yes, they cook for everything. I'll have to bring you over for dinner one night. Mom's food will blow your mind."

"Any home-cooked meal will blow my mind. I grew up eating food made by our chef or the highly talented Marie Callender."

"Talk later, babe," Stella says with a sad smile before pressing the button to end the call.

Turning her focus to me, Stella's lips quirk up as she pats the spot next to her on the mattress. "Come, sit."

I hesitate momentarily before crossing the room and lowering myself down to the edge of her bed. She immediately snuggles into my side. "You survived then? That's good."

"Told you your mom loved me." I kiss the top of her head, debating if I should tell her about my conversation with her mom.

"Yeah, yeah. You're extra loveable. Everyone loves Samson Carter."

"Only one who really matters though."

"And who might that be?" Stella asks, fluttering her lashes.

"I think we both know it's you."

"Yeah." She scoots closer to me. "But I like to hear you say it."

"Then you'll love this." I lean down and swipe my tongue over her bottom lip.

She moans lightly, her tongue tangling with mine as her hands explore my chest.

Reaching around, I palm her ass with one hand while the other slips beneath the hem of her sweater.

"Stella," I groan her name, reluctantly breaking our kiss.

"What?" she asks, her lips still seeking mine.

"This is my first time in your room."

"Mmm." She nips at my lower lip. "And?"

"Your mom," I blurt, immediately feeling like a moron.

"Are you seriously mentioning my mom while your hard-on is digging into my thigh?"

My dick deflates. "Well, you took care of that problem, huh?"

Stella giggles. "I'll make it up to you tonight."

"I'll hold you to that, but for now, your mom needs help in the kitchen."

AFTER DINNER, we're all gathered in the living room with Mom and Dad's wedding video playing on the TV.

It's weird, seeing them both so young and carefree. It's weird to think of them as young period. But the fact that they're just as in love now as they were then makes me feel... *hopeful.*

Like maybe one day, that will be Samson and me—but with a better dress.

Visions of me in white fill my brain, to the point that I hardly notice my phone ringing.

"You gonna get that?" Samson asks.

"Huh?"

"Your phone, Luna."

"Oh!" I slide the still-ringing device from my back pocket and check the screen. *Why is he calling me?*

I drag my finger across the screen to answer the call. "Hey, Sterling?"

"Yeah, it's me."

Wriggling out of Samson's hold, I stand from the couch and pad into the kitchen for a little privacy.

"What's going on?" I ask, pacing the length of the island.

"Listen, have you gotten any weird texts tonight?"

"Yeah." My mind flashes back to the message I received during dinner... *a random link from an unknown number— that's gonna be a nope.* "How did you know?"

Samson creeps up behind me and wraps me in his arms. "Are you okay?"

I shrug and step out of his hold.

"Put it on speaker."

Nodding, I pull the phone away from my face and tap the speaker button.

"Did you look at it?" Sterling asks, his voice tight.

"No." I shake my head, even though he can't see me. "It came during dinner, and Mom hates phones at the table. Plus, I typically ignore unfamiliar numbers."

"Okay, good." The relief in his voice only serves to amp up my worry. Shit has to have hit the fan for him to be calling me.

"You're freaking me out."

Samson pulls me into him again; this time, I accept the comfort he's offering. Something tells me whatever Sterling's about to say isn't going to be good.

"There was an accident," he says.

"What kind of accident?" I curse myself silently when my voice shakes.

"Emmalyn overdosed." And just like that, with those two small words, I shatter.

She seemed totally fine when we talked earlier. I don't... I don't understand.

I look up to Samson, with tears running unchecked down my cheeks, hoping like hell he can somehow make this make sense.

"What?" My knees buckle, and if it wasn't for Samson supporting my weight, I know I would have hit the floor. "Wait, what?"

"We don't know anything yet." Sterling sounds tired... defeated even. "We're at Central North."

"I'm on my way," I tell him, ending the call before he can say something stupid like to stay put.

Samson slides my phone out of my grasp and tucks it into my back pocket before pressing his truck keys into my hands. "Go start the truck. I'll let your parents know we have to go, okay?"

I nod, words completely escaping me.

"I'll be right there, Luna."

"Have you heard from the doctor?" I ask, blazing a path through the waiting room with Samson hot on my heels.

"Not yet," Gabe says, offering Samson a small head nod.

Samson settles into the vacant seat beside Zach, but I'm too worried about Emmy to sit. I can't help but think if I'd have been with her tonight, that maybe this wouldn't have happened.

Four sets of weary eyes track me as I pace, until finally, Samson reaches out and pulls me down onto his lap.

"Let me up!" I twist my shoulders back and forth, trying to break his hold.

"Sit down, Luna." His voice is nothing more than a growl, but I know he's not mad at me—he's worried.

But I am too, dammit. "So help me God, if you don't let me up right now—!"

Samson holds me even tighter, pressing his face into the crook of my neck. "You'll what?"

I don't get a chance to reply though, because a doctor pushes through the double doors and turns toward us. "Are you the family of Emmalyn Price?"

"I'm her husband," Sterling says, his words shocking me mute. *He doesn't mean that literally... right?*

The doctor nods. "Come with me please."

I watch helplessly as the two of them retreat back through the double doors, my heart in my throat as I ask, "Husband?"

Gabe rolls his eyes. "I had the same reaction, but apparently when he told the paramedics he was her boyfriend, they shut him out."

"Okay." That explains that, but I still have so many questions. "What happened?"

Gabe and Zach wear matching looks of discomfort.

"Someone better tell me."

"There was... a video," Gabe hedges.

"A video? What kind of video?"

Gabe mutters a string of curses under his breath, his fists clenching in his lap.

"Shh," Zach murmurs to his boyfriend before turning to us. "It was a... private video of Emmy and Sterling, taken without their knowledge or consent."

All I can do is blink, because *what?*

"Like a sex tape?" Samson asks, giving voice to the question bouncing around in my skull.

Both men nod, and my blood turns to hot lava in my veins. "Who?" I ask. "Who did it?"

"Sterling didn't say. But he swears it wasn't him."

Zach gives Gabe a bland look. "It wasn't and you know it."

"I don't know anyone else that would—"

"Her stepbrother!" I blurt, my voice far too loud for the space.

"Oh, shit," Gabe mutters. "You're right. It has to be."

"Sick fuck." Zach crosses his arms over his chest with murder in his eyes. "I'd like to meet his ass in the back alley."

"Calm down, killer," Gabe groans as he palms Zach's thigh. "And get in line."

"She's gonna be okay, right?" I ask, my voice thick as I try to hold back my tears.

Gabe reaches over Zach and takes my hand in his. "She damn well better be."

"HOW IS MY SUNSHINE?" Gabe asks. If he was anyone else, the nickname would piss me off.

"Stella's good. Still sleeping." She was so exhausted that she fell asleep on the ride home from the hospital and has been out cold ever since.

"Any word on Emmy?" I'm really hoping for good news to give to Stella once she wakes.

"Yeah, Sterling sent out a group text, but I guess he wasn't with us when we exchanged numbers."

"And?" My patience is wearing thin after staying up half the night worried about Stella—and her roommate.

"She's fine. Physically. They're going to do a seventy-two-hour hold."

"Is that all he said?"

"Mostly."

"What else?" I growl, in no mood for games.

"So testy, caveman."

"I swear to God, Gabe."

"Chill. It was a shit night. I gotta get my kicks where I can."

"Whatever." I reposition the phone and peek in on Stella. She's still sleeping soundly. "What else did he say?"

"He said one of the RAs from the building cleaned up their dorm, but that he has mixed feelings about Emmy returning. Things with them are pretty fucked up right now."

"Yeah, I'm with him there. If I could keep Stella here indefinitely, I would."

Gabe snorts a laugh. "Those girls are stubborn."

"Truth." I sigh, massaging my temples. "Keep me posted, yeah?"

"Will do."

I end the call and head into the kitchen to start a pot of coffee and to see about breakfast. Unfortunately, my fridge is pretty bare, so bacon, eggs, and toast it is.

Once everything is cooked, I plate up the food and pour two mugs of coffee. I don't have a fancy tray to carry it on, so I have to make two trips.

And Stella, God love her, sleeps through it all.

I almost feel bad waking her up—*almost*. At this point, my worry is outweighing her need to rest, as selfish as that may be.

"Luna." I gently shake her shoulder. "Wake up."

"Don't wanna," she murmurs, rolling away from me.

"I've got coffee." I lean down and brush her hair away from her face before pressing a soft kiss to her temple. "And bacon."

"Is it crispy?"

I grin. "Damn near burned." The little weirdo likes bacon well-well done.

"Fine." She stretches her arms over her head. "I'll get up."

"You're so fucking cute."

She pouts, only upping her cuteness.

"Puppies are cute. Babies are cute."

"Your point?"

"Grown women don't want to be called cute."

"Fine." I nudge her with my hip and slide into the bed next to her. "You're gorgeous."

"Whatever." Her smile, while small, tells me she's not really mad. "You promised bacon and coffee."

"Gabe called me," I say, passing her one of the mugs of coffee.

"Really? What did he say?" She takes a big sip and then places it on the nightstand on her side of the bed, trading it for her phone. "Oh, it's dead."

"Let me see it." She passes me her phone and I plug my charger into it before passing her a plate of food. "Eat up."

"But what did Gabe say?"

"Emmy's fine, but the hospital is going to keep her for three days."

"What?" Stella's lip trembles. "I thought... I thought it was all a bad dream."

"Stella."

Tears roll down her cheeks. "Em-Emmy... she... really tried to kill herself?"

Fuck. "Yeah, Luna. She did. But she is okay."

"Is she really?"

The look of utter devastation on her face hits me like a punch to my gut. "I..." I trail off, because I don't want to lie to her. "As far as I know. Sterling told Gabe that she was okay."

"Can I see her?"

I shake my head. "Not until they release her. She can't have visitors right now."

Stella whimpers, her breakfast long forgotten. "I feel

like the worst friend ever. I should have been there. I could have—"

"Oh, Luna, baby." I slide the plate out of her lap and place it on the table before pulling her into my lap. "Nothing that happened is your fault. You couldn't have prevented it any more than someone can stop it from raining. Don't blame yourself for this."

"Are you sure?"

"Positive."

"What do I do?" She snuggles into me. "How do I help?"

"Just be you, Stella. You're fucking goodness and light. You're sunshine and daisies. Shine for her."

She glances up at me from beneath damp lashes. "I don't know what that means."

I lean down and kiss her forehead. "Just be there for her —whether it's as a shoulder to cry on or an ear to listen. Follow her lead."

"Okay. I can do that." She nods as if reassuring herself. "Hey, Samson?"

"What's up?"

"Could I... could I stay here until Emmy's released?"

It's on the tip of my tongue to tell her she can stay here forever, but I settle on, "Sure, Luna, as long as you want."

***

"What do you want to do today?" Stella asks, settling down on the couch next to me.

"I'm up for anything, as long as it's with you." I sound like a schmuck, but fuck if I care. Stella's supposed to go back to her dorm tomorrow, and it's all I can do not to chain her to my damn bed to keep her here.

Call me selfish, but I'd be perfectly content for her to never go back.

I know she isn't ready for all of that though—*I know it, but I don't like it.*

Regardless, I don't like the idea of her or Emmy going back to their dorm. And from what Gabe says, Sterling agrees.

"Maybe just chill?" She snuggles in closer to me. "Watch a movie or something?"

"Sure. Whatcha want to watch?"

"Um." She grins up at me.

"*Friends With Benefits*, huh?" I ask, knowing it's her comfort movie of choice.

"If you don't mind."

"Is it gonna make you smile?"

She scrunches her nose. "Yeah?"

"Then I don't mind." I lean forward and grab the remote. "You want some popcorn or anything?"

"Nope." Stella kicks her legs up, laying them on top of mine. "I just need you."

"Alexa," I murmur, hitting play on the remote. "Turn off the lights."

We settle in as the opening credits roll, content to just *be*.

That is until the *tennis scene* happens, touching on the age-old question—*can a sexual relationship really exist without strings or expectations?*

For Stella and me? Hell-fucking-no. I want our strings to be so tangled, so intertwined, that you can't tell where she ends and I begin.

"You know," Stella murmurs. "I know I've only slept with you, but I can't imagine just *sleeping* with someone. Not that I would judge someone else for doing it, you know? To each their own—but for me, I just... I think I would need that deeper connection to let myself be vulnerable like that."

Anger over the thought of her with anyone else pricks at me, but the satisfaction of knowing I'll be her only quickly chases it away. "Good thing I'm it for you, huh?"

She twists in my hold, pressing her lips to my neck. "I wouldn't want it any other way."

"Really?" I draw her lips up to mine, kissing her deep and slow.

"Mmm." She pulls back ever so slightly. "Really."

"That's funny, because I can think of a million different ways I want you."

Stella's cheeks turn my favorite shade of pink. But instead of shying away, Stella does what she does best—and turns it up to fifty. "Oh, yeah? Why don't you show me one or two of them?"

"Fuck, Luna."

"Show me, Samson." She kisses me again, nipping at my lower lip before teasing her way down my jaw. "Right here, strip me down, and show me."

I slide out from under her in a flash, dropping to my knees in front of her. "You gonna do what I tell you to?"

Stella scowls but agrees all the same.

"Good." I pull her hurt leg into my lap and gently undo the straps before sliding it off. The skin is still bruised, but it's more of a yellowish hue, than the deep mottled blue it was when it happened. "Does it hurt?"

"Not too much."

Leaning down, I press my lips to the ball of her ankle and gently kiss my way up to her knee.

"Samson," she sighs my name, and I swear to God, the sound goes directly to my cock.

"Let's get you out of these pants, yeah?"

She nods eagerly. "Yes, please."

I hook my fingers into the waistband of both her leggings and her panties, and drag them down her legs, taking great care when I slide them over her injured ankle.

Her pussy's already glistening with her arousal, and ever the impatient bastard, I can't help but to drag a finger through her folds. "You're so wet for me, Luna."

Her gaze is zeroed in on me, and when I lick her juices from my finger, she moans.

"I'm gonna prop your foot here," I tell her, placing a throw pillow on the coffee table. "And I don't want you to move. Do you understand?"

She nods.

"Words, Stella."

"I understand. Now, please touch me."

Grinning, I lean back onto my haunches. "I don't know... I kind of like you desperate and needy. Maybe I'll tease you until you're begging for my dick."

"You wouldn't!"

I quirk a brow at her. "Wouldn't I?"

"Samson!"

My fingers work the button of my jeans, popping it open as I stand. I shuck off my pants and boxers, leaving me fully naked before her. My dick strains toward her pouty lips, but I want to make my girl feel good before I get mine.

But that doesn't stop me from reaching down and stroking myself, nice and slow, putting on a little show. "Fuck," I groan, twisting my hand as I rub the tip.

"Samson."

"I swear, I'll never get tired of hearing you say my name like that, all soft and wanting." I move closer to her.

"Doesn't seem fair that I'm the only one naked. Lose the top, Luna."

She rips her shirt over her head, tossing it somewhere behind the couch, revealing her perky tits to me.

I lean down and draw one pebbled peak into my mouth, sucking hard before giving the same attention to the other. Stella's soft mewls and moans spur me on.

"Put your mouth on my pussy," she begs, making me grin. Her boldness never ceases to surprise me, but damn if I don't love it.

"When I'm ready."

"Now!" She bucks her hips for emphasis and I draw back completely.

"Didn't I tell you not to move?"

"Are you kidding me?" Her blue eyes glow, a hypnotizing mix of disbelief and lust.

"Does this look like I'm kidding you?" I nod down to my rock-hard dick. "I want to make you feel good, but I don't want you to tweak your ankle. So, stay still and let me work."

"Yes, sir," she says in her brattiest voice. Too bad it only makes me that much harder.

Dropping back down to my knees, I drape her uninjured leg over my shoulder and kiss my way to her slick center.

Her pussy tastes tangy and sweet all at once, like fucking ambrosia. Just for me.

Using my thumbs, I spread her lips wide, dipping my tongue inside of her before licking a hard line up her slit.

"Fuck, Samson!" she whimpers my name in such a desperate way, I can't help but glance up at her.

Her eyes are pinched shut and her hands clenched into tight fists. She wants to move as much as she wants her next breath, but she's doing exactly as I told her, and I fucking love it.

"So pretty," I murmur before latching my lips onto her needy little clit.

I suck and lick and rub at her until she's a panting, trembling mess, bringing her to the edge over and over again, but never letting her fall.

"Samson!" she shouts my name and I retreat—again.

"You want me to get you off?"

"I might die if you don't."

"Okay, Luna." I kiss her pussy, swirling my tongue in soft, teasing strokes. "But only if you say please."

"Please! Oh, God, please. Just... just let me come."

I dive back into eating her like she's my last meal... my *favorite* meal. And this time, when she approaches the edge of her release, I slide two fingers deep inside of her and curl them, rubbing her sweet spot, until she comes all over my face, screaming my name.

FOR THE FIFTH night in a row since she was released from the hospital, I wake to Emmy's panicked screams.

The first time it happened, I tried waking her, but it was no use. There's only one thing that can calm her when she's like this.

I grab my phone off my nightstand and dial Sterling's number.

"Again?" he asks in lieu of an actual greeting.

"Yeah," I reply through a yawn, "again."

"I'm on my way."

Listening to her whimper and scream brings tears to my eyes, and I find myself calling Samson while I wait for Sterling to arrive.

"Luna, is everything okay?" Despite the late hour, he sounds completely alert.

"Emmy's having another nightmare."

"Fuck. That poor girl."

"I don't think being here is good for her," I whisper, my heart aching for her as her garbled cries filter through the walls.

"You're probably right," he grunts. "I don't like you there either. Have y'all given any more thought to moving?"

"I told Emmy that I think it's a good idea. Plus, moving in next to Sterling puts me closer to you."

"Not close enough," he mutters.

"Samson."

"I get it, Luna. I know she needs you. Doesn't mean I have to like it."

The sound of knocking draws my attention. "Hang on, Sterling's here."

I set my phone down and pad into the living area to let him in.

"Thanks for calling," he says, blazing a path straight into Emmy's room.

By the time I make it back to my bed, she's settled and our suite is quiet.

I crawl back into my bed and pull my covers up to my chin. "Samson?"

"Yeah?"

"Tell me a story to help me fall back asleep?"

"A story?"

"I don't know." I yawn again. "Just talk to me. I wanna hear your voice."

"Okay. Um. Do you remember when you were fourteen and Orion and I were going to the lake and you begged to come with us?"

"Yeah, and you told him to let me come."

"That's right. And like the idiot he is, he thought he could impress the two girls he invited by taking them fishing and catching our dinner."

"Mmhmm," I murmur sleepily.

"You wore this yellow bikini, and I remember thinking it was my favorite color. I couldn't focus on anything but you—fucked up, I know—but you've always been it for me. Even before it was acceptable."

"Really?"

"Really. Anyway, he wanted to impress them, but neither of them would bait their hooks because they didn't want to touch worms. But you... you marched right up to that bucket, plucked out the fattest, juiciest worm, and did the damn thing. You didn't balk, or squeal, or nothing. And then, you offered to bait theirs too, because that's just the kind of girl you are."

"What kind's that?" I'm so tired, my words slur together.

"Brave. Caring. Kind. Hell, I probably even loved you then, Stella..."

I sigh contentedly as Samson talks until, finally, sleep takes me.

"But first coffee," I mutter to myself, checking the time on my phone. It's barely eight, but after nearly a week of next to no sleep, I'm tired.

Sterling's deep voice filters out into the kitchen as I scoop grounds into the filter. "...you're serious about getting away for good, maybe while we're gone Gabe and Zach could help Stella move y'all into the unit next to mine?"

"I'd have to talk to Stella," Emmy replies.

"Talk to me about what?" I ask, nudging her bedroom door open. Though, I'm pretty sure I know exactly what they were talking about, and I am absolutely for it.

"Stalk much?" Sterling asks, laughter coloring his words.

"Hey, I was making coffee and heard my name."

"Emmalyn and I were talking about y'all moving in next to me. I suggested Gabe and Zach could help you move everything while I took our girl to my family's cabin."

"And I" —Emmalyn glares at Sterling— "was telling him I couldn't make those kinds of decisions without talking to you."

Called it! "Oh, I am totally down. Let's blow this popsicle stand."

"Are you sure?" Emmy asks, sounding so hopeful my heart feels like it might burst.

"One-hundred-and-ten percent. And I know the guys will be down to help me move our stuff." Samson included. "You just take care of you. Go to the cabin, relax and recharge. Read a book on a bearskin rug in front of the fire."

"I thought you were supposed to make love in front of the fire?" Emmalyn asks, causing both Sterling and me to grin.

"Now, there's a thought," he murmurs in her ear, causing my best friend to blush.

I can't help but smile watching them together. For a couple that had such a rocky start, I'd be hard-pressed to think of two people more meant for each other than these two. You know, except for Samson and me.

"Oh my God! I cannot believe I just said that."

Sterling smirks. "I'm just saying, baby. You want to give that a go, I'm down."

"Okay." Emmy's previously apprehensive look melts into one of pure relief. "Let's do it."

"There's no rug here," Sterling deadpans. "Or fireplace."

I slap my hand over my mouth to suppress my laugh. Never would have thought Mr. Serious could somehow make a dad joke sexual.

Emmy rolls her eyes. "I meant let's go to the cabin. And... let's move."

"Y'all want to get started on packing and I'll head home and pack a bag for the cabin?"

"Yup!" I say, rejoining the conversation. "It's basically just clothes and a few odds and ends."

"Oh! We don't have furniture!" Emmy cries.

"You're in luck. It comes furnished," Sterling says, his voice a smidge too tight to be natural, but Emmy doesn't notice.

But I'm not about to call him on it. Nope. Instead, I smile and say, "Sounds like it was meant to be."

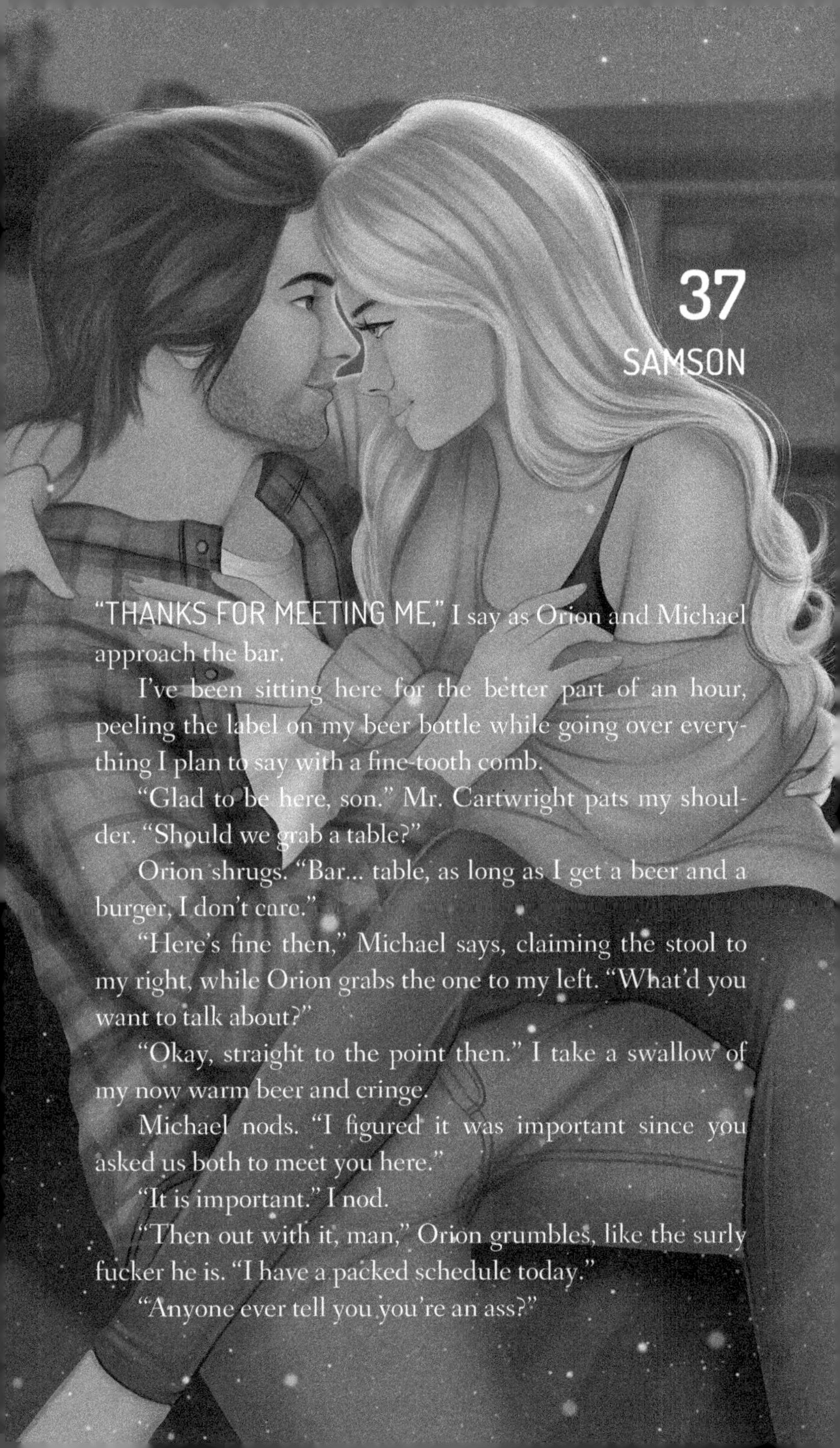

"THANKS FOR MEETING ME," I say as Orion and Michael approach the bar.

I've been sitting here for the better part of an hour, peeling the label on my beer bottle while going over everything I plan to say with a fine-tooth comb.

"Glad to be here, son." Mr. Cartwright pats my shoulder. "Should we grab a table?"

Orion shrugs. "Bar... table, as long as I get a beer and a burger, I don't care."

"Here's fine then," Michael says, claiming the stool to my right, while Orion grabs the one to my left. "What'd you want to talk about?"

"Okay, straight to the point then." I take a swallow of my now warm beer and cringe.

Michael nods. "I figured it was important since you asked us both to meet you here."

"It is important." I nod.

"Then out with it, man," Orion grumbles, like the surly fucker he is. "I have a packed schedule today."

"Anyone ever tell you you're an ass?"

"All the time." He smirks. "Now, out with it."

"I want to ask Stella to marry me."

Orion chokes on air, while Michael regards me stonily.

"I know she's only nineteen and in college—"

"Do you love her?" Mr. C asks.

"I do, and I want to spend the rest of my life with her. To grow old with her. When I picture my future, there's not a version of it without your daughter at my side."

Michael nods. "Then you have my blessing."

"Orion?" I ask, turning to my best friend.

My heart thumps in my chest as he stares me down. I know he said he was okay with us being together, but now, a small part of me can't help but worry he won't be on board with this.

Not that his opinion would stop me. I meant it when I said I would choose Stella over him, every time. I just hope it doesn't come to that.

Finally, he says, "One condition."

"Name it."

"No PDA when I'm around." He shivers. "I don't wanna see that shit. Ever."

Easy enough. "Consider it done."

"Now that that's out of the way," Michael says. "How about we order?"

"Sounds good to me." I redirect my attention to the menu the hostess gave me when I arrived, but my phone buzzes in my pocket before I can make a selection.

I slide it from my pocket and press my thumb to the screen to unlock it.

LUNA

Where are you?

ME

… where are you?

LUNA

Your house. I finished my study group early
and wanted to surprise you.

ME

I'm on my way.

"Gentlemen," I say, as I slide off of my barstool. "I hate to dip before we can even eat, but Stella just texted me—"

Michael waves me off. "Go on. We'll see you for Thanksgiving?"

"Wouldn't miss it."

"Kiss ass," Orion mutters, but I just shake my head, slap down a ten-dollar bill for my beer, and then head for the exit.

"I've missed you," Stella says the second I step out of my truck.

"I've missed you too."

As soon as I'm within arm's reach, Stella wraps her arms around my neck and presses a soft kiss to my jaw. "It feels like I barely get to see you."

She's not wrong either—between her moving out of her dorm, studying for finals, and my job, we've both been busier than ever.

"I don't like it." I speak the words into her hair, content to just feel her body pressed to mine. That is, until she shivers. "Let's get you inside."

I dip low and swing her up into my arms, loving the way she squeals.

"Let me down, you caveman. I can walk."

"I know you can." I slide my key into the lock. "But I like holding you."

"Yeah, yeah sure."

"Whatever. You like it too."

"I certainly don't mind the body heat."

Speaking of... "You have a key. Why were you outside?"

"I was looking at something in the backyard."

"Plants." I shake my head as I move through the house, toward the living room. "I should have known."

"Yeah, well." She shrugs. "Now put me down."

"No thanks." I lower us down to the couch and then adjust her position so that her legs are propped on the empty cushion.

Despite her earlier protests, Stella snuggles into me. "Where were you?"

"Having lunch with your dad and brother."

"Oh! I'm sorry. You didn't leave in the middle, did you?"

"Damn straight I did." How does she still not get that I'd drop anything for her?

"Samson! That was rude."

"So?"

She starts to fuss at me again, but I silence her with a kiss, sucking her plump lower lip into my mouth.

"Fuck, I've missed this," I murmur before tangling my tongue with hers.

"Me too," she murmurs, her lips brushing against mine with every word.

"Oh, yeah?" I nip at her lips. "Show me how much."

Stella grins wickedly before kissing her way along my jaw, down to the hollow of my throat. "Take me to bed and I will."

Hell. Fucking. Yes.

I readjust my grip and stand from the couch, cradling Stella against my chest as stride back toward my room.

She peppers kisses up and down my neck, each one bolder than the last, until finally, she's licking and sucking and scraping her teeth over the column of my throat.

"Fuck, Luna," I groan, setting her on her feet at the end of the bed.

She grins deviously, tugging her sweater over her head. "That's the idea."

My eyes drop to her full breasts. "Lose the bra."

Stella licks her lips. "Make me."

I pull my own shirt off and then take a step closer to her. Her rosy nipples show beneath the lace of her bra, and my mouth waters at the sight.

Reaching out, I trace my index finger over her right collarbone, to the hollow of her throat, and then down the valley of her breasts, to where the ring I gave her so long ago rests on its chain.

"Samson," she whispers my name as I lift the ring to my lips, kissing it before letting it fall.

"I love you." I reach around behind her, unclasp her bra, and then slide the straps down her shoulders. "So much."

She lets the fabric fall to the floor. "I love you too."

I sink to my knees before her and push the button through the loop of her jeans before lowering the zipper and tugging her pants and panties down to her knees.

A deep groan rumbles up from my chest at the sight of her glistening pussy lips.

Unable to help myself, I dip down and press a kiss to the top of her mound.

"Sit," I murmur the words against her soft flesh, already imagining the tangy flavor of her arousal bursting across my lips.

Stella doesn't hesitate, perching herself on the edge of the bed.

She watches me, her eyes dilating with lust, as I tug off her shoe before gently removing her walking boot. Her socks, pants, and panties quickly follow, leaving her completely bare before me.

"I want you naked too," Stella whines, leaning back onto her elbows.

Smirking, I rise to my full height and shove my sweats down my legs. "That better?"

"Almost."

"Almost?" I raise my brows. "Tell me what you need, Luna?"

"You." She slides her arms forward until she's flat on her back and then reaches up to palm her tits, pushing them together. "I need you to touch me."

"Need or want?"

"Need, Samson." She rubs her thighs together. "Need."

"Well, I can't very well leave you *needing*, can I?"

Stella shakes her head, her blonde hair fanning out over my sheets.

I go to kneel at the foot of the bed, ready to tease the first orgasm out of her with my tongue, but Stella stops me. "Please, Samson. I just want to feel you inside of me."

"Luna."

"Look!" She dips two fingers between her legs and pulls her hand away, presenting me with the evidence of her arousal. "I'm ready."

Crawling into the bed beside her, I carefully move her up the bed and onto her side. "Does that feel okay on your ankle?"

"Yeah," she whispers, wriggling her hips.

Moving closer, I slide one arm behind her neck and

drape the other across her middle, so that I'm spooning her from behind. "You're so damn beautiful," I murmur, kissing up and down her neck and shoulder.

"Samson," she exhales my name, and the sound goes directly to my cock.

"Let me take care of you." I trail the hand draped over her waist up to her breasts. Cupping one, I massage the supple flesh as I thumb her nipple. "Fucking love these tits."

"Yeah?" she asks.

"Yeah, Luna." I release her breast with one last pinch to her nipple, and then skim my fingers over her quivering belly, all the way down to her pussy.

"Love this more though." I slide the tip of my finger through her slick folds, parting them before dipping inside of her. "Love how wet you are for me. How you feel gripping me." I withdraw my finger, smear her wetness into the crook of her shoulder, and then suck it off. "Love the way you taste."

Growing impatient with my teasing, Stella pushes back against me, grinding her ass into my painfully hard erection. "Please just fuck me."

"Can't do that, Stella."

"What?" She turns her head, glaring at me over her shoulder. "Why?"

"Because I'm gonna make love to you." I reach between us and drag the head of my dick through her slickness before aligning myself with her entrance. "You told me to show you how much I missed you, and that's exactly what I'm going to do."

I nudge my hips forward, pushing just the tip inside of her, before retreating. I repeat the motion, over and over, feeding a little bit more of my dick into her tight heat with each thrust. Until finally, I'm fully seated inside of her.

"Samson," she moans my name. "I feel so... full."

"That's right, Luna." I flex my hips as I grind against her. "Feel me inside of you. I'm gonna make you feel so fucking good."

"Yes, yes, yes," she chants, reaching over our joined bodies to caress my side.

My free hand roams every inch of her body, from her pussy to her throat; rubbing, touching, playing, and teasing until she's practically vibrating with the need to come.

"So. Close." Her words are choppy as pleasure steals away her ability to speak.

"I love you, Stella." I tug on the chain of her necklace and then slide my hand back down her belly, pressing my index and middle fingers against her swollen, needy clit.

"I-I—*oh my God*—I love you too!"

I increase my pace and apply more pressure with my fingers, rubbing them in time with my thrusts. "You feel so good, Luna. Clenching my dick so tight. *Fuuuuuck!*" I groan, as her pussy walls squeeze my cock. "Like heaven, made just for me."

Stella's entire body tenses as her orgasm crests, her eyes closed tight as she cries my name.

"Goddamn." I press my lips to the soft skin of her neck. "That was..."

"Perfect," she murmurs, her voice soft from her release. "It was perfect."

"We're perfect. Meant for each other. No, fuck that —*made* for each other. You're the best thing to ever happen to me, Stella."

"You are too." She reaches her hand up and brushes her fingers along my jaw. "Sometimes, it's hard to believe that you're all mine."

"I am though. Forever." Her necklace catches my eye,

and an idea sparks. It's probably not my best idea, but I'm still riding the high of my release. "Let's get married."

"What?" She tries to turn and look at me, but I wrap my arms around her, keeping her in place. "You can't be serious."

"Dead serious." I reach up and grab the chain of her necklace. "When I gave you this ring, I meant it. I fucked things up to hell and back, but I. Meant. It. I want to spend my life with you, and I know you deserve a real proposal and a real ring, so consider this your warning, Stella."

"My warning?" This time when she tries to pull away from me, I allow her to, instantly missing the warmth of her body. She pushes herself to a sitting position and glances down at me. "What does that even mean?"

I follow suit, and sit up, propping myself against the headboard. "It means, I *am* going to ask you to be my wife—down on one knee, the whole shebang. It's coming, Stella. I want it all with you."

"Okay, Samson." She rolls her eyes like she thinks I'm talking out of my ass. "Well, why don't we start with a shower and some food?"

"Just you wait..." I stand from the bed and then help her up. "You'll see."

And she will see—not just when I propose—but every day, for the rest of our lives because I'll fucking show her. I'll show her, with my actions, exactly how much I love her. How much I fucking cherish her.

Stella and I may have started as a secret, but our love for one another is too damn strong to deny, and I plan to prove to her, for the rest of our days, exactly how proud I am to call her mine.

"WHERE IS IT?" My heart pounds as I shuffle everything around on my bathroom counter for what feels like the hundredth time. "Where did it go?"

"You almost ready to—" Samson stops short when he sees me. "—hey, what's wrong? Are you okay?"

"No!" My eyes fill with tears as my frustration reaches a boiling point. "It's gone."

"What's gone?" He crosses the room and wraps me in his arms.

"My necklace!" I shake off his hold and drop down to my knees to search through the cabinet one more time. "I took it off last night because the chain had some hair wrapped around it and now it's gone!"

"Hey, it'll be okay. We'll find it."

"But what if we don't?" I ask, my tears falling in fat drops. "I'll never forgive myself if it's lost, Samson. That ring… it means so much to me."

"Luna, baby." He crouches down beside me and tips my chin up so we're eye to eye. "It will turn up. I'm sure of it."

"You think so?"

"I do." Samson nods and stands back up. "But if we don't head out right now, we'll be late."

I stare up at him from beneath damp lashes. "But... my necklace."

Reaching down, he hauls me up. "I promise you, the second we get home, I will tear this house apart with you to find it, okay?"

"I know, but—" Samson silences my protest with a hard press of his lips against mine.

Like always, the second our tongues touch, every thought that isn't of him falls away, until he consumes all of my senses.

I tunnel my fingers into his long hair and crawl onto his lap, needing to be closer, but instead of deepening our kiss, Samson pulls back. "No *buts*, Luna. Come on, we gotta go."

"Fine." I scramble to stand. "Let me just fix my makeup."

"I'll start the truck."

I grab a cleansing wipe and blot away the smudged makeup from underneath my eyes, dust some powder over my cheeks, swipe on a new coat of mascara, and call it good.

Despite it being New Year's Eve—one of my most favorite holidays—my heart feels heavy knowing I've potentially lost something so precious. But I know Samson has plans for us tonight—plans that he's put a lot of work into.

So, with one last look around for my lost necklace, I turn and head for the truck.

"No luck?" he asks, as I climb inside.

I shake my head and readjust the vents so the warm air is blowing my way.

"You're killing me, Luna." He casts a long look my way and throws the truck into gear. "Seeing you so sad is killing me."

"Sorry," I mutter, feeling even worse.

"Hey, no." He settles his big, warm hand on my thigh and squeezes. "Don't apologize to me."

"But I lost—"

"It'll turn up." He sounds so damn sure of himself, but I can't help but feel it's lost for good. I tore his house apart looking for it.

Crossing my arms over my chest, I settle back into the seat. "I wish I had your confidence."

Samson smirks. "It'll be a New Year's miracle."

By the time we make it to our destination, I'm more confused than ever. "Why are we at my parents' house?"

"Figured we'd ring in the new year somewhere special," he says, giving nothing away.

"What does that even mean, Samson Carter?"

"It means, hush your mouth and let me surprise you."

Whatever retort I may have had dies in the back of my throat when he turns down the drive that leads to my special spot. "We're going to the tree."

"We are." He nods. "This place will always be special to me. It's where you fell for me."

"It's where I fell, literally. From a freaking tree."

"So desperate to get my attention, you flung yourself at me from the top of a damn tree."

Laughing, I smack his chest. "You fool. I didn't even know you."

"Love at first sight," he argues.

"I was eight."

He throws the truck into park. "And?"

I shrug.

"Are you saying you didn't love me the second you saw me? Don't lie, Luna. This is a judgment free zone."

"You're an idiot."

"I'm *your* idiot," he says and my heart warms at his silly proclamation.

"So, why are we here?" I ask, once my laughter subsides.

"Figured since tonight is gonna be the first night of the rest of our lives together, we could ring in the new year somewhere special."

"What?" I scrunch my nose. "What's so special about tonight?"

Samson drums his fingers against the steering wheel. "You'll see. But first, we eat."

"What's on the menu?"

"Let me grab the cooler from the bed and you'll see."

Somehow, he manages to run and grab the cooler before I can even fully process his words. He really did put a lot of thought into this.

As he unzips the soft top, the smell of barbecue fills the cab. "Did you get—"

"Purple Daisy?" He passes me a foil-wrapped plate. "Of course, I did. No nachos though, they don't travel well."

"This is amazing!" I tear the covering from my plate and dig into my quesadilla. "Thank you, Samson."

His lips quirk up into a grin as he watches me chow down. "So ladylike."

"Pssh." I reach over and grab a piece of okra from his plate. "You love me."

"I do, Stella. So, fucking much."

We both fall quiet as we devour the barbecue feast before us. And once the last bite is gone, Samson says, "Hope you saved room for dessert."

I sink back against my seat and pat my belly. "I don't know. I'm pretty full."

"Too full for a cupcake?" He reaches back into the cooler and pulls out a pumpkin cupcake.

"I'm never too full for this." I greedily take the baked treat, and swipe my finger through the frosting, except before I can lick it off, Samson grabs my hand and closes his lips around my finger.

"Mmm," he moans. "Tasty."

Heat pools low in my belly, as I imagine his tongue licking the icing off of me instead.

Spurred on by the lust coursing through me, I swipe my finger through the frosting again, only this time, I smear it across his cheek and mouth.

"What the hell?" Samson laughs.

My lips tip up in a devilish smile as I lean forward and flick my tongue over his lips, licking away the cream cheese goodness.

He groans again, and I swear to God, the sound is a direct hit on my clit.

"You're right." I lick his cheek. "So tasty."

"Playing with fire, Luna."

I move back to my seat and gesture for him to slide to the middle of the bench. "Good thing I love the way you make me burn."

"Stella."

"Samson." I pat the seat again. "Slide over here so I can put your dick in my mouth."

"Fuck, Luna." He moves over, working his belt buckle all the while.

I knock his hands out of the way. "It's rude not to let a girl unwrap her gift."

"Your gift?" He lifts a brow.

The whirr of his zipper sliding down fills the cab, and then I free him from his pants. I grip his dick and give it two slow pumps. "Heck yeah, my gift. This thing is a work of art."

"A work of art?" he deadpans.

Leaning forward, I press a kiss to the base of his dick. "Mmhmm."

"How can you be so weird and so sexy all at —*fuuuuuck!*"

His words melt away as I draw his tip into my mouth, swirling my tongue and sucking hard. "What was that about me being weird?"

"Sexy. You're so fucking sexy."

"Damn right I am." I lean over and grab my cupcake from the dash. "Lift your shirt."

I can tell he wants to ask why, but he doesn't. *Because he trusts me*, I think happily.

With one last sweet smile, I drag my cupcake over his abs, smearing the frosting into the hard muscle, before dragging it lower toward his thick, hard cock.

His hips twitch as I scoop the last of the icing and rub it up and down his shaft and then lick my fingers clean. "Dammit, Luna, what—"

I cut off his protest with my lips, licking and sucking the frosting from his stomach. His long fingers thread through my hair, massaging my scalp in time with my ministrations.

His belly quivers and his breathing accelerates as I work my way lower.

"Tastes so good," I murmur just before swallowing his cock whole.

"God—fuck—Stella!" He bucks his hips, shoving his dick all the way to the back of my throat.

My eyes water and I have to force myself to breathe through the urge to gag.

He continues thrusting up from beneath me, until finally with one last guttural cry, he spills his release down my throat and sinks back into the seat, sated and spent.

I slide his dick from my mouth and grab a napkin from his cupholder, wiping away the sticky remnants of the frosting as best I can.

"You gonna let me get you off?" he murmurs.

I shake my head. "Nope. You always put my pleasure first. So, that was all for you."

"I swear I didn't bring you out here just to get some." He tucks himself back into his jeans and cringes. "Still a little sticky."

A bubble of laughter bursts out of me. "Yeah, you're gonna need a shower when we get home."

"You'll join me?" he asks.

I nod.

He smiles, pleased. "Good."

"I love you, Samson." I snuggle into his side.

"Love you too." He presses a kiss to the top of my head. "Was tonight a good way to end the year?"

"It was almost perfect," I answer, sadness over my misplaced necklace creeping in.

"Almost?"

"I just wish I could find—"

"Find this?" He tugs a familiar silver chain from his pocket.

Disbelief and joy duke it out inside of me. "You ass!" I lightly smack his chest. "You had it the whole time? Why did you let me—wait. What's that? Why..." Tears fill my eyes. "...Why are there two rings?"

Samson shifts against the bench so that he's facing me. "I told you when I got you this." He holds up the original ring to emphasize his words. "That it was a promise—that it meant every part of me belonged to every part of you. And that's as true today as it was then. Maybe even more so now. I love you, Luna. I. Love. You."

He lets the ring fall and then lifts the other. It's a simple yellow gold band with a cluster of smaller diamonds ringed around the center stone to look like a daisy. It's dainty and perfect and so totally me.

"I also told you I'd get you a real ring, one with a diamond."

"Samson," I breathe his name, my heart pounding in my chest. *Is this going where I think it is?*

"I also warned you this was coming."

Oh my God. It is. It so is.

"I want to experience every single thing this life has to offer with you by my side. I want you to wear my ring, to have my last name, and then further on down the line, I want you to be the mother of my children. I want it all with you, Luna. I love you. Say yes."

"Stella Carter does have a pretty nice ring to it, huh?" I ask through my tears.

"Sounds like it was meant to be."

"That's because we are. Meant to be, I mean."

"Still haven't heard that yes."

"Yes!" I shriek. "A hundred times yes. A million. All of those things you want, I want them too. You're my everything, Samson Carter. It's always been you."

He unhooks the clasp and slips the new ring from the chain. "Let me see your hand."

It shakes as I hold it out to him, but he slides the ring onto my finger with sure hands.

"Now, let me hook this back around your neck. That way you have both of my promises on you at all times—one for everyone else to see and one right by your heart."

I turn my back to him and gather my hair. His fingers brush against the back of my neck, sending the best kind of chills down my spine.

"Tonight was perfect," Samson murmurs once he's done.

"I can think of one thing that would make it better." I lick my lips. "It would be the icing on the cake, so to speak."

His eyes narrow. "What's that?"

"Let's go back to your place so we can really celebrate. Who knows, if we time it just right, maybe I can scream your name right into the new year."

Samson buckles his seat belt and throws his truck into gear. "Now there's a tradition I can get behind."

I can't help but grin as he tears back down the trail toward the main road. Tonight truly is the first night of the rest of our lives together. And I'll be dammed if I can think of any other man I'd want to spend forever with.

Samson Carter is more than my fiancé—he's my best friend and with him by my side, I know I can conquer anything life throws my way.

All of LK's titles can be read as standalones & are available with Kindle Unlimited. An asterisk next to the title denotes it is also available in audio.

Sweet Little Nothing (an enemies-to-lovers/bully romance)

Pretty Little Thing (a single mom/forced proximity/mistaken identity romance)

Best Laid Plans (an older brother's best friend/secret baby romance)

Best of Intentions (a friends-to-lovers/little sister's best friend romance)

Best of Me (a second chance at love/forbidden twin romance)

Rebel Heart (an enemies-to-lovers jock/tutor rom-com)

Rebel Soul (an arranged baby/friends-to-lovers rom-com)

Rebel Desire (an unrequited soulmates/surprise single dad rom-com)

Coming Up Roses (a small-town/single mom romance)

An Uphill Battle (a frenemies-to-lovers romance)

Weather the Storm (a second chance at love romantic suspense)

Come What May (an age gap/single dad romance)

ACKNOWLEDGMENTS

There are so many people who deserve my gratitude. But instead of naming each friend one by one, I plan to show them—much like Samson did Stella—day in and day out just how appreciative I am to have them in my life, both professionally and personally.

However, a special shout out is in order for my alpha, beta, and editing team. These ladies are forever putting up with my BS. Thanks for not firing me for being such a hot mess.

Kylie and the GMB crew, you ladies work tirelessly and I am so thankful for all you do for not only me, but the book world as a whole.

To my amazing husband for keeping the kids fed and watered while I churned this story out. You're the real MVP, Phoobs.

And last but certainly not least, THANK YOU! Yeah, that's right, YOU! Thank you for reading. I truly believe books make the world go 'round and knowing other people share that love... it just settles my soul. So, from the bottom of my heart, thank you for reading—not only my book, but all of them.

ABOUT THE AUTHOR

Known by Kate to most, LK Farlow is an Amazon Top 40 bestselling author of more than a dozen romances, ranging from sweet, to sexy, to rip your heart out, and everything in-between.

She has a heart built for happily-ever-afters, which is lucky since she found hers at the young age of nineteen. Now, at thirty-something, she is the wife to one hunky man and the mother to four semi-feral humans, three lizards, a chameleon, a tortoise, and a handful of stray cats.

Kate often jokes that her life is all out chaos on most days, but she wouldn't trade it for the world.

www.authorlkfarlow.com